"The alehouse can never be destroyed. Never."

"It will simply move to another place. So the gods have decreed. And I will move with it. I will be an alewife forever. What the gods have refused to give you, Gilgamesh—immortality—they *have* given me."

Then she stepped away, pitcher still in hand. He stood stunned, tall, muscular body unmoving, rigid with shock and pain: Gilgamesh, once-king of Uruk, slayer of Humbaba and the Bull of Heaven.

Then he exhaled. "And the gods mock me still, even here."

She sneered. "Did you not feel their presence in this room? Do you not feel their mantle spread over this building? Over me? Is that not why you came here?"

"No. I came because I had nowhere else to look, nowhere else to search."

Kubaba nodded. Her arms prickled and itched as she said, "Perhaps the gods do not mock you. Perhaps I can help."

—from "An Alewife in Kish" by Benjamin Tate

AFTER HOURS:
Tales from the Ur-Bar

EDITED BY
PATRICIA BRAY
AND JOSHUA PALMATIER

DAW BOOKS, INC.
DONALD A. WOLLHEIM, FOUNDER
375 Hudson Street, New York, NY 10014

ELIZABETH R. WOLLHEIM
SHEILA E. GILBERT
PUBLISHERS
www.dawbooks.com

First Printing, March 2011

1 2 3 4 5 6 7 8 9

ACKNOWLEDGMENTS

Introduction copyright © 2011 by Joshua Palmatier and Patricia Bray

"An Alewife In Kish," copyright © 2011 by Joshua Palmatier

"Why the Vikings Had No Bars," copyright © 2011 by S. C. Butler

"The Emperor's New God," copyright © 2011 by Jennifer Dunne

"The Tale That Wagged the Dog," copyright © 2011 by Barbara Ashford

"Sake and Other Spirits," copyright © 2011 by Maria V. Snyder

"The Fortune-Teller Makes Her Will," copyright © 2011 by K. L. Maund

"The Tavern Fire," copyright © 2011 by David B. Coe

"Last Call," copyright © 2011 by Patricia Bray

"The Alchemy of Alcohol," copyright © 2011 by Seanan McGuire

"The Grand Tour," copyright © 2011 by Juliet E. McKenna

"Paris 24," copyright © 2011 by Laura Anne Gilman

"Steady Hands and a Heart of Oak," copyright © 2011 by Ian Tregillis

"Forbidden," copyright © 2011 by Avery Shade.

"Where We Are Is Hell," copyright © 2011 by Jackie Kessler

"Izdu-Bar," copyright © 2011 by Anton Strout

CONTENTS

INTRODUCTION

SEVEN authors walk into a bar. . . .

No, seriously. This entire anthology began when seven authors—a group that calls itself the Magnificent Seven, for obvious reasons—got together at a bar after a multi-author signing. Drinks were had, alcohol was consumed, and at some point during the conversation someone brought up anthologies, bars, and . . . well, there you have it.

We really didn't think the anthology idea would amount to anything. Thousands of ideas are thought up at the bar by authors; some of them are even good. But the idea was written up as a proposal (a crucial first step that is generally never taken; we were drinking after all) and within the space of five months or so it was pitched and sold.

It's the perfect idea for an anthology: nearly every fantasy novel has a scene in a bar or tavern or inn. It's often where the storyline either starts, takes a major turn (usually for the worse), or where it ends. So why not have a bar as the central theme of the anthology? A bar that's magical in nature, that travels through time. A bar that is the quintessential representation of everything that makes a bar great. The Ur-Bar.

And who better to watch over the Ur-Bar than the immortal Gilgamesh?

So here you have fifteen stories spread throughout time, from the moment that Gilgamesh took over the Ur-Bar into one possible future. All of the stories are set on Earth—perhaps an alternate Earth—and in each, the Ur-Bar is key to how the story unfolds. Pour yourself a drink—or let Gil pour one for you—sit back, relax, and enjoy.

The first round's on us.

AN ALEWIFE IN KISH

Benjamin Tate

KUBABA glared out the door of her alehouse over the sun-baked mud walls of the city-state of Kish and muttered darkly, for the thousandth time, "Curse you, Enlil. And curse this prison."

From her vantage, a maze of streets cut down from the hill through the rectangular houses of the workers, artisans, and merchants that made up this quarter, the pale red clay punctuated here and there by splashes of green from gardens and the occasional glint of sunlight reflecting off of water from a fountain or pool. The land rose again in the distance, houses giving way to the larger temples of the priests and the walls of the king's palace. The temple of Anu rose higher than all of the rest, as befit the god of heaven, but Enlil's and Ishtar's temples were also prominent. Kubaba's glare darkened as it raked across Enlil's shrine and she spat to one side, lip curled. She tossed the contents of the slop bucket she held out onto the side of the street.

"Watch where you throw that offal, you heaping pile of entrails!"

The merchant who'd shouted gestured rudely as he

3

dodged out of the reeking path of slop, then continued on his way up the street. Kubaba bristled and stepped forward, a scathing retort on her lips. As soon as her foot touched the ground beyond the entrance to the alehouse, searing pain lanced up from her sole into her upper thigh. She hissed and lurched backwards, choking back her reply. The man barked out laughter, but she ignored him, focusing on her leg as she ducked back into the shade of the inner room. Hurling curses at Enlil, she hobbled through the mostly empty tables and chairs toward the small room in the back where the urns of barley beer were waiting to be served. The pain faded, but her entire leg now tingled as if it were being feasted on by ants.

"You should be careful cursing Enlil." The slurred voice rumbled outwards from the far corner of the room. "The gods are vengeful, especially one such as he."

Kubaba halted at the edge of the main room, weight on her good leg, back rigid. "I know of the gods and their vengeance," she snapped. "I suffer under their hateful gaze every day." She'd nearly forgotten the man was there, although she wasn't certain how that was possible. He'd arrived early, ducking down beneath the doorway as he entered because he was so tall, possibly the tallest man she'd ever seen. His well-built chest glistened with sweat, streaked with dirt and dust from the road, his finely made fringed kilt also layered with mud. The braids of his beard were loosened, as if he hadn't bothered to groom himself for days, and his face was haggard, lined with age and weariness, even though his entire body strained with subtle strength.

That strength irritated her. He shouldn't exude such controlled danger. Not after the amount of beer he'd drunk.

She turned toward him, toward the shadows where he sat. She could barely see him, although her eyes had already recovered from the blaze of sunlight at the door. The other two patrons glanced between them both warily. They came nearly every day and knew of her foul temper, although today she felt particularly trapped. They'd ordered their beer and settled into their usual chairs with a minimum of words.

Not this man.

"But what of you?" Kubaba asked caustically. "What do you know of the gods? What have they ever done to you?"

The man laughed, a hard sound that reverberated throughout the room, no mirth in it. It was bitter, filled with grief, pain, and a despair so deep that Kubaba, even in her own bitter rage, felt her heart shudder. Her hand clutched at the baked mud of the doorway until the horrid laughter trailed down into silence.

"You ask what the gods have done to me," he said after a long silence. His wooden cup thunked down onto the table top, then scraped across its surface as he pushed it toward her. His eyes caught hers and even in the shadows she could feel his attention settle on her. "Bring me more beer and perhaps I'll tell you."

She drew back a step beneath that gaze, then frowned at herself and straightened her shoulders. Without a word, she slipped into the back room, dipped out a pitcher of beer from the largest urn, and grabbed a bowl of dates. The tingling in her leg had stopped, but it still felt numb. She refilled cups to grateful nods and tentative smiles, before circling back to the man's table. Up close, she could smell his sweat, heavy and dense. His hair glistened with oil. Age radiated from him, although he did not appear old.

She held his gaze, then frowned and set the bowl of dates before him with a clatter. "Would you like a reed straw?" she asked as she refilled his cup, even though he had not asked for one before and this was his seventh cup since his arrival. The quality of his kilt and his bearing spoke of the high caste, but he was no priest. She didn't know what he was.

He grinned, the expression leonine. "I can handle the barley hulls."

She nodded, a little surprised.

"Sit." He gestured toward the nearest chair.

She frowned at him. She hadn't expected him to tell his tale, whatever it was, however wild and unbelievable. She'd been trapped in this alehouse long enough to know when a man came to drink simply to forget. But if he wanted to talk, let him talk. The gods had certainly granted her enough time to listen, she thought with a twisted half-smile.

She set the nearly empty pitcher of beer on the table and sat, arms crossed on her chest. "So talk," she said. She couldn't keep the skepticism out of her voice. "How have the gods assailed you?"

The man leaned back, legs stretched out before him, beer in one hand. He drank deeply from the cup, his eyes never leaving Kubaba, then set the cup down as he glanced around the alehouse. The other patrons stared intently at their own cups and pretended they had not been listening, but the man didn't care. A dark melancholy settled over his shoulders.

"I met him in a place much like this," he finally rumbled, in a voice so low Kubaba had to force herself to remain still. The two others were not so controlled, chairs creaking as they leaned forward. "In an alehouse, at the end of a wedding ceremony. As soon as he entered, I knew he had been sent by the gods to challenge me, a wild man sent to tame me. It wasn't until Shamhat entered behind him that I realized how vicious and sadistic the gods truly were. I had sent Shamhat to find him, to seduce him, to bring this wild man I had heard of to me, not realizing what the gods intended the wild man for. I had summoned my own destruction.

"So the wild man challenged me, there in front of the wedding guests, there in that alehouse. He challenged my right to bed the wife on her marriage night, before her husband. But it was my right, my duty!" The man slammed his hand onto the table, making the boards jump, his cup rattling but staying upright.

Kubaba stirred in her seat. Not a priest, no, but a king. Only kings could bed a virgin bride on the wedding night. But which king?

She scowled and squashed the tiny flicker of hope. He could not be a king. Kings did not squat in alehouses, beard unraveling, covered in sweat and dust. Kings did not drink barley beer without reed straws. It was a story only. A madman's story.

"But the reason for the challenge was meaningless," the madman murmured, calm again. "He would have challenged me over the texture of the rice, or the color of the sky. The true challenge came from the gods, and so I rose to meet it. I shrugged aside the robes of my city, of my station, and I boomed, 'You dare to defy the king?'

"The wild man straightened where he stood. No fear touched his eyes, nor quivered in any muscle. He held himself proud, rigid with anger, and answered, 'I do.'

"The arrogance enraged me. I was the king! I was

god-touched, god-blessed—or so I thought. I roared my rage and charged him.

"The wild man stood, solid as a rock, and met the charge. We collided, grappled with each other, until we struck the far wall. It cracked beneath the impact, chunks of baked mud cascading down. The wild man twisted in my grip, his arm snaking down under my leg and then lifting, toppling me backwards. I roared again as I fell, grunted as my back slammed into the bare earth, rolled away, and surged to my feet.

"But the wild man moved fast, as fluid as a lion, as deadly. He closed and tackled me, drove me back into the feasting table. Wood splintered and food flew. The wedding guests began to scream, but neither of us heard them. I pounded my fists into his back, his arms still latched around my waist, the side of his face pressed into my stomach so tight I could feel his breath hissing through his clenched teeth. He twisted and spun and flung me back. I landed hard, lurched upright in time to catch him as he attempted to leap onto my back, jammed my hands into his shoulder and stomach, knelt and pivoted, and flung him over me with a growl. He slammed into more tables and chairs, scrambled from the wreckage, lithe body tensed with his rage, face twisted and feral. I saw his primal nature then, felt it throbbing in the air, tasted it in the sweat that slicked my face and salted my lips, breathed in its musk with every ragged breath.

"In that moment, the wild man was the most beautiful man I had ever seen. Raw and vibrant. *Alive*.

"Then he charged, plowed into me, lifted me from my feet and carried me out through the open doorway into the street beyond, into the cooling night air. We crashed into a stack of earthen pots on a cart, baked clay shattering around us, unheeded as we wrestled each other across the street, careened into walls, carts, canopies, trampled through empty stalls. Shamhat and the wedding guests trailed after us, and drunken citizens joined them as we staggered past. My muscles began to burn with exhaustion. I tasted blood, my lip split, my body bruised, and yet still we fought, clinging as we pummeled each other with weaker and weaker blows, each trying to break free, neither willing to let the other go.

"Until, seeing the crowd we had drawn, seeing the guests of the wedding whispering to those who had joined them as we fought through the city, my rage overwhelmed my exhaustion. Grasping the wild man's shoulders with both hands, I shoved his torso back, his arms wrapped around my chest, and then pulled him forward as I brought my head down. Our foreheads cracked together and the wild man's grip slid away. Stunned, still I bellowed in triumph and shrugged the wild man's body up onto my shoulder and flung him to the ground, kneeling upon his chest. I'd drawn back my fist to beat his face to bloody tatters when I saw his eyes. Dazed, they gazed up at me in wonder. All of the rage, all of the arrogance, all of the wildness had fled.

"In a raw voice, breath shallow from my weight upon his chest, he swallowed and said, 'I am defeated.'

"And all of my rage vanished."

Kubaba let the silence that followed these words reign for a long moment—

Then she snorted in contempt.

The man turned a heated, narrow gaze on her. "You do not believe my story?"

"You claim that the gods have maligned you," Kubaba said, standing abruptly and grabbing the nearly empty pitcher of beer from the table, "and yet you tell a tale of how you bested them!"

"No, you are wrong."

"You defeated the wild man! The man sent by the gods to challenge you!"

"I did not defeat him. He defeated me. The gods won."

Kubaba stared as the madman took a long draught from his cup. She wanted to throttle him, but he was too calm, too collected. Most madmen, especially those who'd drunk as much as he had, grew incensed if you challenged their tales of woe and misery. This one simply watched her, his broad shoulders slumped, despair still shadowing his eyes. And there was something else, something niggling at the back of her mind. The man's story was familiar somehow, although she couldn't quite place it.

The fact that she couldn't annoyed her. "How, then?" she scoffed. "How did the wild man defeat you?"

Something twisted inside the man, exposed in his eyes, something black and insidious. He grimaced, glanced into his empty cup, then motioned toward it as he said, "He defeated me by befriending me."

Kubaba frowned, confused, but poured the last of the pitcher into the man's cup and then retreated into the back room. She heard the other two patrons stir, murmur amongst themselves, followed by the scrape of chairs. She dunked the pitcher into the urn of beer, the heady aroma assailing her nostrils as it filled. She breathed it in as she thought furiously. Could the man truly be a king? Or was this another drunken tale told by a fool? He wore no robes of state, but his clothing was of finer quality than the workers and merchants of the district. He drank without a straw like a commoner, but his physical presence commanded respect, demanded something more, even though he was disheveled. Yet she could not recall any kings of Kish or the surrounding lands who had abandoned their cities to roam the roads and frequent gods-cursed alehouses.

If she were king, she would rather die.

She grunted in amusement at the thought. Then, pitcher full again, she straightened—

And caught sight of the tablet resting on the shelf of the niche behind the urns of beer. The gods had placed it there to mock her, Ninkasi herself inscribing the recipe for beer upon it before setting it upon the shelf and vanishing with a final laugh, the last lines of power—of the gods' punishment—settling around Kubaba and the alehouse like a weighted fishing net.

Kubaba shuddered, the mesh of that net brushing against her as if in warning. She shrugged aside the tingling sensation and returned to the outer room. She was not surprised to find that only the madman remained, the other patrons gone.

She moved directly to the mysterious man's table.

"I do not understand. How did the wild man defeat you by befriending you?"

The man's glare made Kubaba fidget where she stood, until she could take it no longer and sat. He nodded and poured himself another beer, although he did not immediately take a drink. Instead, he stared into the far distance, cup held in one hand.

"He befriended me, and together we became the terror of the surrounding lands. Nothing could stop us, no one could control us, not even the councilors of the city. We converged on the alehouses of Uruk and drank heavily. We staggered through the streets beneath the white moon, held upright by each other's arms. We challenged every strong man and defeated them, fought lions with our bare hands and killed them, and when those challenges became paltry and trivial, we sought out greater challenges. The elders begged us to stop, but we thought the gods had brought us together for a reason, that they had set these trials before us to test us."

The man's voice had grown rough with memory, the skin around his eyes taut. He paused, drank from his cup and set it aside, and then met Kubaba's gaze. She could see the pain there, and a sudden suspicion lanced through her and clutched at her gut. He'd mentioned Uruk. Her mind turned to the great southern city on the edge of the Euphrates, to the city's great kings—

To one king in particular.

But this man could not be that king. He'd ruled Uruk over a hundred years ago. And yet the story he told, the emotion that throbbed in his voice, the anguish she could see in the tension around his reddened eyes. . . .

"We should have listened to the elders," he continued, and Kubaba found herself leaning forward, eyes narrowed in doubt, searching his face for the truth. "But we were young, and powerful, and we thought we could not be defeated, not together. And so we accepted the challenges we thought had been set before us. And in all of this we offended the gods, although we did not realize it. So the gods exacted a punishment."

The man's voice had grown cracked with anguish, his face drawn and bleak, his bloodshot eyes haunted. He drank from his cup, coughed harshly. Kubaba watched him silently, doubt roiling inside her, even as her chest constricted with echoes of the man's pain . . . with Gilgamesh's pain. She could not believe it, dared not believe it, and yet this man related the tale as if he had lived it. And more. She had heard Gilgamesh's story, but there were subtle differences between those and the story this man told. Yet these differences made it harder to discredit the man before her, not easier.

She leaned forward and in a hoarse voice asked, "What punishment?" Even though she knew the tale of Gilgamesh and the wild man, Enkidu, and how their friendship ended. She needed him to say it, to confirm it.

The man looked up from his cup. "The gods killed Enkidu," he said savagely, face contorted with pain and grief. "They sent him a terrible sickness. It ravaged his body, so that he wasted away. I thought I had met the gods' challenge, there at the wedding. I thought I had won. But the challenge was not to defeat the wild man. It was to resist Enkidu, his friendship, his . . . companionship. We were more than brothers, more than friends. We were. . . ."

But words failed him, choked off by emotions that Kubaba could see warring in the muscles of his face, in the grip of his hand on the cup.

Then, in a voice thick with the lie, he said, "I should have killed him when we met."

With that, all doubt within Kubaba fled. This man—covered in dirt from his travels, disheveled and drunk on barley beer—this man *was* Gilgamesh, once-king of Uruk, slayer of Humbaba and the Bull of Heaven.

And if the tales told of him were true. . . .

Hope swelled up from deep inside Kubaba's chest. She fought it back, even as she felt it tingling along her arms. It exacerbated the prickling sensation of the gods' net that enfolded her and the bar, raising the fine hairs along her arm. The urge to scratch made her fingers twitch, but she stilled, eyes narrowed at Gilgamesh. She had met many would-be heroes since the gods had laid down their punishment. None of them had agreed to help her escape.

She had to tread carefully.

"But if you had killed the wild man then, you would never have enjoyed those battles, never have experienced as deep a bond as you did with Enkidu."

Gilgamesh slammed his wooden cup onto the table, beer sloshing out from its sides, the cup itself cracking. Kubaba flinched as he roared, "I would never have experienced the pain of losing him! I would never have felt the fear of death that has consumed me since!"

He lurched to his feet, chair scraping across the floor before tilting and clattering to the ground behind him. He planted both of his huge hands onto the table, the wood creaking beneath his weight, and leaned toward Kubaba, so close she could smell the beer on his breath. "Do you know what I've done since his death?" he growled. "I've traveled to the underworld to speak to Utnapishtim, blessed by the gods with eternal life. I've swum the Great Deep and found the spiny plant that grants those who eat it youth. I've climbed the highest peaks of Zagros so that I could breathe the air of the gods. And at every turn, at the height of every triumph, the gods mock me and snatch immortality from my grasp."

He thrust back from the table, arms raised to heaven. "I have traveled the length of the Great Valley, to the edges of the world, to its greatest heights and fathomless depths, and at every step I can hear the gods' laughter." He crossed his arms over his chest and glared downwards. "Now, alewife, tell me that you know of the gods and their vengeance. Tell me that you have suffered as much as I have. How do the gods punish you?"

Kubaba stared up at the king of Uruk for a long moment, then slowly rose. "You fear death, and so the gods punish you by keeping you from immortality. I. . . ." She paused, clamped her jaw together, then grudgingly continued. "I wanted more than the gods thought I deserved. I wanted to become a god myself." She snatched up the pitcher of beer and Gilgamesh's cracked cup and filled it, thrusting it into his hands. "For that presumption, they thought it fitting that I be forced to endure life as I began, as an alewife, catering to the workers and the merchants I sought to leave behind, serving them for all eternity." She nearly spat in disgust, but caught herself.

Gilgamesh grunted, then laughed. "That's it? That's how the gods have punished you?"

Kubaba spun and the sharp look she gave him cut his laughter short. "You don't understand," she hissed. "I'll be an alewife forever. At this alehouse for a while, because it is the best in this district, because it is the essence of the life I led before. But when the city of Kish begins its decline—as all cities do, even your great Uruk—when this district begins to fall into ruins, then this alehouse and I along with it will shift. It will appear in another city, in another district like this, and there I will serve the workers and the merchants yet again, until time passes, until the essence of the alehouse shifts yet again, and again, and again." She moved a step closer to Gilgamesh, satisfaction snaking down into her gut when he flinched back. "The alehouse can never be destroyed. Never. It will simply move to another place. So the gods have decreed. And I will move with it. I will be an alewife forever. What the gods have refused to give you—immortality—they *have* given me."

Then she stepped away, pitcher still in hand. He stood stunned, tall, muscular body unmoving, rigid with shock and pain.

Then he exhaled. "And the gods mock me still, even here."

She sneered. "Did you not feel their presence in this room? Do you not feel their mantle spread over this building? Over me? Is that not why you came here?"

"No. I came because I had nowhere else to look, nowhere else to search."

Kubaba nodded. Her arms prickled and itched as she said, "Perhaps the gods do not mock you. Perhaps I can help."

It took a moment for her words to sink in, but when they did, Gilgamesh's eyes flared with hope. "What do you mean?"

The gods' net blazed across her arms and her fingers clamped down so hard on the handle of the pitcher of beer that her knuckles turned white. But when she spoke, her voice was deceptively calm. None of the eagerness and hope and desperation bled through at all.

"Come now. You've dealt with the gods before. You know they play games." As she spoke, she shifted forward and lowered her voice. Gilgamesh watched her, eyes narrowed skeptically now, mouth a tight frown. She halted a step away, pitcher of beer lowered to her side. "They gave me a way to escape. All I need to do is find someone who will willingly take my place."

Gilgamesh's frown deepened. "I would think that task easy."

"Ha!" Kubaba scowled. "Do you think I haven't

tried? But while most men claim they want immortality, few really mean it. Fewer still will accept it at nearly any cost." She stared up into Gilgamesh's eyes. "So what of you? How badly do you want your immortality? Have you searched long enough that you would willingly take my place here, in this alehouse, serving the men and women you ruled over for years?" Then, in a soft voice, with a subtle shift closer to his dust- and sweat-smeared body: "How much do you fear death, Gilgamesh?"

Their tableau held, the only sounds their breaths, the clang of a bell, and the muted bleat of a goat from outside.

And then, finally, Gilgamesh muttered, "Enough."

Kubaba nearly leapt for joy, managed to contain it enough to step backwards and motion toward the table where Gilgamesh had been seated before. "Then sit. I will make the appropriate preparations."

He stared at her a long moment, doubt that she was telling the truth still lining the edges of his eyes, but then he turned. She waited until he was settled, then grabbed the cracked cup he'd drunk from earlier, tossed the dregs of the beer still left to one side, and retreated into the back room.

Muttering to herself—prayers to the gods, prayers to herself—she set the empty pitcher to one side along with the cracked cup, then scrambled through the urns into the back corner where her pallet lay, along with all of her worldly possessions. She drew a leather satchel from beneath the pallet, dug through it until she found the vial Ninkasi had left with the stone tablet. She held it up to the shadowy light, read the inscriptions on its sides, noticed that her hands were shaking. Gripping the stone vial tight, she shoved everything she owned into the satchel, then climbed to her feet and tossed it to one side near the door to the small room.

Then she turned to the stone tablet in its niche against one wall.

"Ninkasi, I pray you spoke the truth that day or I shall curse you until the day I kill you myself."

She reached up into the niche and grabbed both sides of the stone tablet. She swore as she lifted it—it weighed more than it should—then staggered into the outer room. Gilgamesh did not move to help her as she crossed to his table and set it down. He frowned down at the inscription, reached out to touch it, but she caught his forearm.

"Don't touch it," she said. "Not yet."

She returned to the back room, grabbed her satchel, Gilgamesh's cracked cup, and the vial, but left the pitcher. If this worked, she wouldn't need it any more.

Trying to control a wild grin, she crossed the outer room and set the cracked cup onto the center of the tablet. Arms prickling with the sensation of the net and her own excitement, she pulled the stopper from the vial and poured the liquid within into the cup. It came out clear, like water, but smelled of cedar and mint, and continued to pour forth even when it became clear that the tiny vial could not possibly contain the amount of liquid already in the cup. But Kubaba did not hesitate, pouring until the cracked cup was full, then sealing the vial once again. She set it down on the tablet as well. It was still full.

"Now drink," she said.

Gilgamesh reached for the cup, then hesitated, his hand held still in mid-air. Kubaba's breath caught in her throat, a fist-sized lump of despair lodging in her chest.

"That's it?" he asked, his voice a low rumble.

Trying not to show her tension, knowing that she failed, she nodded. "That's it. Drink, and the alehouse . . . and immortality . . . are yours."

He grunted, lowered his head as if in deep thought, then picked up the cracked cup.

He held it before him, long enough she wanted to strangle him. The lump in Kubaba's chest tightened, so hard she thought her heart would burst.

And then he drank, tipped his head back, throat working as he downed the entire draught, not stopping for breath.

When he finished, he sat forward, breath coming in a harsh gasp as he set the cracked cup back onto the tablet. For a long moment, his face was flushed. He coughed once, twice. "It burns," he said, voice hoarse. "Burns in my throat. I can feel it inside, in my gut."

Kubaba said nothing. The net still prickled against her skin. The despair lodged in her chest began to seep outwards into her shoulders, down into her gut, followed closely by seething anger. Ninkasi had lied to her! She'd told her she could escape! She'd told her—

But then, without warning, the prickling sensation began to fade. A weight she hadn't realized had covered her sloughed off her shoulders, like cloth pulled from a statue's head. She straightened, and the despair that tightened her chest lifted.

Snatching up her satchel, she moved toward the alehouse's door.

"Wait!" Gilgamesh growled, and shoved up from the table. "Wait! Did it work? I feel nothing! Even the burn has faded."

Kubaba didn't stop, didn't turn. "Let's see."

She stepped out of the shadows of the alehouse and into the glare of the sunlight slanting down into the street. Her foot landed in the dirt, solidly, without hesitation—

No pain shot up her leg. Not even a twinge.

Laughter burst from her, a harsh sound, but triumphant, wild and exuberant. She took another step, and another, emerging completely into the sunlight. She flung her arms up to the sky, danced briefly, to the annoyance of the workers and merchants and shepherds trying to pass by, one with a ram in tow. "Bless you, Ninkasi! And curse you, Enlil!" She spat onto the ground, eyes narrowed in rage. "Curse you for cursing me. But I am released! I am free!"

Behind her, Gilgamesh came to the alehouse's entrance, began to step outside as he said, "What do mean? What are you say—"

As soon as his foot touched the ground he roared in pain and flung himself backwards, back into the shadows of the alehouse, where Kubaba couldn't see him. But she could hear him, fumbling among the tables and chairs as he regained his balance, as the pain in his leg began to fade into the tingling numbness she had grown to know so well. She'd stopped cackling and dancing in the street. She stood now, clear of the alehouse's doorway, and watched its blocky shadow in silence.

When Gilgamesh appeared again, balanced on his good leg, the numb one held carefully to one side, he said through gritted teeth, "What have you done, bitch? What have you done to me?"

She snorted. "What did you think, once-king of Uruk? That immortality came without a price?"

"You lied to me!"

She shook her head even before his roar ended. His hatred was palpable, like the heat of the sun against her flesh. "I told you the conditions. You have your immortality, and you have the alehouse. You can never leave, can never step beyond its doorway. But the alehouse . . . and its keeper . . . can never be destroyed. You will live forever, Gilgamesh. Or at least until you find someone like yourself, someone so desperate or so afraid that they will willingly take your place." She paused, watched the rage roil in Gilgamesh's eyes, and felt no pity. "I've left you the vial and the tablet. You have everything you need. The alehouse will provide the rest."

Then she turned, stared up into the sunlight through squinted eyes, then lowered them toward the city of Kish and smiled. She began moving into the city, toward the hills where the temples and the king's palace lay. Behind her, Gilgamesh spat curses at her back, called upon the gods to strike her down, to slay her where she stood. But she ignored him.

The gods had taught her something after all. Perhaps aspiring to be a god was too great a goal for now. She needed something more reasonable, something attainable, no matter what the cost.

Perhaps if a king could become an alewife—

Then an alewife could become a king.

WHY THE VIKINGS HAD NO BARS

S. C. Butler

THE old man leaned on his staff. Yesterday, the long-house had been abandoned. Today, through the magic of hard work and a little silver, it almost looked like a jarl's mead hall.

Maybe he could find a way to use the change to his advantage.

A raven flapped down to perch on the peak of the sod roof as the old man crossed the yard. A second raven followed him through the door. In the shadows inside, the few idlers who were always the first to discover this sort of establishment drank their way through the afternoon. The sweet, sour, too-familiar smell of ale cloaked him as heavily as his own garment.

He recognized the proprietor. Word of the man's fate had preceded him, even here, where little was known of the world beyond ice and blood, and even less of the past.

The question was, would the proprietor recognize him?

He brought his staff down heavily on the plank table at the back of the hall. The raven settled in the rafters.

"It'll never work," he declared.

The proprietor ignored him, continuing to wipe the table. Like most of his type, he was stoic, but not bright.

"What will never work?" the proprietor asked.

The old man swept his staff at the longhouse behind him. "You can't run a public ale house in Daneland."

The proprietor shrugged. "I have worked rougher towns."

"I doubt it."

"We shall find out soon enough." Hanging his dish-rag over his shoulder, the proprietor began setting out a fortune in small glass cups on his wooden bar. "To tell the truth, I have been looking forward to coming here for some time. You Norsemen have quite a reputation."

He laced his fingers and stretched ostentatiously. The muscles in his arms and shoulders rolled like whales on the surface of the sea. "I look forward to finding out if the reputation is true."

Despite himself, the old man was impressed. Even Thor would have his hands full with this one. Still, he liked that the man was so sure of himself. It would make him that much easier to use.

"You like causing trouble?" the old man asked.

"To tell the truth, I am starting to prefer the quieter towns. My name is not as famous as it once was. In Cordoba, only a few scholars recognized me. The last thing they wanted was to fight me. An interesting town, Cordoba."

A sow stuck its snout through the door. One of the men at the front of the hall heaved an empty bowl at it. The sow squealed, and disappeared.

"Hedeby isn't Cordoba," the old man said.

"I knew that before I got here."

The old man leaned forward with his hands on his staff, bringing his face closer to the proprietor's.

"You don't recognize me, do you," he said.

He caused what little glamour he was using to fall away. The proprietor stared back at him stupidly. The old man threw back his tangled gray hair to reveal his empty eye socket, and summoned the raven.

The proprietor shrugged. "I have met gods before." He began piling his glass cups into a small ziggurat. "Your Norsemen will be no different from any other drunkards."

"That depends how drunk they get." The old man held out a hand. The raven hopped from his shoulder to the end of a knobby finger.

The proprietor shook his head. "It is always the same. In every place and every century, whether I serve beer, wine, or mead. Or ambrosia."

The old man pointed his staff at the small casks on the shelf behind the table. "What about those? You think it'll be the same when you serve them?"

The proprietor gave him a curious look. "You know about those?"

"I do. We're not all ignorant in Daneland."

"Care to try a glass? Your good opinion would make my establishment an instant success."

"No, thanks. I only drink wine."

"Will Andalusian do? It is the only vintage I carry."

The old man did not resist. He sipped the offered glass unwatered, enjoying its fullness. His thoughts drifted to the warriors he had left carousing in his own hall. They would like this place.

"I could help you settle in, you know."

The proprietor looked at him suspiciously. He had some experience with gods, after all.

"Why would you help me?"

The old man shrugged. As usual, the lie came easily. "Hedeby could use a little sophistication. It might be good for my people to learn there's more to life than blood and beer. But even you'll find it hard to control them without my help."

"You wish to join me behind the bar?"

The old man snorted, and drained his cup. When he was done, he wiped his mouth with his sleeve, picked his nose, and offered what he found to the raven.

"The last thing you need is me hanging around, stirring up trouble. A pretty woman or two would be much better. And good for business. A proper Dane or Gotlander likes to have a pretty woman pour his ale for him. Or whatever else he's drinking."

"I like a pretty woman." The proprietor winked.

Yes, the old man thought, this one was still true to the type. A few more centuries might pound some sense into him. In the meantime, his predictability might provide some amusement.

And some reward.

"Uncle, is it true the Sons of Odin turn into bears when they fight?"

Abjorn looked down at his sister-son. Almost seven, the boy was old enough to learn the truth rather than the hearth-tales he heard from his mother and the skalds.

"Calling the Sons of Odin bears is a kenning, Tyrvi. When the mood comes upon them, they fight more like bears than men. But they never actually turn into bears."

"Snurri says his father can turn into a bear any time he wants."

"Snurri is mistaken. Perhaps Snurri is not old enough yet for his father or mother-brother to tell him the truth the way I tell you."

Tyrvi poked the fire with his wooden sword. Thin gray smoke curled up toward the roof, where a patch of sky showed through a small square hole. Clearly the boy prefered being able to turn into a bear to the truth.

"Snurri is two months older than I am," he said. "He says his father told him he could turn into a bear. He says the Sons of Odin go into the woods at night and sing songs and eat mushrooms and then Odin One-Eye turns them into bears. And no swords can cut their skin, or anything."

Abjorn thought before replying. He did not want to say that Snurri's father was a liar. At best, that meant Tyrvi would end up in a fight with Snurri. At worst, it meant that he or Tyrvi's father would end up in a fight with Snurri's father. Joffur was the largest man in Hedeby, the largest and strongest man Abjorn had ever seen. He was also one of the slowest-witted, and quickest to take offense at any perceived slight. The last thing Abjorn wanted was to spend a week avoiding Joffur until he and Leiknarr had a chance to ambush him. The notoriety would not be worth the trouble.

Besides, Joffur was just ignorant enough to think he *could* turn into a bear.

"Perhaps Snurri and his father know something your father and I do not," Abjorn said. "But if they do, it is a secret, which means it might be better not to talk about it with them any more at all. If Snurri brings the matter up again, you should talk about something else. You could ask him how old he thinks each of you will be when you make your first voyage, or fight your first battle."

Abjorn hoped the boy was listening as Tyrvi swung his sword back and forth across the room. His imaginary cuts were so ferocious, the thin plume of smoke wavered before him like a coward.

"When I grow up," Tyrvi said, "I will be a Son of Odin. I will win a score of battles, and die fighting over a heap of gold."

Abjorn laughed. "Yes, and the Valkyries will carry you off to Valhalla, where you and I, and your father and grandfathers, and all our grandfathers before us, will fight and die again together like true men."

Tyrvi gripped his sword more firmly and attacked the fire pit even more vigorously. Abjorn watched him proudly. From the room next door he heard the sounds of his sister singing to his sister-daughter as they baked and churned. It was a good life they had here in Daneland. Farms and fields for wives and cattle, the sea close by for voyaging, and fresh lands to raid and settle everywhere. He was only just back from his own first voyage, silver pennies jingling in his pocket from the treasure he had sold to the smith and slaver, but it was good to be home again all the same. Next spring Hastein would call for ships to sail to Mercia, so that they could conquer that country the way they had conquered Northumbria, but in the meantime Abjorn could spend the winter at home. Tomorrow he would set off for his father's farmstead, where his mother would make much of him, and his father would put him to work with his brothers and thralls in the fields.

The door to the street opened. A blast of cold frightened the flames more thoroughly than Tyrvi's sword.

The boy attacked his father's legs viciously as he entered the house. Leiknarr allowed his son his triumph, then packed him off to his mother with a smack on the backside. Helping himself to a bowl of ale from the cask in the corner, he joined Abjorn.

"I have heard some interesting news," he said. "A Frisian told me there is an ale-house south of town."

Abjorn fetched a bowl of ale of his own. "What is so special about an ale-house? The Saxons have scores of them."

"This is no Saxon ale-house. The owner is a Saracen."

"A Saracen?" Abjorn spat in the fire. "I do not accept drinks from thralls."

"The Frisian says this Saracen is no thrall, but a free man doing business like any merchant. Only his trade is not furs or slaves, but hospitality."

"Hospitality is no trade."

"If a man can buy a bed slave, why not a cup of ale?"

"Why should I buy a cup of ale when I have good drink brewed by my sister right here?"

Leiknarr looked at Abjorn over the top of his bowl. "Ale is not the only thing the Saracen offers."

"I have no need to pay for mead, either."

"It is not mead. The Saracen serves a special brew. The Frisian says he brought it all the way from Baghdad."

Abjorn's eyes widened. Leiknarr had sailed with Bjorn Ironside when that brave jarl had sacked Algeciras and Rome, and had brought home many tales. As a boy, Abjorn had always enjoyed the stories of djinnis' caves and magic rings.

"Even you have never been to Baghdad," he said.

"It is called al-kuhl."

"Al-kuhl? It sounds like the name of one of their djinnis."

"Al-kuhl is not a djinni. Though from the way this Frisian describes it, like as not it was a djinni who first brewed it. He says it is a drink fit for Odin himself."

Abjorn waved a dismissive hand. "It is probably just some sort of wine."

"Whatever it is, I would like to try it. And if we do not hurry over to the Saracen's establishment right now, we are unlikely to get our chance. Everyone was talking about it on the dock—they say the Saracen has brought a limited supply. You can stay here if you want, but I do not intend to miss the opportunity. Even when I sailed the Middle Sea, I never heard of al-kuhl."

Leiknarr wagged a finger, then placed it on the side of his nose. "They say it tastes like fire."

They started at once. The sun had almost fallen, and the sky had gone the color of steel. A breeze from the Schlie iced the town. The two men's feet clomped heavily on the wooden boards that covered the half-frozen streets.

The guards at the gate laughed when they saw them. "Better hurry up," one said. "Half a dozen Franks just passed through ahead of you."

The other hiccupped and rubbed his head. "It was worth every silver penny I had, but you will feel like you spent the night inside of a drum tomorrow."

Abjorn and Leiknarr left the two guards arguing about who had drunk more and followed the road into the countryside. A pair of ravens pecked at the dirt in front of them, flying ahead whenever the two men approached too close.

They heard the ale-house before they saw it. A crowd stood drinking and quarreling outside. Abjorn recognized most as the sort of men who rarely saw the inside of a jarl's hall, let alone a king's. Landless men not so good with their arms that they had won places for themselves in Normandy or Northumbria, but not so bad that they had been outlawed either. Though they were drunk, they knew better than to challenge Leiknarr, who had done great things in his day, or Abjorn, whom everyone knew would do great things in his. Instead they eyed the two men as they approached, and fiddled with their drinking horns and ear spoons.

A maiden greeted the new arrivals at the door. Abjorn was surprised, as much by the fact that she was both beautiful and richly dressed as by her presence. So beautiful, in fact, that he almost lost his tongue. Her hair, pale as the whitest gold, was pulled back behind her head in long braids knotted like a crown. Her blue robe was richly embroidered, and the silver brooches that clasped her apron were intricately worked. Beneath her white throat hung a necklace of perfectly matched beads and stones.

"Welcome, brave heroes," she said. She offered them a smile and a golden bowl. "May my gift of ale grace you with strength, wealth, and manly vigor."

"Well said, maid." Leiknarr took the bowl.

Abjorn sniffed its contents after his sister's husband was done. "It is only ale," he said.

The maiden laughed. "In Gisl's establishment the ale is freely given. The Saracen al-kuhl, however, you must purchase from Gisl himself."

Extending a graceful arm, she led Abjorn and Leiknarr inside.

There was hardly room for them. A mass of Danes and Franks, Norse and Rus, Wends and Gotlanders, packed the hall as tightly as a hull full of Sami furs. Every one of them glared belligerently at the newcomers, cups and horns in their fists, daring them to pass.

They parted for the maiden. Abjorn and Leiknarr followed in her wake. Past the fire pit, at the back of the hall, they found a large Saracen standing behind a wooden table ladling what looked like pure water from a small cask into tiny glass cups. He bore himself like a jarl, or a hero out of some tale more used to battling giants and draugr than serving beer. Nearly as tall and broad as Joffur, his neatly groomed dark hair and beard clung to his head in tight curls. Clearly this man was no thrall.

"Welcome, heroes," he said. He refilled the maiden's bowl from a larger cask on the floor. "Have you come for the fine ale, or do you seek rarer tastes?"

"We hear you have brought something new to the north." Leiknarr eyed the smaller barrel.

The Saracen tapped the cask with a thick finger. "One of the wonders of the modern world," he said. "I have brought it all the way from Baghdad, the center of wisdom and learning. Frankish priests call it aqua vitae. The Arabians who invented it, al-kuhl. Would you care to try it?"

"It is why we came," Leiknarr said.

"It is expensive. One silver penny will only get you enough to fill one of these small cups."

The Saracen held up one of the tiny glasses set out beside the cask. In his large hand it looked no larger than a thimble.

Abjorn had seen glass cups at King Helge's hall, but

had never actually held one, let alone drunk from one. His mouth watered. The Saracen must be a wealthy man to display such treasure so freely, let alone share it. A silver penny, however, was a lot to spend for less than a mouthful of anything.

"Leiknarr," he said, "perhaps we should content ourselves with our host's good ale. He is right. The price is too high."

The Saracen smiled. "I do not barter." Turning to the maiden, he said, "All the good things in life are expensive, is that not right, Sigrun?"

"Loyalty to one's comrades cannot be bought," the maiden answered. "And that is the best thing in life of all."

The Saracen's dark eyebrows pinched. "Clearly you have not seen much of the world. Loyalty can be bought and sold like anything else. And it does not require a dragon's hoard, either."

"That is not true in Daneland," Abjorn declared.

The maiden lifted her chin. For a moment it seemed she was taller than the Saracen. "The sort of loyalty you describe has not the worth of that which is given freely, from foster-son to foster-father, or wife to husband."

Leiknarr pounded the table in approval. Abjorn's blood stirred. He wondered who the maiden's father was, and how much silver and cattle it would take to purchase his favor.

"Well said, fair maid," Leiknarr declared. "For that, I ask that you pour the first round. Abjorn, give her a pair of silver pennies. It is a custom I learned in the wine shops of Rome after we sacked the place. The youngest always buys the first round."

Abjorn fished two silver pennies from his purse and

handed them to the Saracen. The Saracen nodded to the maiden. With her own hands she poured out two small glasses of al-kuhl, and two large cups of ale.

"It is also the custom," the Saracen explained, "to follow a measure of al-kuhl with one of ale."

Leiknarr raised one of the tiny glasses in a toast. "To Odin," he cried. "May he bring all of us to Valhalla."

Sigrun smiled.

Abjorn's heart beat faster.

Leiknarr gulped the contents of his glass. He blinked, his eyes watered, and he shook his head like a dog killing a squirrel. Without taking a breath, he grabbed his mug of ale and downed that, too.

Wondering how bad the al-kuhl could be, Abjorn sniffed his glass. The smell of the drink tickled the back of his nose, sharp and almost sweet. Whatever al-kuhl was, it was not water. But a mouthful could hardly kill him, so he followed Leiknarr's example and swallowed it all at once.

It was like drinking fire. For a moment he thought he was going to spray the entire mouthful like a seal coming up for air at a hole in the ice. Even after managing to force it down his throat instead of out his nose, he let loose a gigantic sneeze.

"Here! Get your filth off me!" A large Rus with a mustache like a pair of oars wiped his tunic and reached for his knife.

Leiknarr pounded Abjorn on the back and offered the Rus an apology. "Our pardon. My friend here is not used to al-kuhl. He meant you no disrespect."

Eyes tearing, Abjorn wiped his nose and reached for his ale. But, even after draining his cup, his mouth still tingled. He felt strangely alive, and expectant. He was ready for anything, from battle to another glass of al-kuhl.

The Rus slapped a silver penny on the table. The Saracen served him a measure of fire. With a sneer for Abjorn, the Rus placed the glass at his mouth and, throwing his head back, tossed its contents down his throat.

"It takes a little getting used to," Gisl offered as the Rus wiped his mouth with his sleeve and pushed his way back into the packed hall. "It is not distilled for the taste, but for how it makes you feel. Can I pour you another?"

Abjorn's chest heaved. The feeling of alertness and invincibility was increasing with every breath. He reached for his purse.

Leiknarr pushed him back. "My turn."

Abjorn was glad to see that his sister's husband was also still blinking back tears.

"I feel as if I could row all the way to Wessex on my own after one taste," Leiknarr said as he placed two more silver pennies on the table. Then he winked. "While bedding three Saxon maids at the same time."

Three rounds later, they pushed their way back down the hall. The Saracen would not allow them to take the tiny glasses with them, explaining they were too valuable to let out of his sight. Instead they each carried a large horn of ale, most of which they lost in the jostling as they crossed the hall. Abjorn nearly got into a fight with a Gotlander who made him spill the most, but there was no room to throw a punch so he just glared at the man instead. The Gotlander glared back, and their chins came closer and closer until finally Leiknarr pulled Abjorn on past the fire.

"This is no place to start a blood feud," he said. "If you cannot hold your drink, go home."

"Speak for yourself, brother. I never felt better in my life."

It was true. What Leiknarr had said before about rowing and Saxon maids was exactly how Abjorn felt. He wondered if Sigrun, or one of the other two beautiful maidens helping her, would be interested in taking the imaginary Saxons' place.

He was not the only one wondering that. A Frank slapped the backside of one of the women as she passed. In response, the maiden slammed the Frank's head into a post so hard he slumped to the floor.

The crowd roared.

The door opened. More men pushed their way inside. The heat and noise grew. Even the maidens had trouble pushing their way through the press. A Danelander and a Frisian began arguing about who was buying the next round. The Danelander pulled his knife. Before he could strike, the Saracen jumped between them. The crowd fell away on either side of him like birch trees bent back by an angry bear. The Frisian, enraged at the Saracen's interference, bashed him in the ear. The Saracen grabbed the Frisian by the chin with one hand and lifted him off the floor. The hall went quiet. Still using only the one hand, the Saracen carried the Frisian to the door and threw him out.

The crowd roared again.

Abjorn slapped his leg. "That man is no thrall. I would like to have him with us next spring when we sail to Mercia. We should ask him to drink with us."

Leiknarr beckoned the nearest maiden. Three men at the next bench smashed their drinking horns on their foreheads and laughed. The maiden went to fetch the Saracen.

"Begging your pardon, Gisl," Abjorn asked as their host arrived clutching the precious barrel of al-kuhl. "But why are you wasting your time in a place like this? Clearly you are a leader of men."

"It is a long story."

"We have plenty of time."

Leiknarr plunked down three more silver pennies. "And you have conveniently brought the al-kuhl with you. Drink with us."

"That is exactly what I wish to do." The Saracen poured three glasses, one for himself, and two for his new friends.

"To Odin!" Leiknarr cried, and drank his down.

"To Odin!" everyone around them agreed.

Pleased with the acceptance of his toast, Leiknarr essayed another. "To the fair maidens of this hall!"

"To the fair maidens!"

The Saracen got into the spirit of things as well. "To Shamash!" he proclaimed.

"To Shamash!" the crowd answered.

Leiknarr blinked several times and leaned forward. "Who's Shamash?"

The Saracen poured another round for himself and his friends. "It does not matter."

"To King Helge!" shouted a voice from the back.

"To Helge!"

"To Harald Fairhair!"

"To Harald Fairhair!"

A man with a wolf's head cowl glared at Abjorn. His eyes glittered. "Hail, King Harald!" he repeated.

"I just did," Abjorn answered.

"Then do it again."

Abjorn had nothing against King Harald. But he did not like being told what to do by any man.

"Who are you to tell me whom to hail?" he demanded.

The man's eyebrows disappeared into the wolf's upper jaw. "I am Botni, and Harald is my king. Do you dishonor him?"

"I dishonor no one," Abjorn answered. "I hailed your king. If you did not hear me, here is my spoon to clean your ears."

Botni started forward with an oath. Abjorn knocked him sideways. The Norseman fell, his head cracking against the edge of a bench. He slumped to the floor. Abjorn was sorry he did not rise so he could hit the man again.

"Well struck," said the Saracen.

"Abjorn! I knew I would find you here!"

A giant appeared, looming over the heads of the other men in the crowd. Abjorn wondered why he had not noticed Joffur before—there was no mistaking the man. Perhaps the al-kuhl had distracted him more than he thought.

Joffur shook his fist. "You told my son I am a liar."

"I have not spoken with your son."

"It is the same thing. You told your sister-son to tell my son I told him lies about the Sons of Odin. And my son told me! Since Tyrvi is just a child, the insult comes from you!"

Leiknarr gave Abjorn an irritated look and started to rise. "What exactly did my son say?"

Joffur pushed him back onto his seat. "This is not your affair, old man. It is Abjorn I accuse, not you."

Abjorn was in no mood for bullying, and knocking

Botni down had hardly satisfied that mood. If Tyrvi had
paid no attention to what Abjorn had told him, so much
the better. Joffur was large, but he was no swordsman.
But Abjorn would have to get him outside first, where
there would be room to move.

He got to his feet.

The Saracen was between them at once, the barrel of
al-kuhl left on the bench. "Warriors, please. This is no
place for quarreling. This house is for drinking and singing songs. If you have to fight, go outside."

Joffur glared at him. "Go away, thrall."

The Saracen's eyes narrowed. "I am no thrall. My
name is Gisl."

"You have no name here, thrall."

The Saracen lifted Joffur off his feet as easily as he had
lifted the Frisian. Joffur, however, kept himself from being carried to the door by grabbing the roof beams beside
his head. The roof creaked as Gisl tried to pull him free,
but the two men were equally matched. The Saracen let
Joffur go before the roof came down around their ears.

Joffur let go the beams. He landed heavily, and the
moment he did the Saracen tackled him. In the middle
of the hall the two men strained, arms locked, their feet
scuffing for advantage. Joffur used his greater height
and weight to try and force the Saracen to his knees. The
Saracen leaned left and right, hoping to throw the larger
man off balance. Neither budged. They stood still as a
pair of runestones, the rest of the hall just as motionless
around them.

The frieze broke. The Saracen gave beneath the giant. Falling backward, he pulled Joffur with him. They
rolled head over heels toward the door, and when they
stopped the Saracen was on top, his knees pinning Jof-

fur's arms. Two quick, stunning blows followed. Joffur's head snapped back at each, then the Saracen picked him up, lifted him over his head, and threw him out the door.

He looked back at the hall. Sigrun regarded him with open admiration. Abjorn seethed.

"Anyone else have a problem with drinking and singing songs?" the Saracen asked.

The door blew open behind him. Frame and lintel followed. An enormous bear, with eyes as bright as coals and strips of shredded clothing hanging from its shoulders, burst inside.

It roared. Canines sharp as daggers and twice as thick gleamed.

Apparently Joffur had not been lying.

Danes and Franks, Norse and Rus, Wends and Gotlanders all reached for their knives. The bear charged. The Saracen met it unarmed, throwing it the same way he had when it had been Joffur. The bear rolled down the hall with men jumping on it from either side. It shook them off as if they were fleas; they bounced off benches and walls. One of them hit the barrel of al-kuhl and knocked it to the floor. Leiknarr grabbed for it but missed, drink splashing his tunic and trousers. The barrel rolled toward the fire.

"Stop it!" the Saracen shouted. But, instead of the bear, he threw himself at the al-kuhl.

These southerners, Abjorn thought. Barely winter, and already they were afraid of the fire going out.

The barrel rolled into the flames. Like a sap-filled pine cone, it exploded. Mouths of flame clamped onto the beams, walls, and nearest men. The Saracen, who had dropped to the floor with his hands covering his head, jumped up and ran for the back as sparks caught in the dry turf of the roof. The hall went up like parchment in a bonfire.

Abjorn faced the bear. Small tufts of hair smoldered on its back and shoulders. He dodged its blows and plunged his knife into its ribcage. The bear grunted and pulled away as two more men stabbed it in the back. Abjorn was just barely able to hold onto his blade as he pulled it free.

The bear backed toward the door. Several men began hammering at the walls with their hands as they saw their escape was blocked. Several more faced the bear. It was every northerner's worst nightmare, to be trapped in a burning house. No chance of Valhalla, in that death. Odin only took those who died as warriors.

The bear charged again. The men stabbed and slashed at it, but what they really needed were swords. The bear brushed their weapons away. Blood spouted from its chest and arms, but none of the wounds were deep or fatal. Its small eyes blazed with rage.

Abjorn joined the attack; the bear knocked him down. He fell over a bench as its jaws crunched the head of the man beside him. He hacked at its flanks, but it was hard to do any real damage while lying on the floor.

Sigrun appeared, hovering in the air like a swan. Her hair unwound in pale, floating wings behind her. The bear ignored her. Smiling, she reached down for the man who had died. His spirit, ghostly and green, rose to meet her. Gathering it into her arms, she jerked to one side and disappeared in the dark like a bat.

Abjorn's heart filled. "A valkyrie," he whispered.

Jumping to his feet, he waved his blade. "Odin is with us!" he cried. "The Valkyries are here! The road to Valhalla is open!"

Leiknarr raced by, his body enveloped in flames. The bear snapped his neck with a blow. Botni staggered to his feet and began to shake. His mouth lengthened into a wolf's snout, and his ears grew. His cowl crawled over his head. Falling onto all fours, his jaws fastened on the leg of the man beside him.

The Saracen appeared from the back, his arms full of blankets. "If we hurry and smother the fire," he said, "we can deal with the berserkers after."

Abjorn ignored him. His heart blazed hotter than the al-kuhl or the hall.

The Saracen looked at him as if he were mad.

The wolf leaped, jaws gaping. Abjorn caught it in the chest with his knife. With strength greater than he had ever known, he held it on the blade before him. It squirmed like a spitted rabbit, all four legs clawing. Abjorn flicked it away and looked around for the Saracen, but the Saracen had disappeared. If he could only find him again his entrance into Valhalla would be assured.

Smoke swirled. Heat blistered. Knives and fangs thrust and bit. The Valkyries swept back and forth above it all, happy men in their arms. Leiknarr, the flesh burnt from his face but not the smile. The Rus, the stumps of his arms draped and dripping around Sigrun's neck. Botni, his great red tongue lolling.

With an ecstatic shout, Abjorn hacked his way through the flames. A man rushed at him out of the smoke. Abjorn chopped off the man's hand. The man bashed him with the stump. Abjorn ripped open his belly. Blood sheathed in yellow flames pooled across the floor.

He dropped his knife when his nails turned to claws. The blood on his teeth and tongue was sweet as honey and hotter than al-kuhl. He ripped and rent and tore at the men and beasts around him. They ripped and rent and tore at him in turn.

It was glorious. The skalds were right. Dying in battle was the finest thing a man could hope for. Teeth clamped onto the back of his neck. Breath hotter than fire burned his ear. His long claws mauled an eye from the muzzle in front of him. Other claws sliced his belly.

His heart poured out his life. He looked up into Sigrun's eyes. His blood stained her robe.

She smiled.

"Thanks for the help," Gisl said sarcastically.

"I have my own interests to look out for," the old man answered.

They surveyed the ruin of the longhouse. For the second time in as many days, the place had changed completely. Now it was a pile of charred wood and sod, smoke rising from the wreckage. The collapse of the roof had made sure no one survived.

"I never saw a group of men so eager to die."

Gisl kicked at the smoldering timbers as he spoke, looking for something. Hacked and blackened corpses caught at his feet and ankles. He, of course, looked no worse than he had two days before.

"You haven't lived through one of our winters," the old man said.

"Why did you let them do it? You could have stopped them at any time. You were the one who turned the big fellow into a bear."

"You have your curse, I have mine. And it's what they expect. Blood and honor is the stupidest code in the world. Someday they'll see the light and throw me over for someone better, perhaps that Galilean. But until then, they're mine. I need them."

One of the ravens flew up from the rubble with something white and bloody in its beak. An eye. The old man examined it with his one good one, then handed it back to the bird. The raven gulped its prize.

"You might try Beijing next," he said, regretting how quickly Gisl's sojourn in Hedeby had ended. The man might even have felt at home here. "The Chinese are even more civilized than the Moors. They already know how to distill, too, so that shouldn't be a problem."

Gisl bent to pick something up from the wreckage at his feet, frowned, and tossed it away.

"I have no control over where I go," he said without looking up.

"I'll put in a good word for you. In the meantime, good luck. You need it."

He offered Gisl his hand. Gisl ignored it. Instead, he gave a cry of delight as he found the stone he was looking for and picked it up. Snow and smoke swirled, then both he and the old man were gone.

THE EMPEROR'S NEW GOD

Jennifer Dunne

A small party approached from the shelter of the trees, their boot steps muffled by the fierce storm. Otto squinted, trying to make out the face of his friend, Peter. It had been years since they had last seen each other, during Otto's first trip to Italy to be crowned Holy Roman Emperor, but his godson's father could not have changed so much.

One of the men stepped forward. "Otto?"

It was no surprise his friend did not recognize him, disguised as he was in the costume of a junior member of the ambassadorial party. Only Peter's most trusted aide, John the Deacon, who had arranged the secret trip, knew Otto's real identity. And not even he knew the real reason for Otto's visit, believing instead that the emperor was here to conduct secret negotiations between the Holy Roman Empire and the Republic of Venice, while receiving inspiration from Venice's saintly relics.

Otto took a step forward and held out his arms.

"Peter." He could not make out his friend's face, but he recognized the voice.

They embraced, clapping each other on the back, and

giving the kiss of peace. Putting his lips to Otto's ear, the Doge of Venice muttered, "You are late. If you wish to see the monastery of San Zaccaria, you had better go there at once, so that you may be safely received before dawn within the walls of my palace."

Otto's heart leapt at the thought that finally, his destiny was almost at hand. Soon, he would be taking the first steps toward the greatness that was his due. He just had to fool everyone a little while longer.

"I understand. We will follow you back to San Marco. But pray, keep your lanterns shuttered and your oars muffled."

Peter grunted, his appreciation for Otto's desire for secrecy clearly not extending to standing in the pouring rain in the middle of the night. But he bent his head in acquiescence, and led his men back to their boat. John the Deacon helped Otto back onto their boat. Both boats slipped silently away from the dock, and into the lagoon, Otto gripped the rails at the front of his boat as if he could force it to move faster through the sheer power of his will.

The crossing to San Marco was accomplished safely and in silence. Soon, their boat was sliding up the canal behind the Doge's palace to his private dock. Peter offered to have one of his men guide Otto to the monastery, but Otto had memorized the way.

"See that my companions are taken inside and settled. I will make a private pilgrimage, and return to the palace before first light."

"A room has been prepared for you in the east tower. I will post a man by the door to guide you to it on your return. We will speak tomorrow."

A few of his companions made half-hearted offers to

accompany him, but Otto turned them all down, claiming a desire for solitary prayer and reflection. He had not chosen anyone for this journey that would actually be interested in making a pilgrimage of his own. They were far more interested in experiencing Venice's legendary luxuries, and happily left him to visit the monastery alone.

And he would visit the monastery tonight, since the Doge was bound to ask the abbot about the Emperor's visit. But first he had somewhere else to be. His destiny awaited.

No one else was braving the storm at this hour of the night, so Otto had no worries about being seen. The narrow lanes and alleys between Venetian buildings left no room for stealth. They also left little room for the rain water sluicing into the canals. His feet in their simple rope sandals were soon chilled to the bone. But he barely noticed.

He followed the directions he had memorized, turning left at the first intersection, then turning right when he reached a street large enough for four men to walk side by side. He stayed in the shadows of the buildings, more for the protection from the rain than for concealment. Soon, the street arched up and over a canal. *The river of wine.*

Otto smiled grimly. He could see the corner of the monastery in the distance, the oil lamps guttering in the wind.

He turned away, heading down the narrow path along the canal. He found what he was looking for at the next intersection: a narrow building, shutters closed against the driving rain, a sign swinging back and forth on its chains with each gust of wind. *The Golden Amphora.*

There should be trumpets, fanfare and spectacle; something to acknowledge that his glorious future was about to begin. The incessant patter of rain sounded nothing like the rolling thunder of drums or a cheering crowd, but it would have to do.

He opened the door and stepped inside.

He was struck immediately by the very ordinariness of the place. The bar itself was a simple L-shape, the top inlaid with marble slabs of all sizes and colors. The red-brown clay mouths of the amphorae poked through regularly placed holes in the bar, where the barkeep could easily dip a measure of whatever a patron required. Simple wooden stools were tucked neatly against the mosaic sides of the bar, depicting the gods pouring wine from a golden amphora to welcome a hero who had slain a lion.

Venice being a cosmopolitan city, there were also bottles along the wall behind the bar. Small tables were scattered throughout the rest of the room, for those who preferred to see the faces of those they drank with. Unsurprisingly, given the weather and the hour, the tables were empty.

Otto's heart plummeted, his chest filling with a cold far worse than the frigid water he'd walked through to get here. He was too late. This meeting had taken months to arrange; to find a way to slip away from his court and prowl the side streets of a foreign empire, without sparking a diplomatic disaster. He'd paid a heavy price for the secret knowledge that led him here, and had been warned that he could only visit once. Everything needed to be arranged perfectly. This tavern was the only place in the world where man and gods still mingled, and he'd been given a specific time and date to be here. He cursed the storm that had delayed him for crucial hours.

A giant of a man stepped out from behind a curtain. His curly black hair gave him a Greek look, but his braided beard added a barbarian cast to his features. His faintly accented Italian did nothing to clarify his origins. "How can I help you, traveler?"

"I was supposed to meet . . . someone."

The giant nodded, and waved toward the empty tables. "One can never predict how long it will take to defeat an army. Sit. I will bring you wine."

Otto's eyes widened at being ordered about by a mere barkeep, but he obediently sat. Did the man somehow suspect Otto was here to meet Mars? Perhaps he was a demigod himself, pretending to be a servant.

Otto wondered what his entourage would think if they knew that, far from praying devoutly at a Christian shrine, their Emperor was in a bar, consorting with a pagan god. He doubted the nobles would care, unless their shocked outrage could somehow elevate their standing among their peers. Even the bishops and priests could give the satyrs and sybarites a close race, although they would use his digression as an excuse to wring more money from his treasury. Piety was for the little people; Christianity, the goad to keep the serfs in line with promises of endless riches after death. The ancient religions understood that men needed rewards in this life. And Otto intended to be extremely well rewarded.

He quickly reviewed likely candidates for a god of wine. The barkeep was clearly a man, with no softening, so he wasn't Bacchus. He showed no sign of Priapus's eternal erection. Was he perhaps Liber? But, no, Liber was the height of a normal man.

His thoughts racing, Otto didn't see the barkeep dip a glass of wine from one of the amphorae. The man was suddenly at his table, wine glass extended. The Venetian glass caught the light, giving a subtle glow to the deep red wine within.

Otto accepted the wine and took a generous swig, determined to appear strong before the mysterious barkeep. It was no cheap watered wine, but a rich and flavorful wine blended with honey and a touch of pepper, warmed to ward off the chill of the night.

He sighed, and took another deep swallow. The warmth spread throughout his body, banishing the chill from his feet, and replacing the cold fear in his chest with radiant confidence. Doubts were for lesser men. With Mars's help, Otto would become Emperor of the World, as was his destiny. It was too bad that his mother had not lived long enough to see her son on the throne over Byzantium. In time, he would reclaim Rome's lost colonies in Africa, Egypt, Arabia, and Gaul. None would dare to compare him to his father and find him wanting.

Another curtained alcove caught his attention, as flashes of red and gold light bled out around the curtain. A man's muscled arm pushed the curtain aside, and a warrior clad in boiled leather and gold plate stepped into the wine bar. Far from ceremonial, his breast plate was thick with dust and flecked with blood. The god of war had come directly from a battlefield.

He paused to accept a glass of wine from the barkeep, a pale white with a slightly greenish tinge to it, then strode to Otto's table. Otto was puzzling over whether or not to stand—he outranked every man on Earth, including God's representative on Earth, the Pope—but Mars was a god in his own right.

Mars solved the puzzle by dropping onto the seat across from Otto, the stool groaning at the sudden increase in weight. His gaze flicked dismissively up and down.

"You don't look like an emperor." He sipped his wine, his eyes going soft with pleasure, and relaxed his militant posture.

"I am on a pilgrimage."

"A pilgrimage that includes sharing a glass of wine with Mars? Your God has grown generous with his followers."

Otto shrugged. He followed no one, although it would never do to admit as much. "The end days were upon us, and we were not called home to our Father's house. We must do what we can now with the Earthly world."

Mars smiled. "And what would you do with the world, that you seek my help?"

"Rule it, of course."

Mars laughed. "Of course. You are twenty years old, and have been emperor for seventeen of those years. How far has your empire expanded in those years? Oh, wait, it hasn't. In fact, you lost France."

Otto's face flamed. "France was lost when I was but an infant, with my mother and grandmother holding the throne for me. I commanded an army at the age of thirteen, restoring the northern borders and beating back the Wends."

"A noble battle, to be sure." Mars swirled his hand lazily in the air, and an image coalesced above the tabletop. With shock, Otto recognized himself at age thirteen, stalking around the fine pavilion that had been set up for him in the field. The image sharpened, and Otto could hear his own voice.

"*. . . power cannot be exercised in paltry campaigns in an empty country of miserable bogs against wretched Slavs.*"

Mars flicked his fingers, banishing the image. "You conquered an empty country of bogs, driving off an invading force of wretches. And it took you three years."

Otto clenched his fists, but knew better than to argue with a god. His own petulant words had damned him.

"At twenty, your father was called Augustus, Imperator, and Lord of the Universe. He held France, Italy, and Germany in his fist, and kept them against hardened warriors. His defeat of the Emir was a crushing blow to the Saracens." Mars took another sip of wine, then waved away Otto's father's glories as unimportant. "You are not unaccomplished. Your skill at learned debate has been praised throughout the empire. Even Apollo has taken note of you. Why do you beseech me?"

"Words will not conquer an empire. I need strength of arms. And as you have pointed out, that is not my natural skill. If I am to succeed in achieving my destiny, I must have help."

"What of the lance I gave your grandfather? The one that was enchanted to always give victory to he who holds it in battle?"

"The Holy Lance? Was a gift from you?" Suddenly, the first Otto's ability to unite all of Germany under his leadership became much easier to understand. "My father did not see fit to share the truth of it with a swaddling child. No doubt if he had lived, he would have told me of its power. I carry it for ceremonies of state, not into battle."

"Do so, and you shall triumph. On the field of battle, at least. Holding cities once you have conquered them ... is also not a natural skill of yours."

Otto forced his teeth to unclench. "The nobles who drove off the man I made Pope were dealt with. I executed Crescentius for his treason, and suitably punished his puppet antipope. I held Rome."

"That is why the people of Rome rose up against you not three months past?"

"I spoke to them. They understood their mistake, turned on their ringleaders and beat them nearly to death before throwing them at my feet and begging my forgiveness."

Mars shook his head. "Words, again. You are a man of words, not deeds. So where has this desire to be a warrior come from?"

Otto hesitated. He suspected Mars already knew the answer, and his reply was a test of some sort. It was a test he dared not lose, or his destiny would never become a reality.

"Last year, I ordered Charlemagne's crypt at Aix-la-Chapelle opened; the marble slabs covering his burial place removed. I asked for his guidance, and was given a vision of myself as the new Charlemagne. My empire will be greater even than his, encompassing Germany, Italy, and Byzantium."

"An empire you can only gain by the sword."

"Yes." He had been raised on tales of his father's glory, drinking in stories of someday ruling his mother's homeland in fulfillment of his father's promise, as well as the empire whose crown he had been given in his cradle. He would be greater than either his father or his grandfather before him. But the path to glory led through steel and blood.

Mars gulped the last of his wine, and placed the empty goblet on the table. The barkeep reappeared from the shadows and instantly removed it. No replacement was offered, as Mars leaned forward and braced his forearms on the tabletop, staring intently at Otto.

"I can give that to you. Your armies will be undefeated, and the cities you conquer docile as lambs after you leave them. What are you offering in return for my help?"

"What are you asking?"

Mars laughed. Otto fancied he heard the sound of clashing swords within. "That's not how it works. The gods can only make demands of those who are sworn to our service. Anyone else must petition our aid. You make an offer, and I accept or refuse. There is no negotiation."

No negotiation. Otto's stomach clenched painfully. Prior to their meeting, he'd mentally calculated all of the things he could offer to Mars, as well as rehearsed different strategies for reaching an agreement. He was, after all, highly skilled at philosophical debate, and had negotiated a fair share of treaties. He'd expected this to be a similar encounter.

Mars lifted a hand and summoned the barkeep. The giant returned with another glass of the pale green wine.

"Your ambrosia, exalted one."

Mars claimed the goblet and sipped from it. "You have until I finish my drink to decide."

Otto's thoughts raced. He knew what he could offer. But what did Mars want? Clearly the god wanted something, or he wouldn't have agreed to this meeting. Boredom and a predilection for interfering in human affairs didn't seem enough reason to obligate himself to an agreement with a mortal. If all he wanted was carnage and bloodshed, he didn't need to ally himself with Otto for the battles ahead. No, Mars seemed to want the Holy Roman Empire to be triumphant over Byzantium.

He considered their conversation, sifting through Mars's comments for clues. He'd made a point of questioning whether or not Otto's Christian God would share one of his followers with an ancient Roman god. And he'd focused on Otto's troubles holding the city of Rome.

Could the god have been echoing his own problems? The people of Rome had turned to the Christian God. In fact, the Pope, the representative of that God on Earth, lived in Rome. Did Mars want the city back? To have the people worshipping him and his brethren again?

But Otto could not demand that the people worship the pagan gods. His power was tied to the church's power. The German bishops did much of the work of holding the united factions of Germany together, while he was the Holy Roman Emperor only because he'd been crowned by the Pope. It didn't matter that he'd elevated the man to his position mere days before the coronation.

He glanced at the god, and saw with dismay that his glass was half empty. He was running out of time. He felt the reins of his destiny slipping through his hands.

But what if Otto could encourage the people to turn to Mars on their own? What would prompt the people of Rome to embrace the god of war instead of the Prince of Peace?

He would have to make an example of Rome. Show them that their prayers could not save them. And it was only fitting that they suffer for their disloyalty. Their rebelliousness had forced him to flee Rome. If not for his clever negotiation, he would have been forced to fight them just to get free of the palace where they had trapped him under siege. But it had still galled him to load his goods into wagons and depart the city under their watchful eyes, like a guest who had overstayed his welcome. He'd vowed that he would one day return in triumph.

With a single stroke, he could have his revenge and deliver a sacrifice worthy of purchasing Mars's aid. Once Rome was secure, he would go on to unite all the empires under his rule. Even the haughty Venetians would bow to him.

Mars swirled the last spoonful of liquid in the bottom of his glass, and lifted it to Otto in a challenging toast.

"This is my offer," Otto said, rushing to speak even as the half-formed plans were coalescing in his mind. "I will mount an attack on the city of Rome, the holy seat of Christianity. Those who survive will be sworn into my army of conquest, dedicated to your cause, and bringing the rest of the world to heel. They will learn that the only god who can protect them is the god of war, and the blood of our enemies will pour forth in sacrifice."

Otto held his breath as Mars drained the last ambrosia from his glass. He turned the goblet over and set it upside down on the table, the glass chiming as it struck the marble surface.

As the last echo of the chime faded, a golden disk appeared on the table. Otto could not read the upside-down Latin incised into the disk, but spotted his own name, Mars and Roma. Air filled his lungs. It was the terms of his offer. That must mean—

"I accept."

Flushed with triumph, Otto was in a daze as he visited the monastery of San Zacharia, although fortunately the monks misconstrued his befuddlement for religious rapture. He made his way back to the Doge's palace unseen, and changed into the garments of a mid-level court appointee for his presentation to the Doge the next morning as part of the diplomatic party. He congratulated himself on his cleverness, as none of the Venetian court save Peter and his aides knew that the humble man at the back of the party was really the Holy Roman Emperor. Knowing it was vital that no one suspect the true reason for his visit, he met in secret with the Doge as planned, and still put on his poor pilgrim's clothes to make his visits to the churches and monasteries that the members of his court thought he'd come for. After two days, he slipped back onto John's boat to return to the monastery at Pomposa where he'd supposedly been taking a health cure on the shores of Lake Comacchio.

Once back in Ravenna, Otto redoubled his ostentatious religious devotion, making barefoot pilgrimages, kneeling on stones until his knees bled, and allowing chosen courtiers to discover him wearing hair shirts beneath his court raiment. His devotion had always been at least as much pageantry as piety, but now he put on a show that no one would forget.

The people and religious leaders must have no cause to question his faith. They must never guess that he had made a deal with Mars.

He sent messages to his vassals, ordering them to send troops. First he would have his revenge on Rome, and then he would embark upon his destiny. But the wait was excruciating. His messengers had to travel over the Alps and throughout the length and breadth of Germany, summoning men from the fields where they labored.

But after all, why should he delay? He had the Holy Lance. He could not lose in battle. The troops he had at hand would be sufficient to retake Rome, and from that victory he would launch a campaign that would strike terror into the hearts of his enemies.

By June, his patience had worn completely through. Despite his advisors' warnings, he gathered those troops who had already arrived and led them to Rome.

His small army crested the hills surrounding the city, and he paused, struck as always by the city's beauty. The travertine buildings gleamed a warm white in the sun. There was the parkland where Roman gladiators had raced their chariots. There was the now empty Coliseum, open to the sky, whose seats would once again be filled with cheering throngs beneath graceful awnings of sailcloth when he returned in triumph from Byzantium. Towering columns and domes of cathedrals dotted the city, erasing all memory of the Romans' pagan temples.

He did not sound the charge.

Instead, he rode slowly back and forth across the hilltops, watching the shifting play of light and shadow on the city as the sun wheeled through the sky, and remembered the speech he had given only last January.

"Are you not my Romans, for whose sake I left my fatherland and friends? Whose fame I would have carried to the ends of the earth? I have preferred you to all others. ... However, I find it monstrous that my most faithful followers, in whose innocence I triumph, are mixed together with the evildoers."

How many of those glorious edifices would fall when he attacked? How many of those innocent people who were loyal to him would die in the bloodbath that followed? How could he start the conquest of his empire with the destruction of his own capital city? He would not become the next Charlemagne, he'd become the next Attila.

The problem was the size of his army. The people of Rome did not realize that his divine mandate ensured his victory, so would stand and fight against his troops. The resulting massacre would have no glory to it. It would not be a fitting sacrifice to Mars. There would be no cowed and obedient people, worshipping at the war god's altar, only piles of corpses.

No. He could not do it.

He summoned his captains to him. "We do not have enough men. We will ride back to Ravenna, and wait for the rest of the soldiers. When the full army is here in the fall, then I will return and crush Rome beneath my boot heel."

The captains shifted restlessly, and traded sidelong glances with each other, but raised no objections. A few mumbled agreement, while the rest knew better than to question the dictates of their Emperor. The only one he had to explain himself to was Mars, and he was confident that the god would understand his reasoning.

Otto turned and led the army back the way they had come, glancing over his shoulder to see the city of Rome disappearing behind the hills. A trick of the setting sun bathed the hills in blood.

He called for another fur cloak to protect him from the sudden chill that settled into his bones.

A soldier he didn't recognize rode up, his arms filled with heavy furs. Otto took a cloak, and swung it around his shoulders. It didn't help. The cold he felt emanated from within, and no amount of furs could keep it at bay. Still, he took the second fur as well.

"You retreated from the battle without firing so much as a single arrow," the soldier accused.

Otto lifted his head, shocked at the man's temerity. How dare he question—

Dimly, like a ghost, the image of Mars's features flickered over the soldier's face.

He stiffened, inwardly cursing the lack of time to prepare an eloquent and reasoned defense. He hated having to depend upon mere facts. "I did not bring enough men. Why waste their lives attacking now, when I will need them to attack Byzantium later? I will come back in the fall, with a full army, and show Rome the folly of her ways."

"There will never be enough men to give you the courage you lack. With my spear in hand, you could have taken Rome with only your standard bearer at your side." A golden disk appeared in Mars's hands, covered with deeply incised Latin words. The god snapped it in half, releasing a blinding spray of golden light. "You have broken our agreement. You will never stand on the far shores of Byzantium, knowing that it belongs to you. You turned your back on your own God, and the worship of a coward means nothing to me. You will not have the world. You will have nothing."

Mars rode off, waiting for neither response nor dismissal. Otto thought about calling him back, but he lacked the strength, instead huddling deep within his furs.

The world spun around him, and it was almost more than he could manage to keep his seat on his horse. His bones ached, as if a bevy of blacksmiths had tried to temper them on their anvils.

He had made a serious mistake. But if he could deliver Rome, perhaps Mars would relent and deliver Byzantium. That thought sustained him in the months that followed, when it seemed his very body was determined to betray him with weakness.

Finally, at the end of the year, all of his vassals' soldiers had arrived, and he was able to march on Rome with a force large enough to terrify them into submission. But he would never see the city.

He took shelter in the castle of Paterno, consumed by fever. His dear friend and former tutor, Pope Sylvester, came to comfort him, but his words of Christ's divine forgiveness meant nothing to Otto.

A soft summer breeze blew through the room, although the window was shuttered against the January cold. Golden sunlight seemed to stream from the ceiling, illuminating a patch of lush grass growing from the stone floor. A beautiful woman wearing silver armor stepped out of the light.

Otto struggled to sit up, but she placed a cool hand against his forehead, pressing him back onto the bed. Amazingly, no one else reacted to a woman being in his sickroom.

"They can neither see nor hear me, Otto. Only you."

"Who are you?" he whispered.

"You know who I am. Minerva."

"Goddess of learning." If he had the energy, he would have laughed. His heart had always belonged to the scholarly pursuits. After all he had done, trying to force himself to be a warrior, she was the one who had come to him.

"I am also the goddess of war." All gentleness faded from her expression. "You should have appealed to me instead of Mars."

"Have you come only to tell me what a fool I was?"

She shook her head, her features once again softening. "I cannot heal you from the curse of Mars's soul fire. But have no fear. You will be remembered. Not for your conquests, but for your mystery. A thousand years from now, scholars will still be arguing over the meaning of your secret visit to Venice, and what you hoped to accomplish."

"I failed. . . ."

"Only because you ended your studies too soon. If you are willing to learn another lesson, I will take you to drink of the river of forgetfulness, and be born in a new body. One born to poverty and squalor rather than an empire. If you can succeed there, you may yet achieve the glory you desire."

At least he wouldn't have to see his mother in the afterlife, and admit how he had failed her, or explain to the father he'd never known why the line of Ottonian emperors ended with him.

Struggling against the weight of his unresponsive body, Otto lifted his hand to Minerva.

Her fingers closed around his.

THE TALE THAT WAGGED THE DOG

Barbara Ashford

AS Michael, Rona, and I enter Gil's establishment, a familiar voice calls out, "Stop me if you've heard this one. A priest, a selkie, and a talking dog walk into a bothy...."

The fur on my neck instinctively bristles. Although I usually smile at Thomas' lame jokes, my transformation has rendered me understandably sensitive to those about talking dogs. Before I can concoct a clever retort, a tankard soars through the air. Still smiling, Thomas the Rhymer falls backwards off the bench, landing with an audible crunch of rushes.

Every head in the place swivels towards Gil. Slowly, he lowers the wooden cup he is wiping and leans on the trestle table, staring at the corner from whence the tankard was launched.

I think Wallace gives a half-shrug—all he can manage since he has yet to unearth the final quarter of his body from its unmarked resting place in Perth—but it's hard to tell. The peat fire smoldering in the center of the bothy lends a lovely aroma to the place but little light.

When Gil continues to stare, Wallace calls out, "Sorry."

Gil resumes his meticulous cleaning. The faeries flanking Thomas help him back onto the bench. Every head swivels towards Rona.

Although my companion is dressed in a sober kirtle and gown, there's no mistaking her otherworldly origins. Her face glows like the rising moon. Her linen kerchief merely accentuates the silky black hair that cascades down her back. And when that dark gaze rests upon you, you feel the warmth from toes to belly and your pintle grows hard as a stave.

Needless to say, she's quite popular with the largely male clientele at Gil's. Even Robert the Bruce stops picking at his scabs when she comes in.

It's a pretty good crowd for a Saturday. The usual mix of dead heroes, enchanted folk, and curious locals line the three trestle tables. The scent of roasting lamb emanates from the central fire pit, combining with a dizzying bouquet of peat smoke, wet wool, and stale sweat. My nostrils quiver with delight and my tongue flicks out to intercept the thin line of drool oozing down my muzzle.

Rona and I head towards our usual table, leaving Michael to linger before the stone tablet. Like all those who find their way to Gil's, Michael desires the magical elixir. So far, the only elixirs I've seen Gil serve are ale and whisky. However, Michael remains convinced that the small stone tablet hanging near the doorway holds clues and spends countless hours attempting to decipher the queer scratchings etched upon it.

When Wallace first pointed Michael out to me, I naturally hurried over to make his acquaintance. If the famed Wizard of the North could transform copper into silver, he might be equally adept in returning me to my natural form. I made it as far as "My name's

Tam Lin and the Queen of Faerie transformed me into a Border collie and I was wondering. . . ." Whereupon Michael launched into a tirade about his non-magical credentials—theologian, mathematician, philosopher, astrologist, confidant of Frederick II—and I politely excused myself.

Thomas is far easier to talk to, and I am especially eager to talk to him tonight. My hope that he has finally convinced the Queen to lift her curse far outweighs my pique over his taste in jokes.

As Rona and I approach, the faeries rise and make their way to another table, ostentatiously snubbing me. Thomas rises as well and bows to Rona. For all his eccentricities, he has retained the fine manners of a laird. Maybe that's why the Bitch Queen dotes on him no matter how many times he leaves her, while my desertion sent her into a rage.

As I leap onto the bench, Thomas suddenly bellows, "On the morrow, afore noon, shall blow the greatest wind ever heard in Scotland."

A hush descends. The last time Thomas uttered those prophetic words, Scotland's king died the following day.

Several things happen in rapid succession:

Robert the Bruce shakes his fist at Thomas, shouting, "You'll not prophesy the death of the last heir to the House of Bruce!"

Michael strides towards our table, shouting something about substance, potentiality and actuality.

William Wallace jumps to his feet. His head rolls across the rushes, shouting, "I'll give you a great wind!" His body rips out a tremendous fart.

Gil leans over the table to murmur something in Thomas' ear.

"Oh, dear," Thomas replies. "Well. That would explain. . . ." He waves his hand vaguely at the shades of Wallace and the Bruce, still gesticulating angrily from their respective corners. "Sorry. Sorry, everyone! Still a little flummoxed from Faerie. Starting to prophesy backwards like Merlin."

Wallace retrieves his head. I've always wondered how he manages to find it when his eyes are looking elsewhere, but being transformed into a dog and cursed to spend eternity in that form encourages one to accept the unexplainable.

Before I can ask whether the Bitch Queen has relented, Thomas whispers, "Forgive me for prying, Tam, but surely Janet cannot approve of a liaison with a selkie."

Knowing that Thomas' memory is always a bit hazy in the days following his return from the Otherworld, I remind him that my wife moved back to her father's hall seven years ago. This after clinging to me like a leech on that harrowing flight from Faerie, during which I was transformed into any number of horrible beasts as well as a vessel of burning iron.

"But after I threw you down the well, you were a man again," Janet remarked as she briskly packed up her belongings. "For a while."

"It's not my fault the royal bitch held a grudge."

"Maybe not. But you can't expect me to have carnal relations with a dog. It would be sinful. Besides which I don't much like you."

After all I'd been through. Even now, it galls me.

Thomas gestures for Rona to sit. She pays no attention, of course. Webbed fingers idly braiding a lock of hair, she stares east, her head cocked as she strains to hear the sea. She's always doing that. Even when I'm humping her leg. It's a bit off-putting.

I bark to attract her attention. Her gaze focuses on me. When I see tears forming in those dark eyes, I look away. She seats herself, sighing.

"Your lovely companion seems melancholy tonight," Thomas notes.

"Selkies are a melancholy lot."

"Only if someone steals their sealskins and they are trapped in human . . . ah."

There is much to recommend Thomas. Beautiful singing voice, beautiful ballads, beautiful manners, but definitely not the sharpest scythe in the shed. Another reason the Bitch Queen dotes on him.

I can't hold a tune or write one, and my manners are only so-so, but I was an incredibly handsome man. Faery or human, queen or serving wench, women couldn't get enough of me. Even now, I attract more than my share of feminine attention, although these days, it's generally from hounds and collies and the odd lapdog. Since Janet left, I've had most of the bitches betwixt Dryburgh and Galashiels. Rona takes little notice of my infidelities. Even when I recount them. Too busy sighing and staring east towards the sea.

The threatened tears now ooze down her flawless white cheeks. Each time Thomas dabs at one with his handkerchief, another spills over.

"You had to mention the skin."

"Sorry," Thomas mumbles, still trying to stem the flood. "Can't seem to do anything right tonight."

"I don't suppose you know where it is?"

Thomas' eyes widen. "You mean to say you lost it?"

"I didn't mean to!"

I don't mean to snap at him, either, but his appalled expression makes me feel nearly as guilty as Rona's tears.

A dozen times a sennight, I apologize. I tell her that I was overcome by her beauty when I saw her sunbathing naked on that boulder. I tell her that I was lonely. That I wanted to feel flesh under my tongue instead of fur. That I fully intended to return her skin after a bit of firkytoodling.

Back in my cottage, we firkied and toodled the day away. And the night. All right, so I didn't go back to the river the next day. Or the day after. It was raining fit to drown us. And Rona was having as much fun as I. Smiling and laughing and performing all manner of carnal acts that Janet wouldn't consider even when I was a man.

The morning after the storm, the River Tweed was in full spate. Took two days for the waters to recede. The alder I'd buried her sealskin under was gone, but I nosed around, digging under every branch and log and uprooted tree littering the riverbank.

Come to that, Rona bears some of the blame for swimming so far upriver. Imagine thinking Selkirk was a church for selkies. If she'd stayed at Berwick, none of this would have happened.

Now she's bound to me. Every morning, we walk the banks of the Tweed, searching for her skin. Every evening, we return empty-handed to my cottage. Every night, I have to listen to her weep.

Most women become ugly when they cry. Faces all scrunched up, noses dripping snot, eyes red-rimmed and swollen. Rona becomes more beautiful, dark eyes huge and liquid, pear-shaped breasts rising and falling with each sigh. And those sighs . . . so soft and tremulous that it's hard to choose whether to comfort her or tup her.

Sure enough, my pintle peeks out, pink and perfect. I merely lick her arm again; I can be as gallant as Thomas if I've a mind to. Then I notice two of the Kerr brothers drifting our way. Hard to say which ones; they're all big and bluff and red-haired.

My lips curl back in a snarl. A growl rumbles in my chest. My fur rises.

"There's no cause for that," one of them protests.

"Gentlemen."

Hearing the edge in Gil's voice, the Kerr brothers slink back to their table.

"Horny bastards," I mutter.

"You're no better."

I lower my tail, cringing. For a big man, Gil moves very quickly. One minute, he's wiping a cup. The next, he's towering over you, glowering. And since he's a good eight to ten feet tall (his height seems to vary according to his mood), the towering glower is quite effective.

He looks unusually tall at the moment, a sure indication he is displeased.

"I didn't do anything," I whine.

I'm forever whining and cringing around Gil. My canine aspects come to the fore when I'm nervous.

As Gil continues to glower, I belly forward on the trestle table, ears folded back.

"If it weren't for Rona, I'd ban you from my place."

I roll onto my side to expose my groin, the ultimate act of submission.

"Put your leg down and get back to your seat."

I edge backwards, quivering but relieved; the last time Gil reprimanded me, I'd pissed all over the table.

Gil turns to Rona and offers one of his rare smiles. Her face lights up as if he had proffered her sealskin instead.

"Evening, Rona. The usual?"

"Thankee, Gil."

It's been more than a sennight since she's spoken to me. The mere sound of that soft, husky voice encourages my pintle to reassert itself. Gil shoots me a dark look, and it quickly retreats.

"He couldn't possibly have seen," I grumble aloud.

"Seen what?" Thomas asks.

"Nothing. Thomas, did you ask the Queen about lifting the curse?"

Thomas grimaces. "She became very wroth. Thought she'd turn me into a dog as well."

"It's not fair. You're always leaving and she adores you."

"I always ask permission. You just bolted."

"Because I suspected the bitch meant to sacrifice me to Hell as a tithe!"

"Still, there are niceties to observe. Especially with faeries. You know how touchy they are."

I stare across the fire pit. The faeries are watching me, sniggering. Little beasts.

"Perhaps if you came back with me," Thomas suggests. "Begged her pardon. Humbled yourself."

"She'd likely turn me into a newt. No, it'll have to be the elixir."

Thomas strokes his beard and surveys me, doubt writ plain on his face.

"Maybe if *you* ask Gil," I suggest.

"Not after what happened last night. One of the Kerr boys made the mistake of asking for the elixir and Gil . . . ejected him."

"Threw him out, you mean?"

"I mean lifted him off the bench and hurled him through the doorway. I could hear his bones snap from here. Ah, wonderful!"

At first, I think he means the Kerr boy's snapping bones. Then I see Gil striding forward with two wooden plates in his hands.

He places the lamb chop before Thomas and the herring before Rona. I wag my tail, but he simply walks away.

Thomas—kind soul—slices off a piece of lamb for me and lays it on the table. Rona picks up the raw herring and rips the head off with her teeth. Her table manners are disgraceful. It is my only complaint about her. That and the endless weeping. And sighing. And staring seaward when I'm humping her leg.

Thomas' knife clatters onto the table. He stares intently at his plate.

"Meat a bit overdone for your taste?" Ever since I became a dog, I prefer mine rare.

His head comes up. He's wearing that glazed "I feel a prophecy coming on" expression. He shoves back the bench, nearly unseating me, and rises.

Another hush descends on the bothy.

"Look to the sacred tree, for in its branches shall the magical fleece be found."

A long silence greets this pronouncement. Then Wallace shouts, "That was Jason and the bloody Argonauts, you great nit!"

"Sorry! Sorry." Thomas shakes his head and resumes his seat. "What were you saying? Ah, yes. The elixir." He spears a chunk of lamb on the point of his knife. "Sorry, Tam. Don't see much chance of that happening."

The lamb halts midway to Thomas' mouth. He gasps. For the third time that evening, all conversation ceases.

Gil walks towards us. The rushes crackle with each slow step. He cradles a chalice in his hands, the glint of bronze barely visible between his thick fingers.

Around the trestle tables, mouths gape open like congregants about to receive the Host. My tail wags so violently that my hindquarters are jigging back and forth. I have to dig my claws into the wood to keep from tumbling off the bench.

I hear Thomas murmur, "I'm frightfully off tonight." No one else dares speak. It is so quiet I can hear Rona crunching herring bones.

My tongue lolls out as Gil draws nearer. I cannot suppress a soft "woof." The last time I will ever make that sound. Or walk on four legs. Or view the world from the level of a man's knees.

Gil halts in front of me. Then places the chalice before Rona.

A collective sigh eases around the bothy. I barely hear it over my anguished howl. Gil's eyes—the gray-green of the Tweed in spate—fix on me before returning to Rona.

My howl must have startled her. Concern etches two small grooves between her dark brows. She strokes my head, her hand gentle. Only then does she look at the chalice.

Fear of Gil is all that prevents me from leaping onto the table and plunging my muzzle into it. Rona's fingers trace the patterns on the shallow bronze bowl, the short, curving neck, the conical base. A hesitant smile curves her lips. She glances up at Gil, then leans forward to sniff the brew. Her snub nose wrinkles.

"Thankee, Gil. 'Tis a lovely cup. But I'm not much for strong drink."

The incredulous gasps are still drifting skyward when she pushes the chalice towards me.

"But, my dear," Thomas says. "You don't understand. One sip of that elixir and your most heartfelt wish—"

He breaks off as I turn on him, snarling.

I dare a glance at Gil. He is watching Rona.

"Are you sure?" he asks.

She nods and rips off a piece of the fishtail.

Gils turns to me and I cringe, waiting for him to snatch the cup away. Instead, he shrugs.

I cannot believe it. I've talked of little else for the last few months except the possibility of acquiring the elixir. Granted, Rona pays scant attention to my ramblings, her mind consumed by her desire to find her sealskin. But when she is offered the drink that would ensure that, she foolishly passes it to me.

I laugh aloud at the irony. At my incredible good fortune. I forgive Rona for her inattention when I am humping her leg and vow that, when I am restored to my true form, I will give her the best swiving man ever gave woman.

My laughter captures her attention. She ruffles my fur affectionately. Her smile—rarer even than Gil's— fills me with warmth.

And shame.

The warmth settles in my groin. The shame niggles at my mind. I recall one of Janet's annoying maxims: "If you thought more with your head and less with your cock, you'd be a better man."

Which is nonsense. I am like any other man, only more so.

Can I fulfill Rona's heartfelt desire without sacrificing mine? If I make two requests, I'm liable to get neither.

In addition to being incredibly handsome, I am also exceptionally clever. If I choose the words carefully, I might succeed in gratifying the desires of both our hearts.

I form sentences in my mind, adjust the phrasing, discard a few words and choose others. Wallace and the Bruce leave their corners and edge closer. Wallace raises his head between his hands for a better view.

The tension in the bothy is palpable. So is my arousal.

I concentrate hard, willing my errant pintle into submission. But the aroma from the chalice maddens me. Sweet honey and tangy beer. Strange spices that tickle my nostrils. Saliva fills my mouth. Images of my manly self fill my brain.

I hastily mutter, "I wish to make Rona happy by becoming a man," then scramble onto the trestle table, thrust my muzzle into the bowl, and frantically lap up the contents.

My mouth burns. My eyes water. But I cannot stem my frenzy. No Israelite wandering the desert had a greater thirst, no man mounting a maid a greater desire. My tongue plunders the dregs, and I shudder at their bitterness.

I'm not sure what to expect. Skin stretching uncomfortably? Bones creaking as they elongate? Instead, there is only a sickening wave of dizziness. I snap my jaws shut lest I vomit up the elixir. When the chalice melts into a puddle, I squeeze my eyes shut as well.

Something tickles my nose, and I sneeze. I open my watering eyes to discover a dark veil obscuring my vision. At first, I think it is Rona's hair, but when I shake my head, the veil moves. Only then do I realize that it is my hair, my thick, glorious waterfall of black. Between the wavy locks, I see two hands. Small, perfect, wonderful hands, fingers splayed atop the wood of the trestle table.

I raise those trembling fingers to my face and discover the noble brow of legend. The long, feathery lashes that made women sigh. The boyishly smooth cheeks Janet stroked. The full lips that the Queen of Faerie called two pink rosebuds. The determined chin that lends strength to a visage that might otherwise be too beautiful for a man.

The laughter that fills the bothy imbues me with love for my gracious comrades who can set aside their disappointment at being denied the elixir to share my delight.

I shake the hair out of my eyes. Wipe away the tears obscuring my vision.

That's when I see the fur.

Thick doggie fur, patched with black and white, covering my arms, my chest, my belly. I fall back on my haunches, only to discover they are haunches still, my legs short and crooked as a dog's and ending in two large paws. Worst of all is the fast-wilting pintle that peeks out of my furry groin. It is still pink and perfect, but smaller than my thumb.

My screams and curses fail to drown out the laughter. Thomas' face betrays sympathy. Rona's is streaked with tears. Gil's is expressionless.

"I wanted to become a man and you've turned me into a monster!"

"Becoming a man is harder for some than for others," Gil replies.

Rona's gaze sweeps the bothy, and the laughter subsides. She pushes back the bench and rises, then holds out her hand to me.

"Come, Tam. Let's go home."

I scramble off the table, claws scrabbling on wood, and land on my hands and paws. Rona has to help me rise. Even then, my crooked legs prevent me from walking out like a man. I have to totter, bent over, my gaze helplessly directed towards the nub of my once-proud pintle.

How Janet would crow.

I spend the Lord's Day alternately lamenting my fate and banishing all thoughts of it with the whisky jug. Occasionally, I remember to pray.

The following morning, Rona kneels before the wooden chest and begins extracting articles of clothing. The moths have feasted on my woolen hose, and the linen braies hang in rotted shreds, but the fine lawn shirt and doeskin tunic presented to me by the Queen look as if I had tucked them away yesterday. With a sigh, Rona pulls out her spare chemise and fetches her sewing kit.

At midday, she holds up the loose-fitting braies for my inspection. In spite of my black despair, I have to admire her neat stitches.

I slip the braies on and secure them with my belt, another gift from the Queen. There are three gaps among the gems studding its length; likely, I'll have to wrest another free in order to purchase more garments to cover my shame.

"I'll go to the Clothmarket on the morrow," Rona says as if reading my mind. "But now, we must go to the river."

I wipe my streaming nose and nod. It is the least I can do in return for her kindness.

Our cottage is half a day's walk from the nearest town, but I wait for Rona to wave me out the door lest some wayfarer or shepherd glimpse me in my newly monstrous condition. The isolation can be depressing, but it serves me well during the regular invasions of the English and shields me from the notice of the ecclesiastical authorities that undoubtedly would have ordered a talking dog strangled and burned at the stake.

After years guarding the dark pinewoods of Carterhaugh, the open meadow around my cottage has always provided relief to eyes and spirit alike. Today, consumed by my misfortunes, the scarlet poppies and yellow buttercups seem gruesomely cheerful. Thistle stands knee high among the browning grass; I must swing my head from side to side to avoid scratching my nose.

The languid air trembles with the hum of bees and the trills of pipits. Garbed in clothing and fur, I am wretchedly hot and heave a grateful sigh when we enter the small woodland. All too soon, the path emerges above the Tweed, a vista I can only enjoy by twisting my neck up and sideways.

I hobble down to the river, rip off my clothing, and plunge into the cool water. I dare not linger long; the Tweed is a popular fishing spot. As I reluctantly don my garments, I watch Rona scouring the riverbank. I know I should join her, but my body aches from its unnatural contortions.

I scramble up the bank and rest against the trunk of a towering beech tree. The stump of my tail makes the position uncomfortable and I must fling myself flat and stuff my tunic beneath my rump to achieve a modicum of ease.

Late afternoon sunlight makes the leaves sparkle like

the emeralds adorning my belt. The spreading branches carve out a mosaic of green, brown, and gold. The ever-shifting patterns lull me into drowsiness. I close my eyes and pray that the elixir stole my immortality along with any form recognizable to God. To live forever as a dog is curse enough; to spend eternity as a monster would be unbearable.

A jay screeches, startling me into wakefulness. It pecks at a misshapen squirrel's nest in the notch of the tree. Fragments of dead leaves drift onto me, and I shout irritably to drive the bird off. As I sweep the detritus away, my fingers brush something soft.

I bring my hand close to my face and examine the tiny piece of fur. My mind refuses to believe what my fingers and eyes tell me.

"Oh, Thomas!" I cry.

He might have gotten the tree wrong, but the rest of his prophecy was accurate. I can only shake my head at the foolishness of searching the riverbank when the waters had raged high enough to flood the countryside for a mile.

I open my mouth to call out to Rona, then close it again.

If I were the young man I should be, I could easily scramble up the ladder of branches. In my present form, I must leap skyward, hands desperately scrabbling for the lowest branch while my back screams in protest. Twice I fall to the ground, jarring the breath from my body. The third time, my fingers close on the branch.

I hang there, feet helplessly churning the air, vision failing along with my strength. I pray to God and the Blessed Virgin. To Margaret and Andrew and Columba, patron saints of Scotland. To Francis of Assisi, patron

saint of animals. To Giles, patron saint of beggars and
cripples. To Jude, patron saint of impossible causes. To
Christopher who bore Our Lord across a river. I cannot
remember the name of any saint who climbed trees.

I swing my feet to the side and rake the trunk of the
tree with my claws. They grip, hold. I dig the claws of my
left foot free, swing my leg over the branch, and leverage
myself up until I am straddling it.

My bollocks ache for all the wrong reasons.

By this slow and arduous method, I finally come close
enough to seize the dappled sealskin. I drape it around
my neck and sink back upon my perch. It seems impossible that I am a mere fifteen feet above the earth. Surely,
my exertions must have taken me to the very gates of
Heaven.

I hear a splash. Through the branches, I spy Rona's
head bobbing above the water. A salmon flops between
her jaws. She slowly emerges, the lush curves of her body
plainly visible beneath her chemise. Incredibly, given my
recent ordeal, my pintle stiffens.

She cannot see me. She cannot know that I have
found her treasure. It would be easy to leave it in the
notch. Or find a more accessible hiding place.

Why should she get her wish when mine was denied?
Why shouldn't she remain with me, a lover to warm
my nights, a companion to share my days? What other
woman would have me now? Even the friendly bitches
that guard the sheep will turn up their noses at me.

Rona tosses the fish onto a rock and climbs the bank.
No time now to clamber down. I can only shrink back
against the trunk, hoping to remain hidden.

She pauses when she reaches the tree, searching the
landscape.

"Tam?"

She cups her long fingers around her mouth.

"Tam?"

She sucks at her thumb like a child. A third time, she calls.

"Tam! Are you hurt?"

It would have been kinder had she stabbed me through the heart.

I stare down at her for a long moment, memorizing the sheen of her wet hair, the contours of her sweet, plump face, the worry in her sad eyes.

Then I brandish her sealskin and call out, "I'm up here!"

Our farewell is tender and tearful. She is generous enough to allow me to mount her. It frets me that my stubby pintle offers her so little pleasure, but I make up for this by employing my fingers and mouth to better effect.

We wait until dusk to make our way back to the river, lest anyone observe her transformation. Even I am not permitted to watch. She ducks behind a boulder near the shoreline and emerges a few moments later. Only her eyes are the same, huge and dark and liquid. I kiss her whiskery snout and stroke her head, hoping to prolong the moment, but she trembles with the urgency to begin her voyage.

I do not begrudge Rona her happiness. If I'm honest—and I rarely am—she deserves it. She is a good-hearted creature and I . . . I am a rogue. A once-handsome and oft-times clever rogue, but a rogue nonetheless. Little wonder after spending my formative years among faeries. But it was I and I alone who demanded the payment of a maidenhead from every virgin passing through Carterhaugh forest. None of them complained—Janet surrendered hers with alacrity—but I could have asked for a kiss. Or a rose. Or a lamb chop.

Rona looks back only once. Her deep bark echoes across the water. Then she turns eastward and glides effortlessly away, a dark form slipping through the moon-streaked silver of the river.

I stand on the shore long after she has vanished. Then I turn homeward. The sight of my dark cottage is so depressing that I keep walking. The ache in my back subsides a bit. The ache in my bollocks persists. As does the less familiar one in the general vicinity of my heart.

As I walk into Gil's, a familiar voice cries out, "Stop me if you've heard this one! A man walks into a bothy. . . ."

Every head in the place swivels towards me. Overcome by a wave of dizziness, I lean against the door-frame until it passes.

The faeries brush past, ostentatiously gaping. Conscious of their gazes, I straighten, wincing with the effort. I walk unsteadily towards Thomas, who leaps to his feet and embraces me. I wonder why he is crying. Perhaps he misses Rona, too. Then I realize that, although I must look up into his face, I no longer have to twist my neck to do so.

I run my hands over my hips, my thighs, my knees, marveling at the graceful contours, the rippling muscles, the long, straight, beautiful bones cracking with gleeful abandon. I long to race out of the bothy, to race across the grasslands, to race all the way to the sea and cry, "Look, Rona! I am becoming a man!"

But of course, she knew that when I held up her sealskin.

I ease myself onto the bench, mindful of my bruised bollocks. Shielded by the table, I surreptitiously examine myself. My left foot is still a paw. So is the right. Fur still swaddles my body. And when I slip my hand into my braies, my pintle feels as small as ever. But the fur feels a bit sparser. Coarser, too. Like pubic hair. This is encouraging.

Gil wanders over, a wooden cup in his hand. I meet his gaze without cringing.

"Evening, Tam."

"Evening, Gil."

"Where's Rona?"

"Nearing Kelso, I expect."

"Nice night for a swim." Gil places the cup of beer before me. "On the house."

I clear my throat. "Any idea how long this process will take?"

Gil shrugs. "Becoming a man takes longer for some than for others."

Thomas saves me from a precipitous descent into gloom by urging me to share the tale of my adventure. I describe the long days digging under logs and tree roots, nosing through shrubbery, peering into the low-hanging branches of saplings before finally discovering the sealskin hanging high in the branches of the beech.

Enthusiastic cheers greet the conclusion of my tale. As they subside, Thomas calls out, "Little wonder it took so long to find what you were seeking, Tam." He pauses dramatically and surveys the room. "You were barking up the wrong tree!"

There is a general groan. A few curses. Gil heaves the sort of enormous sigh only an immortal can heave.

Wallace calls out, "Gil? You mind?"

When Gil shrugs, I seize Thomas' arm and drag him under the table. We lie there, giggling, while tankards and cups clatter onto the tabletop like hailstones.

"I shall write a song," Thomas shouts over the din. "'The Ballad of Tam Lin: Part Two.' Or something."

I hope he will leave out the part about my tiny pintle. I hope Rona will make it safely to the sea. I hope I will not have to live like a saint in order to become a man.

When you come right down to it, every man is a bit of a dog. And I am just like other men. Only more so.

SAKE AND OTHER SPIRITS

Maria V. Snyder

THE paper lanterns swung as cold air gusted from the open door. A group of traders bundled in furs hurried into the sake-house. Flakes of snow swirled around them. Azami noted the lack of excited chatter and boisterous calls to Gilga-san, the owner of the establishment. Concerned, she stuffed her bar rag into her kimono and helped the men remove their heavy coats and leather boots.

She caught Saburo's gaze. Usually so quick with his smile, his lips were pressed tight. His movements were stiff with tension as he shrugged off his fur. His fellow traders kept their somber expressions as they ordered sake and shabu stew.

"What happened?" Azami asked Saburo in a whisper.

"Two traders have died and Toshi's caravan is missing. I'll tell you more later," he said as he joined the men around a low table, dropping onto a cushion as if defeated.

Gilga-san, always alert to the mood of his customers, crossed the room with a seasoned fighter's grace. He managed to fold his tall body into an open space at the table. Even sitting he towered over the traders.

As she served bowls of steaming stew and cups of sake, Azami heard snippets of the traders' conversation.

". . . white as snow, not a drop of blood . . ."

"Disappeared for days, then . . ."

". . . on the western bank . . ."

". . . Toshi and four others . . . gone . . ."

Each word caused her greater alarm. Besides being horrified for the men and their families, these strange happenings might bring the samurai to town. And if they came, Azami would need to flee.

When the night grew late and only a few customers remained, Gilga-san assisted in the clean up despite her protests.

"This is what you pay me for," she said. "Go and entertain your guests."

Gilga-san enjoyed regaling his customers with stories that put the best Rakugo to shame. But tonight he seemed preoccupied, and his gray-green eyes peered through her. "Not tonight. No one is in the mood for frivolous stories."

"Is it because of the traders who died and the missing men?"

"Yes. The first two disappeared three days ago from Yukio's caravan while they traveled around Lake Biwa. A fisherman found their bodies today, washed up on shore."

"Drowned?"

"Hard to tell. Their lungs were full of water and their throats were shredded."

Azami's hand went to her neck as she glanced at Saburo. Since the snows had closed the mountain passes, his caravan also passed the lake. He remained at the table with three others. The rest had gone home.

"Murder?" she asked.

"Perhaps."

"The other five?"

"Toshi's caravan was due back this afternoon."

"That's terrible. Their families must be upset."

"They are. You should keep your kaiken close at hand when you leave tonight," Gilga-san said.

She jerked in surprise. No one knew about her dagger. Or so she thought.

He shot her a slightly amused smile. "We've been working together for over a year."

A year? Already? She had taken the job in his sake-house to earn enough money to leave Hokuga. Azami needed to increase the distance between her and her former life. The small fishing village of Hokuga had just been a temporary stop. Except Gilga-san treated her as an equal, and his bookkeeping had been an utter mess until she had taken it over. Then there was Saburo with his kind heart, good intentions, and sweet smile.

As if he could read her thoughts, Gilga-san said, "Saburo won't let you go home tonight unaccompanied. But he has no fighting skills."

Azami searched his expression. Most men would forbid her to carry a weapon. Did he suspect her former identity? He must, otherwise he would send along another protector who could defend them both.

Aware of her assessment, he waited. His foreignness used to unnerve her. With his oval eyes, black curly hair, pale skin and muscular build, he stood out among the locals who were mostly thin with straight black hair, olive-colored skin and brown slanted eyes. Like her.

She glanced away, stacking clean cups under the bar. "Why didn't you mention my kaiken before?"

He gestured to the room. "Men inebriated by sake plus a beautiful serving girl equals trouble."

She snorted. "You can handle trouble."

"But I can't protect you when you leave here."

Gilga-san lived upstairs and had never been seen outside the building. Azami stifled the desire to question him. He hadn't pried into her past so she would respect his privacy as well.

Saburo, on the other hand, had been curious. She had told him a fire killed her family and she wished to start a new life someplace else. As Gilga-san had predicted, Saburo insisted on walking her the few short blocks to the room she had rented. They bundled in heavy coats before muscling their way through the icy wind. No others walked the streets of Hokuga, which was odd, considering the town was a popular stop-over for caravans traveling to the western sea ports.

"Until the criminals are caught, you shouldn't be out on your own," Saburo said.

"Did you know the men who died?" she asked.

"Only in passing. Do not worry." He took her hand in his. "I will protect you."

She kept her tongue as frustration boiled. Years of tradition could not be undone by one outburst. Women were wives and mothers. They were protected and cared for. As Saburo talked of other topics, Azami realized if she truly desired independence she would need to disguise herself as a man.

It was a prospect she had toyed with this past year, but it galled her to no end. She had been taught how to fight and defend herself. Yet her skills could only be used to serve another—her future husband. To keep his house and children safe when he was away from home.

Azami hated the need to be connected to a man—a father or a husband—in order to be accepted as a member of their society. Women without a family had no rights. They were frequently arrested and sent to be yūjo in the walled pleasure cities.

But she didn't hate men. In fact, some, like Saburo, treated her almost as an independent person. He also didn't act stoic and emotionless, mimicking a samurai. She wished she could spend more time with him.

Wished she could stay in Hokuga.

Wished to no longer be afraid.

Two days later, the five missing men surfaced in Lake Biwa. Their bloodless corpses and shredded throats matched the first victims. To add to the general panic, Saburo's caravan had been attacked in broad daylight. A few traders had been injured and others taken, but no one who came into the sake-house could name them.

When she heard the news, her chest felt as if she'd been skewered by a katana. Time slowed and each breath she pulled hurt.

Azami kept busy, serving stew and sake to customers. The hushed conversations had turned from speculation of robbers and murders to the belief that a malevolent water spirit had taken up residence in the lake.

". . . greenish-yellow skin like seaweed . . ."

". . . scales and webbed toes . . ."

". . . misshapen head . . ."

". . . small, like a child but stronger than a sumo . . ."

". . . kappa . . ."

This last comment stopped Azami. Did they really believe a kappa haunted the lake? Gilga-san had told tales about the creature before. She glanced at the far corner of the sake-house. Gilga-san had drawn the screens around his biggest table. The town leaders had assembled to discuss the situation.

She fretted about Saburo until he strode through the door late into the evening. He sported a deep gash and a nasty bump on his forehead.

The tightness in her heart eased and she rushed to him in relief. She remembered her place, stopping short and stifling the desire to crush him to her. Instead she bowed politely and took his coat. They locked gazes for a moment.

Near closing-time, Gilga-san gestured for Azami to follow him. He pushed open the screen and offered to bring the leaders fresh food. They declined.

"Have you made a decision?" Gilga-san asked.

"We will appeal to the daimyo and request help from his samurai," Moyama, the oldest and therefore wisest man of Hokuga, said. "We cannot fight a kappa."

"If a water vampire does prey on your shores, then all you need to do is—"

"What do you know of fighting a kappa?" Moyama asked, but he didn't wait for a reply. "You're gaijin. And too afraid to leave your sake-house. Let the samurai deal with it."

Gilga-san bowed to the men and retreated. Azami collected the used stoneware and carried them to the kitchen to wash. Once again, Gilga-san helped her, but his sour mood and frequent outbursts about the stubbornly traditional locals made her wish he had chosen to brood in his office.

"How long until the samurai arrive?" she asked him.

"Three days at most."

Azami had to leave Hokuga. The only way to avoid

the incoming samurai would be to head west—past the water vampire. If it existed. Yet Saburo and the survivors of the attack had been convinced a kappa haunted the lake. Azami couldn't risk leaving now. That was the reason she clung to, and not because of her reaction to seeing Saburo alive. She would endeavor to blend in and hope the samurai wouldn't recognize her. They shouldn't as they lived in another district than her hometown.

Despite his injuries, Saburo walked her to the inn that night. Azami's kimono flapped in the cold wind. The night sky sparkled and a three-quarters moon illuminated Hokuga's wooden buildings. The weathered structures huddled together like lost children.

When they neared the Ryokan, Saburo paused. "Azami, I. . . ." He played with the toggles on his coat. "The attack made me worry about the future. I'd always assumed I had more time."

He turned to face her, taking her hands and pulling her close. Her heart thumped against her chest.

Saburo's intense gaze met hers. "Today I learned the future could be gone without warning. Time has become precious and I do not wish to waste it. Will you do me the honor of becoming my wife?"

She had known he cared for her, but respectable traders didn't marry kojis. Or liars either. They married the daughters of other traders. These thoughts weren't helping her sort out her chaotic feelings, but they gave her a place to start. "Your family—"

"Already approved."

"But I—"

"Not anymore. Gilga-san has offered a dowry for you."

Shock silenced her. Then fury at her boss's presumption warred with affection for the meddling man. She pushed those emotions away. Marriage had been the reason she ran away in the first place. Granted it was a different type of union, but still.

"I would wish to continue my work for Gilga-san," she said.

"You won't need to. I will provide—"

"For me, I know. I love you, Saburo. I do. But I cannot be a traditional wife."

He stiffened as if she'd slapped him and dropped her hands. "You'd rather be a serving girl than a respectable member of this community?" His harsh tone cut through her.

"I'd like—"

"Do not say another word. I will inform Gilga-san his offer was rejected." He strode away.

The desire to run after him and explain pulsed in her chest. However if she told him the truth, he would no doubt report her to the daimyo, his honesty another admirable quality. Deep down, she'd always known nothing could come of their relationship. But it had been nice to delude herself for a little while.

The samurai's' arrival injected hope back into the terrified townspeople. The sake-house filled with relieved traders, fishermen, farmers and a company of samurai. Saburo wasn't among the customers. No surprise.

"The boy's an idiot," was Gilga-san's only comment to her regarding the marriage proposal and he ignored her questions about the dowry.

Azami wove her way through the crowded tables, but kept clear of the warriors. Gilga-san waited on them. They livened the mood with their boisterous laughter and confident manner. And the best part was, she didn't recognize any of them.

But they lingered until the other customers had gone. Gilga-san told her to go home; he could handle a dozen men. Before she left, the door swung open and the rest of the samurais entered. Azami returned to the kitchen with dread pushing up her throat. They were the warrior elite and by law the sake-house would remain open until they chose to leave.

Thirty men gathered. They kept her and Gilga-san busy with orders. Their conversation focused on the village's rumors and the survivors' stories, comparing information to create a plan of attack.

Gilga-san approached the leader. He bowed slightly and introduced himself. The men shook hands.

"May I offer a suggestion on killing this kappa?" he asked.

Azami suspected he was being polite for her. This was his place and if he wished to speak his opinion, he could.

Amusement quirked at the samurai's lips, but he invited Gilga-san to join them.

"The water vampire is strong and quick. Before engaging him, I suggest you show him the proper respect and bow to him. The lower the better."

Laughter rippled through the men.

"We do not honor a malevolent spirit," the leader said.

"In this particular case, it is vital that you do."

The leader scoffed. "Ridiculous advice, gaijin. Samurais do not bow to evil."

"Then you will die." Gilga-san walked away as another wave of mirth erupted.

Azami hurried after him. In the kitchen she asked, "Will they succeed?"

"No."

"How do you know?"

"These things are not limited to the waters of Nihon."

"Can it be killed?"

"No, but it can be . . . reasoned with."

"You need to tell the samurai."

"I tried. Twice."

Her stomach twisted with fear. "Try again."

"They will not listen to me. I'm gaijin."

Late into the night, the samurai meeting finally ended. As the warriors filed out, Gilga-san asked his chef to accompany Azami back to her room. The pre-dawn silence chilled her more than the air. The wind had died. An ill omen.

Azami thanked the chef and entered the quiet inn, surprising since the samurais filled every room except hers. Too bad they didn't pay for their lodging or their meals. Then again, they had come to help. And if she had thought about it beforehand, she should have spent the night in the sake-house. Now who was the idiot?

She crept up the stairs, slipped into her room and shut the door without incident. The floor creaked behind her. She spun, pulling her kaiken.

A dark shape stood near her window.

Brandishing her weapon, she said, "Get out or I'll make the kappa seem kind."

He chuckled. "Well said, Runaway."

Caught. Her insides turned to stone. No one to blame but her own fear.

"Did you really think we wouldn't notice you? A beautiful koji? Our brothers in the north had sent us a message months ago to keep an eye out for you. We will return you to your proper home when our business with the kappa is finished."

She stepped into a fighting stance and held her weapon close. "No."

With a ring of metal, he drew his katana. The sharp blade reflected the weak moonlight. "Do you think you can refuse me?"

If she had her naginata, her odds of beating him would be much higher. The long pole and curved blade would keep his katana from reaching her.

"No." She returned her dagger to her belt. Azami had been forced to train in tantojutsu, the skill of the knife. The intended wife of a samurai needed to protect his home and children from his enemies. Educated as well, she'd been taught how to run a household and, in the process, how to think for herself. Unfortunate since she realized she had no desire to become a samurai's wife. To be, in essence, owned by another.

The samurai pointed to the floor with his katana. "You will remain here. There will be a guard at your door." Confident she would obey, he didn't wait for a reply. He left and ordered a colleague to stand watch.

No need to confiscate her weapon. She had earned the right to carry it, and it was useless against a skilled warrior. Sitting on the edge of her bed, she considered her options. Azami had prepared for an escape, but her plans hadn't included an evil spirit. She would bide her time. For now.

The next morning the warriors talked and laughed as if they faced a kappa every day. When they left to hunt it down, Azami didn't waste a moment. She pulled a box from under the bed. Emergency escape supplies had been packed inside.

She changed into the loose pants and tunic that the local fishermen wore, tucked her kaiken into the belt, and wrapped her hair in a tight bun. Donning a fur hat, she grabbed a heavy coat.

The inn's owner had been asked to provide a guard outside her door. However, she didn't plan to use it.

Taking the rope from the box, she secured one end to the sturdy bed frame and tossed the other out the window. Azami removed the last item from the box—a satchel already filled with all she would need on the road. She dropped the bag and coat out the window. They landed with a soft thud.

Not waiting to see if the guard noticed the noise, she climbed out the window sill and wrapped her legs around the rope, sliding to the ground. She collected her belongings and ran to Gilga-san's sake-house.

Slipping in through the back entrance, Azami surprised the chef, who ordered her to leave. Gilga-san, though, recognized her right away. He brought her to his office and closed the door.

Exotic antiques and strange metallic objects filled the shelves of the room. Keys of all shapes, sizes, and metals—gold, silver, iron—littered every surface.

As she perched on the edge of the chair facing his desk, Azami marveled. The room shouldn't be big enough to hold the massive collection, yet it did.

Gilga-san half-sat on the edge of his desk. He tugged his braided beard while she explained her predicament.

When she finished, he rested a hand on her arm. "I can hide you. You do not need to leave."

His offer touched her, but the risk was too great.

"This town is too small. Even disguised as a man, they would find me. You would be arrested."

He laughed. "I'd like to see them try."

"No. You've been so kind to me, I won't endanger you."

"But what about that kappa? I doubt the samurai killed it today."

Icy fingers of fear stroked her back, but she considered the alternative. "I would rather lose my life than my freedom."

Gilga-san sobered and stared at the red clay tablet that hung on the wall opposite his desk. Pictures had been scratched on it and it appeared as if someone had used a chopstick to poke round dents into the clay before it had hardened. According to Gilga-san, it was an old drink recipe. No one was permitted to touch it.

He played with the braid hanging from his chin. Then he surged to his feet. "I agree. Losing your freedom is a hardship you do not deserve. Before you go, I have something for you. Wait here."

Unable to remain sitting, she paced. She hoped to leave before the samurai returned. If they were busy fighting the kappa, they wouldn't notice a fishing boat leaving the dock. And if the kappa remained engaged in battle, it wouldn't bother chasing after her.

Gilga-san returned with a plain white cup. He handed it to her. She sniffed the warm contents. It smelled like jasmine tea but resembled milk.

"Your features are too elegant to pass for a man," he said. "If you truly wish to live as a man, drink the . . . tea and you shall be transformed. However, once done, it cannot be undone."

Azami's hand shook. An impossible offer. A jest? She

had never known him to play pranks. No. Deep down in her heart, she felt it. He meant it. She sank into her chair and clutched the cup with both hands, resting it in her lap.

Afraid to spill it. Afraid to drink it. Afraid to refuse it.

A knock broke the silence. Gilga-san cracked open the door.

"The samurai have returned," a voice said.

"Stay here," Gilga-san said to her. "No one will find you." He left.

Azami's thoughts swirled. To transform into a man. To have the freedom and the privileges men enjoyed. To no longer be afraid someone would force her to marry and bear children. She could walk among the samurai in the sake-house without worry. Her problems solved.

Then her musings went deeper. Would her personality change? Would she desire women? Or would she still desire men?

It had been easy to wish, but making a choice wouldn't be as straightforward. Gilga-san slipped into the room. His expression troubled.

"What happened?" she asked.

"Six samurai died, ten injured and the kappa remains at large."

"You were right."

"Poor consolation, considering the cost." He eyed the cup in her lap. "They're searching for you. If you become a man, you can stay here and work for me. Otherwise, I'll hide you."

She stared at the white liquid. Hiding was another form of imprisonment and it didn't sit well with her. Transforming felt wrong as well. As if she cheated.

"What do you truly desire, Azami?"

"A partner." The words popped out without censure and kept coming. "Someone I can share my life with and who won't direct my life. Someone who treats me as an equal despite my gender." Like Gilga-san did. Why? Because she had worked hard for him, sorted out his messy bookkeeping, and helped create a few new drink recipes. She had earned his respect and friendship.

Sudden understanding zipped through Azami, energizing her. She thrust the cup into his hands. "Thank you for the offer, but I don't deserve it. And I'm not hiding any longer."

A strange expression crossed his face. Not quite amusement, although gladness did spark in his eyes. He seemed proud and that added to her determination.

"What are you going to do?" Gilga-san asked.

"Go fishing."

"And you will show this fish the proper respect?" he asked.

"Unlike the samurai, I do not have a delicate male ego," she said.

His deep laughter followed her out the door.

Her bravado and determination leaked from her as she crept from shadow to shadow, heading west through Hokuga. The idea she could prevail when the samurai could not seemed ridiculous in the cold darkness. Doubt and terror swirled in her chest.

She scanned the small town, committing its quirks—Toshi's half completed fence, fishing nets hanging from Futsu's back door, and the family of cats living under Oda's bamboo hut—to memory. Fondness for these people pulsed in her heart. She would have been content to serve customers and listen to Gilga-san's stories until the end of her days.

When she reached the last building, she gauged the distance to the thin cover of the winter woods. Could she do this? She considered the alternative—dragged back to Yamakage, punished and forced to marry.

Gilga-san believed in her. It was time to trust herself. Azami shoved her misgivings away.

As she dashed to the tree line, hurried footsteps sounded behind her. She spun in time to see a figure running after her, hissing her name in a loud whisper. Drawing her kaiken, she slid her feet into a fighting stance. But the man skidded to a stop and held his hands out, showing he was unarmed.

"Azami, I need to talk to you." Saburo puffed.

Bad timing. She lowered her weapon. "Go home, Saburo."

"Not until you listen."

"No. I lied to you about everything. I'm not koji. I ran away from Yamakage because I did not wish to marry a samurai. Now they have found me, I need to leave."

"Then I will come with you," he said, stepping closer.

"But I do not—"

"Wish to become a traditional wife. I understand. All I desire is your company."

She sheathed her kaiken and crossed her arms in suspicion. "Have you talked to Gilga-san?"

"Yes, he told me where to find you."

That explained it. "Did he give you a special drink?" Meddling again, Gilga-san was worse than the local matchmaker.

"No time. He urged me to hurry."

This threw her. "Why did you change your mind?"

He sucked in a deep breath. "I considered the reasons why I love you. You are independent, intelligent, and brave. If I had done this before asking for your hand, I would have realized my error. Rather than lose you, I wish to accompany you."

"What about your life and home here?"

"It is of little concern to me."

"I—"

He rested a cold finger on her lips, silencing her. "You are all that matters." He cupped her chin and drew her toward him for a kiss.

Heat spread from her lips and she pressed against Saburo, deepening the kiss and tangling her fingers in his long hair. Her heart beat its approval.

Shouts intruded. Azami spotted two samurai pointing in their direction and calling to others.

"Time to go." She grabbed Saburo's hand and they raced down the path to the lake.

With six dead and ten injured, she hoped the warriors wouldn't follow them right away. Hoped they'd assume the kappa wouldn't let them escape. A smart assumption.

Moonlight lit the trail, and, while glad to be able to see, Azami worried they would be visible to the samurai.

They ran until the sounds of pursuit died. When her breath no longer huffed so loud in her ears, the crash of the waves reached her. Arriving at the lake, they paused. Silver moonlight flashed and danced on the water. The surface undulated as if restless and irritated. Foaming curls of water rushed and pounded on the shore.

"All those windy days combined with a big moon have increased the tide," Saburo explained. "I hope the northern path is not underwater."

By his nervous glances toward the lake, Azami knew he didn't voice his true fear. Hand in hand they followed the road that ringed the vast lake, keeping away from the surf.

"Saburo, I've one more . . . confession," Azami said.

He squeezed her hand in encouragement.

"I'm not running away. It is a life full of fear."

Slowing his pace, he looked at her in confusion.

"I came here to challenge the kappa."

Jerking to a stop, he peered at her in utter astonishment. "But . . . you will . . . it. . . ." He drew in a deep breath. "You'll die. It's jisatsu!"

"It remains the only way I can *earn* my freedom."

He stared at her for so long Azami wondered if she'd lost him.

"And I cannot leave the people of Hokuga to the mercy of the kappa," she said, and meant it. "The samurai are unable to see past their code of honor. They will continue to die."

Saburo's shoulders relaxed. "And you won't?"

"All I know is I have to try."

The gradual infusion of color into the black sky announced the dawn's arrival. As sunlight swept across the lake, the pressure in Azami's chest relaxed a bit. Until she spotted a child playing in the rough surf.

Terrified for his safety, she waded into the chilly water, calling and gesturing for him to leave the water before he drowned. The young boy laughed, but he walked to the bank and sat on the edge, waving her over.

Saburo caught up to her as she neared the child. She stopped a few feet away and gaped. Not because delight shown on the boy's face, but because he had greenish-yellow scales instead of skin. And he had a dent on the top of his misshapen head that was filled with a white liquid. Fear's icy teeth bit into her.

"Oh, what a glorious morning! No longer boring." It splashed its webbed toes in the water. "I smell love in the blood. Yummy!"

Saburo grabbed her arm and tugged her back. "I cannot . . . let's run."

The kappa chortled. "Yes, yes! Run, run. Make it fun."

Azami sorted through the story Gilga-san had told months ago, when he had been entertaining guests. Her frantic pulse calmed. "No." She pulled her kaiken, wishing again for the long reach of her naginata.

"Oh, what a delight. A fight." It jumped to its feet.

Saburo stepped in front of Azami, protecting her.

Huffing with annoyance, she pushed him aside. "Trust me."

To her relief, he nodded and backed away. Azami joined the kappa on the narrow bank. They faced each other. At five feet five inches in height, she never considered herself tall, but compared to the four foot kappa she towered over the creature. The height difference was all part of its game, luring its opponents into a false sense of security. It also waited for her to make the first move.

She bowed deeply to the kappa.

"Oh, a proper warrior." It returned the bow. As it dipped its head, the white liquid poured from the indentation and pooled onto the ground. When the kappa straightened, it didn't appear to be concerned about its loss.

Azami prayed Gilga-san's story had been accurate. Their lives depended on it. She lunged at the kappa, slicing at its neck with her kaiken. The blade narrowly missed as it jumped back. She advanced, thrusting the tip toward the kappa's chest.

It retreated a step, but then blocked the next jab. The blow was hard, but not strong enough to dislodge her grip on the kaiken. Confidence flowed through her veins, energizing her. Without the white liquid, the kappa's supernatural strength and speed were gone. For now. It would regain its powers in time. Already a small amount of fluid had returned.

She increased the intensity of her attack, striking and slicing without giving the kappa a chance to get close to her. It blocked and dodged. When she swung her dagger a little too wide, it darted in and latched onto her forearm—the one holding the kaiken.

It dug its claws deep into her flesh as it pressed close. A burning agony sizzled on her skin. A snap vibrated through her bones. Pain exploded in her arm. The kappa squealed with joy. With one hand, it raked its claws, slashing cuts. Then the kappa clamped its mouth over the bloody wounds. The level of white liquid inside its dent rose at a faster pace as it sucked her blood.

The horrifying noise galvanized Azami into action. She stomped on its foot and slammed the edge of her free hand into its temple. It jerked with the blows, but hung on. She transferred her weapon to her left hand and jabbed the tip of the blade into the kappa's ribs. It let go, staggering back.

Hugging her injured arm to her stomach, Azami changed tactics and kicked it in the chest. It stumbled. She kept after it, using a variety of kicks. So used to being faster and stronger, the kappa couldn't adapt to this new attack. When its gaze slid to the water, she knew it considered escape.

Feinting left, she shuffled forward and to the right, hooking the kappa around the neck with her uninjured arm. Azami pressed the edge of the blade against its throat. The scales felt thick, but red blood welled under her knife.

"Oh, please, don't kill," it cried.

"Why not? You have killed many."

"Must eat."

"Not good enough."

"Do anything for you," it said.

"Always?"

"Yes, yes."

"Give me your word."

"Oh, my word is yours."

Satisfied, she released the kappa.

"Azami, no!" Saburo yelled, running over to her.

"It will be fine. He is an honorable opponent; his word will never be broken."

"How do you know?"

"Gilga-san. Despite his matchmaking tendencies, he's quite knowledgeable."

Gilga-san had also been correct about another one of the kappa's unique powers. The spirit was skilled in mending broken bones, and in reattaching severed limbs without leaving a scar.

When asked, it healed Azami's arm. Once she regained her energy, the three of them headed back to Hokuga. It didn't take long to encounter the samurai.

"Remember, do not kill anyone," Azami said to the kappa as fourteen warriors surrounded them with their weapons drawn.

"Must eat," it whined.

"Human blood? Or can you drink animal blood?"

"Oh, both. And like cucumbers. Yummy."

"You will be fed in exchange for protection."

It perked up. "Protect now? Fun? Make men run?" The white liquid completely filled the kappa's dent.

"Only if they attack us." She took the kappa's hand in hers. Then she turned in a slow circle and met each samurai's gaze, holding it until the warrior acknowledged her with a nod and sheathed his katana.

"What now?" Saburo asked.

"We go home."

THE FORTUNE-TELLER MAKES HER WILL

Kari Sperring

"FIRE," whispered the angels. "Fire is falling."

Their voices slipped between her daughter Madeleine's lips, silken and sweet, some high, some low. And the fire followed them, long ghost banners of it. It licked the tips of her fingers, rolled out across the table top, danced and pranced and spun out on every side. On the other side of the table, the fortune-teller shivered, her eyes fixed on her daughter's face. "Fire". No matter how she phrased the question, the answer was always the same. Fire. Fire for the fortune-teller and her associates. Fire for the pretty wife of the councilor, with her hunger for beauty and money and freedom from marriage. Fire for the complacent priests and the perfume-sellers; fire and pain and darkness. It reached its fine red fingers for the rakish *comtesse* in her web of plots, for the dashing *duc* with his hopes and hidden hatred, for the peerless *marquise* in her royal *boudoir*. It limned the slim silhouette of sweet Madeleine as she sat at her mother's table to channel the angels, blue eyes blank and empty, fixed on nothingness. The future was full of fire and it would consume them all. It rolled and danced about the room,

threw hot shadows across the vials and bottles, the jars
of herbs and the heavy bound books. It ran its hands
over the fortune-teller's face, down her throat, closed its
fingers about her, hot and heavy. She gasped and shuddered from it, breaking the spell.

Madeleine's eyes snapped shut as her head dropped
forward. The red light winked out, leaving the workroom pale in the inferior glow of the candles. For long
moments the fortune-teller sat in silence, calming her
breathing, swallowing down her fears. Fire and only fire.
There was no way out for her, then: the angels had spoken. She must face that, head high, and make of it what
she must. But Madeleine. . . . Rising, she went round the
table to her daughter, who had slumped forward. Madeleine's skin was soft with sleep, her breathing low and
regular. The fortune-teller stroked back the long curls.
The angels had touched her. The angels, surely, would
want to save her, this vessel, this innocent through whom
they worked? She patted the girl's cheek and returned
to her own seat. Opening one of the drawers of her work
table, she took out three sheets of the finest paper.

She was not, perhaps, the most gifted of the diviners of Paris. There were others more apt with the arts
of conjuring or the skillful manipulation of smoke and
mirrors. But in the art of presentation, none surpassed
her. Her bower was the most fragrant, her consulting
room the most opulent and alluring, her person—if not
by nature attractive—the cleanest and most reassuring.
And then there was Madeleine, with her blue eyes and
blonde curls and wide sweet smile; Madeleine, through
whose soft pink lips the spirits spoke—angels, most certainly, for no demon could find foot-hold in such an innocent vessel. Madeleine brought the clients in, to sit on

soft settles and hear the words of the otherworld. No matter that the words were often garbled or unclear. Her voice was soft and bell-toned and her face guile-less. And her step-mother, the fortune-teller, was always on hand to offer explanations and translations alongside other, more practical services.

Fire on all sides. But not, the fortune-teller told her-self, for Madeleine, the agent of angels. Dipping her quill into her purest ink, she bent her head and began to write.

The fortune-teller thought long and hard about these letters, to be delivered should anything befall her. She crafted each word with exquisite care. No outsider, read-ing one of them, must catch so much as a glimmer of what they contained: a warning, a threat, a wish. Under the seal of each she placed a strand of her thin grey hair, whispering words to the soft wax she placed over it. Her will. Her will. Her will be done.

Thaïs stalked into the cabaret and flung her hat down onto the long counter. The bartender, Monsieur Gilles, cast a knowing look at her, before setting a small cup of something thick and potent before her. She drank it off without looking at it, coughed, wiped her mouth with the back of her hand and swore.

"Your *marquise* wouldn't like to hear you talk like that," said Gilles, moving the nearest bottle out of easy reach.

"The *marquise* can dance on a sharpened spike." Thaïs glared into the cup. "What *was* that? The contents of your pisspot? Give me another."

"You don't need it." Gilles took the cup away and re-placed it with an earthenware goblet which he half-filled with red wine. "Try this. The *chevalier* de Lionne sent me two barrels to clear his tab."

The cabaret was situated on a low corner, where the Rue Servandoni met the Allée de St-Paul, in the damp undercroft of a print-shop. From outside there was nothing to distinguish it—no sign, no welcoming flambeau, only a short flight of stone steps and a rather battered door. It had no formal name: it was known simply as the *bar de l'heure*, from the great clock of the Église St-Paul opposite. It was seldom more than a quarter full. "Those who need us find us," said Gilles, when customers asked. Thaïs had stumbled across it one day some three years earlier—quite literally, when her ankle gave way and she tumbled down the steps. The door had opened just quickly enough to conceal her from the young nobleman who had stepped, quite unexpectedly, out of the book-shop three doors down. Chances were he would not have been able to place her, but she did not like to take such chances. Not when one filled one's pockets in the fashion she did.

Her employer knew Thaïs could read: that was part of her value to Madame. She had no idea, however, that Thaïs was one of those who supplied the print shop over the *bar de l'heure* with its steady stream of satires and filthy songs on courtiers, ministers, mistresses, and the king. Madame was rich and spoiled and expected her maids to be loyal.

Now, she sipped her wine and pulled a face. Too sweet and too thin, like the young women the *chevalier* preferred for his bed. Like Madeleine, the little witch who haunted too many of Thaïs' dreams. Gilles picked up a cloth and began to polish a pewter tankard. He said, "Give it time to breathe. We're all the better for a little breathing."

She threw him a dusty look. He went on, "I take it your latest work was too hot for my neighbor?"

"He doesn't want to offend *too much*." She mimicked the mincing tones of the printer. "Not in the current climate, with La Reynie and his policemen hunting up trouble all over the city."

"Ah." Gilles set the tankard down and wiped imaginary dust from the top of the squat clay tablet mounted over the back of his bar. For any other man, it would have been a reach. Gilles was not any other man. He was the tallest man Thaïs had seen, taller even than the giant musketeer who went by the name Porthos. If La Reynie came here with his men, he'd have a real fight on his hands.

Not that La Reynie, the Lieutenant-General of the Paris Police, was remotely interested in cabarets, however odd. Or printshops, not right now. The word on police lips everywhere these days was "poison."

The house of the *marquise* was in uproar when Thaïs returned. Madame could not find her preferred fan— some careless servant must have misplaced or broken it. Madame's chicory water was too sour, too warm, too dusty. Madame's creditors were daring to contact her: had they no idea who she was? Nothing and no one was pleasing to her in any imaginable way. The king, murmured a tiring maid to Thaïs, had been late to arrive and early to depart, and had, moreover, dared to raise with Madame the matter of her spending. Madame had raged and ranted for fully two hours before finally finishing her *toilette* and sweeping out to soothe her spite by exercising it on those she professed to call friends. Shedding boots and breeches and male doublet in the narrow room she shared with three others, Thaïs murmured quiet thanks to her guardian angel—if she had such a thing—that today had been her *jour de congé*.

Madeleine believed in angels. "As beautiful as your Madame," she had whispered to Thaïs, on one of the visits Madame had paid to consult with her mother the fortune-teller and, through her, with Madeleine. Madeleine's angels visited her regularly, at her mother's command, and used her lips to speak to the elect, promising—or so the fortune-teller swore—every kind of benefit and earthly advancement. "Your Madame is blessed," said Madeleine, who could not credit that angels might have truck with any but the good, the pure.

If angels spoke to her Madame, then Thaïs had no faith in angels—or else the angels who came to Madeleine were of that company no longer welcome in heaven. If Madeleine understood the questions Madame put, she, too, might be more ready to doubt. But Madeleine remembered nothing, once the angels settled upon her. It was her mother who called them down into residence, her mother who decoded the strange sweet words they spoke.

Angels. Demons. Or perhaps just Madeleine's private madness. Thaïs neither knew nor cared overmuch. It was Madame's gold that went to pay the fortune-teller, not hers, and Madame's interests that the visits sought to serve. Now, Thais wriggled into her dress, tied her hair into a perfunctory knot and went downstairs in search of food.

Madeleine was waiting for her in an antechamber, nibbling on one of the dainty pastries rejected earlier by Madame. Her long pale hair fell forward over one shoulder in lustrous curls; her blue gaze examined the delicate porcelain plate from which she ate. If Madame knew she came here. . . . It was one thing to consult soothsayers in their Parisian lairs. It was quite another to admit them to the gilded precincts of Versailles. The king had no love for such creatures, whom he regarded as charlatans at best. And as for those who consulted them. . . . Not even Madame's beauty and her long sojourn in his regard would help her if the king chose to believe her guilty of seeking to influence him through sorcery.

Madeleine looked up and every part of her face smiled as she saw Thaïs. Thaïs pressed her lips together, fighting the wave of pure delight that threatened to rise in her at the sight. She would not be softened by blue eyes and curls and that endless, guileless innocence. She plumped herself down at the table opposite Madeleine and grabbed a handful of pastries from the platter. "What are you doing here?"

"Maman sent me." Madeleine's voice was as sweet as her exterior. "She has sent a new lotion for Madame."

"Madame won't be pleased. She doesn't like your mother sending people here."

Madeleine's lips drew down. She never seemed to know what to do with contradiction or complication. She looked back at the plate, small fingers playing with the remains of her pastry. Her mother, the old witch, would have told her to deliver the message personally, of course. Thaïs sighed. "Give it to me, then, and I'll make sure Madame gets it."

Madeleine looked up and once again that smile was written across her face. "I knew you'd help me."

"Well." Thaïs shrugged and held out her hand. "The lotion?"

"Oh!" Madeleine reached into the bodice of her dress and drew out a tiny phial. "Here it is." Thaïs took it and tucked it into a pocket without looking.

She said, "You'd best be going, then."

"Oh, but. . . ." Another pout. "One of the other maids told me Madame was out. I had thought. . . ." Her fingers traced the bright borders of the plate.

It would not do. It would never do. The whole thing was hopeless, stupid. If they were caught. . . . Thaïs swallowed her last mouthful and stood. "Very well, then. Come on."

It was her own fault, of course, for telling Madeleine about Madame's lovely gowns and fine furnishings. The trouble was, Madeleine loved to hear of such things, and Thaïs loved to tell her of them and watch those blue eyes grow round with delight. And as to her promise to show them, should Madeleine ever visit the palace. . . . Foolishness, from start to finish, and all too like to draw upon her precisely the kind of attention she did not desire. They were bought with blood and lies, all those beautiful things: tricked or wheedled out of the king, who should know better than to squander his tax revenues on his spoiled mistress. Of course, Madeleine would never think of that. Madeleine saw only the prettiness.

Thaïs led Madeleine along the narrow back corridor that led to Madame's *boudoir*. She listened carefully at the door before opening it and ushering them both inside. This was the heart of Madame's lair, where she entertained the king and displayed herself to choice friends and rivals.

The room was a treasure-box of gilded wood and rich fabrics, mirrors and crystal, fine-turned and decorated furnishings, fine porcelain and gold and silver *objets d'art*. Madeleine's breath caught and her mouth opened on a silent "Oh," as she took in the Turkey carpet and the great carved bed, the heavy tapestries depicting goddess and nymphs at their sport, the silver candelabra and the great crystal chandelier. She put out a hand towards the nearest object, an inlaid cabinet, and drew it back, shaking. She said, "Madame lives like a queen."

"Better than the queen." Thaïs said. She took hold of the closest edge of the bed hangings and gave them a tug. "The queen has to make do with old cloth and dust. These are new." They were crimson, these hangings, and richly damask: a whole village could have lived in comfort for a year on what they had cost. Thaïs herself had earned three times a month's wages with a ballad written on what they witnessed every night.

Not that Madame knew about that, of course.

"So many pretty things," Madeleine said. She had advanced into the center of the room. "I wish I was you, to see these every day." There was a great portrait of Madame, dressed in a loose robe and with her hair unbound, hanging on the wall opposite the bed. "Madame is so beautiful."

Madeleine would not think Madame so lovely if she saw her in a rage. But Thaïs did not say that. She picked up one of the silver-backed brushes from the dressing table, and said, "She knows how to make herself look well, I'll grant you." Crossing the room, she set her hands on Madeleine's shoulders. "But your hair is lighter than hers, and longer, too. Sit down." She gave Madeleine a little push, guiding her to a straight-backed chair. "Hers is coarse, these days, and her hairdresser has to help her with the color." She tugged the cord from Madeleine's hair and began to draw the brush through it. "You'd look much better than she does in most of her gowns." Under her fingers, Madeleine's hair was silk. Thaïs closed her eyes. She should not be doing this, if she was caught it would be her job, and worse.

"I wish I lived here, like you," Madeleine said. "I'd love to look after all these things."

Thaïs shook her head, opening her eyes. "It's harder work than you think."

"I'd like it. I could dust and wash and mend. I like to do all those. Much better than what Maman has me do."

The angels, or whatever creatures it was that the fortune-teller conjured from those soft lips, that was not a safe profession, not in these days. Thaïs said, "I'll speak to Madame. Perhaps she'll have work for you. But your mother. . . ."

"I don't like it," Madeleine burst out. Under Thaïs' hands, her neck was suddenly rigid. "It makes me feel dizzy and strange when Maman calls them. The voices make my throat hurt and when they leave, I have a headache. I don't know what they make me say. I don't like it. I want an ordinary life, like yours. To work for someone like Madame. Some day a husband and babies. But not the voices."

Louis Vanens was the heart of a network of poisoners, who had accomplished the death of the Duke of Savoy. The rumor started in the depths of Vincennes, as those rounded up by Monsieur de La Reynie prolonged their lives by naming names. It traveled fast, on the lips of gaolers and guards, clerks to the inquiry and officers of the police. Monsieur de La Reynie was vindicated, it seemed, in his conviction of the corruption that engulfed France. Vanens, sanguine, wrote to the king offering to share his occult knowledge of the philosopher's stone.

The king did not trouble himself to reply. Another captive, Madame Bosse, knew nothing of Vanens, but she had her own tales to tell, of the four hundred or more diviners who plied their trade in Paris.

La Reynie and his men listened to them all, accounts of spells cast to find treasure or secure the love of a desired person; descriptions of confused, semi-Christian rituals designed to make husbands less cruel, of fortune-telling sessions to uncover the death-dates of those gentlemen, of potions and magics designed to hasten those deaths. The stories spun out and out—black masses here, animal sacrifice there; aphrodisiacs and perfumes; abortifacients and skin creams. The names mentioned reached higher and higher, closer and closer to the king. Husbands began to look askance at wives, lovers at their mistresses. Highborn lords dismantled the alchemical equipment in their cellars and burnt their correspondence. Court ladies smiled too brightly at one another as they proclaimed that they, of course, had never had recourse to the perfumers and magicians of the city to aid complexions and love affairs. With each new revelation at Vincennes, La Reynie added another diviner to his public list and another aristocrat to the more private list he shared only with the king. With each new arrest, the blame spread further and further. The king ordered the creation of a special court to try the magicians and poisoners, the *Chambre Ardente*. Officers of the police force came by night to capture the fortune-teller's associates. And, at last, one night, they came for her.

At first light the next day, her letters were delivered.

The first letter was carried to the doors of Madame de D___, a society beauty whose cousin was one of the officials of the *Chambre Ardente*, well-loved and well-connected at court. A maid brought the letter to her as she took her breakfast: she glanced at the seal, then waved a hand for the maid to throw it into the fire. *Really, the audacity of those creatures. Chasing her for debts, no doubt.* She was popular, she was young, her lover was one of the highest peers of the land. She was above debts and duns and those silly rumors about black magic. The king knew her. He would never permit her to be touched.

Within two weeks, she would follow the fortune-teller to Vincennes.

The recipient of the second letter was wiser, or perhaps more afraid. The *Comtesse* de S____ had once enjoyed the favor of the king, and she had never forgotten. In the long years that followed, she had made constant attempts to recapture it, with her charm, her wit, her beauty. With dark magic and poisons, said the prisoners at Vincennes.

Perhaps it was true. Before the letter was delivered, the *comtesse* was in her carriage, heading for the border. The letter lay forgotten on a marquetry table in her antechamber, gathering dust alongside bills and notes and *billets doux*, until her son swept the whole batch away and threw them out, months and months later.

The third letter came to Madame.

She was at her *toilette*, admiring her white throat in the mirror while her personal maid attended to her hair. A footman came in with her letters on a silver tray, which he set on a small table at her elbow for her to contemplate. She flicked through them idly, alternating with taking small bites out of a sweet pastry. Notes from friends—or those who passed as such. Notes from supplicants hopeful of catching her attention, and through her, that of the king. Notes from merchants—jewelers, tailors, traders in fine furnishings—wishful of acquiring her patronage. Tiny notes in wobbly writing from her children, which she opened at once and smiled over. A note from their governess, which made her frown. Nothing, today, from the king. It had been years since he had last found it necessary to write her little letters, since so much as an hour apart from her was a torture he found hard to bear. These days, his attentions were born more of habit than passion. His passion, it was whispered, was more and more directed to the beautiful young Mademoiselle de Fontanges. Angelique, as lovely as her name, as enchanting—and, said Madame, as stupid as the stupidest of the fancy fowls that lived in the palace gardens.

Mademoiselle de Fontanges' health had been poor, this last week or two, despite her youth and the royal favor. *Poor child,* said Madame in public. But in private, where once she had raged, now she smiled a creamy smile.

It was, of course, mere coincidence that the new beloved's health had begun to fail the very day that Madeleine had delivered the new lotion for Madame. Coincidence that Madame had had Thaïs take that same lotion, in a fine silver bottle, as a gracious gift from her to Mademoiselle de Fontanges.

Laying out garments for Madame to wear, Thaïs spotted the fortune-teller's seal at once. Her eyes met Madame's in the mirror. Madame frowned, and her fingers moved away to select another note instead. Thaïs went back to her task, unfolding and shaking out the fine silk. Did Madame suspect her hand in the never-ending stream of satires that were printed in the capital?

Perhaps. Yet Madame must also know how much else Thaïs knew about her, after twelve years of service.

She was Madame's confidential maid. That meant she was well-enough paid, relatively speaking, and trusted, up to a point. It did not mean she had to like Madame. A maid's feelings were of little account, as long as she could maintain the appearance of loyalty and restrain her venality to petty things. She had never known why Madame had chosen her, out of all her servants, to be her companion on those furtive visits to the soothsayers and sorcerers of the capital. It had been an adventure at first, slipping through the streets in cloaks and hoods to watch odd women read the future in Madame's palm, and recommend perfumes to tempt a king. But the perfumes had not worked for long. The king had a roving eye and little sense of loyalty, and Madame's lovely figure lost some of its appeal through repeated child-bearing. That was when the excursions grew darker and the rites performed became more desperate. Perfumes gave way to aphrodisiacs, while the courtiers watched and smirked and counted up the small humiliations endured by the fading favorite.

Madeleine would have pitied her. Madeleine was soft-hearted and foolish. Thaïs did not pity Madame. One could not pity such a woman. Madame could scent pity from a league away and uprooted it without mercy. It was not the king—bloated and selfish and arrogant— that held Thaïs, though many of her colleagues professed to love him. It was not the court, in all its vainglory. It was not even Paris, with its cabarets and bookshops and protests. Perhaps it was simply that she could think of nothing else to do.

Perhaps she was bound by Madame, complicit in her

activities. She had said that, once, in her cups, to Gilles, who had looked at her, his eyes narrowed, and said nothing in return.

And then, there was Madeleine. A child when Thaïs first saw her, gazing round-eyed over the rim of a cup at her mother's lovely visitor. She had been pretty even then: Madame had exclaimed over that, cupping the child's face in her hand. Ten years ago, or more: it had not been until she reached puberty that the angels had first spoken through Madeleine.

She finished smoothing out the gown and turned to go. Madame's sharp voice called her back. "Thaïs."

Thaïs turned again and dropped a curtsey. "Madame?"

"Wait. I'm not happy with the neck of that dress. I shall want you to adjust it."

"Yes, Madame." Thaïs retreated to the door while the other maids finished with Madame's hair and the cosmetics for her face, and wound her into the lush layers of her garments. Jewels were hung in her ears, about her white throat, slid to glitter on her fingers. Musky perfume clung to her skin as she revolved slowly, examining her reflection in the longest mirror. Finally, she nodded, waving a hand to dismiss the maids. They filed out past Thaïs, one or two casting sharp glances at her from under their lashes. She looked away. They knew Madame used her to carry messages to her less savory friends. It had not made her popular.

Well, and she could live with that. The last girl left, and, at a nod from Madame, Thaïs closed the door behind her. Madame said, "This neckline. . . ." She plucked at the lace, fretful, frowning. "It doesn't lie properly. I told you to fix it."

Thaïs peered at the lace, patting it into place with her

fingertips. She could see nothing wrong. But it did not do to contradict Madame. Instead, she fetched needle and thread from her pocket and set a tiny stitch at one edge, to hold the lace flat. "I beg your pardon, Madame. I trust that's now acceptable."

Madame gave herself a perfunctory glance in the mirror. "It will do, I suppose." She stepped backward. "Be more careful next time."

"Yes, Madame."

"I'm not sure about these earrings." Crossing to her toilette table, Madame re-opened the jewelry box and began to pick through it.

Thaïs followed her. The fortune-teller's letter still lay on the tray. Carefully, she said, "Madame, the angel-speaker...."

"That woman does not know her place. And in the current circumstances...." But Madame was distracted, holding up a new pair of earrings against her cheeks to try the effect. "Read it to me, will you."

"Yes, Madame." Thaïs picked up the letter and turned it over. The seal snapped easily beneath her fingers: a shiver ran through her, and despite herself she looked over her shoulder. Nothing there. A draught. Versailles was full of draughts. She unfolded the letter, faint unease still spilling down her spine. The letter was short, little more than a note, scrawled in the fortune-teller's clumsy hand. She read it quickly, voice low. "Esteemed Madame, finding my health declining, I send this letter to express my gratitude for your care for me and to commend to you my daughter Madeleine, in the hope that you will aid her as you have aided me." The chill laid tighter hold: Thaïs dropped the letter back onto the tray and stood there, shivering.

Madame looked up at her and frowned. "What is it now, silly girl? The woman wants money, I daresay."

"Yes, Madame."

"It can wait." And, in a swish of brocade, Madame swept from the room.

By noon, the news of the flight of the *Comtesse* de S_____ had spread across Paris and the court. Other great ladies began to censor their dressing tables and burn their correspondence. The following morning, the diviners La Vigoureux and Marie Bosse were first put to the question and then burned at the stake.

Two days later, the police came for Madeleine.

"She won't do anything." Thaïs set her cup down on the counter and pushed her hair back out of her face. "She has the ear of the king. It's easy for her. And she won't do anything." She shoved the cup back towards Monsieur Gilles. "No one will touch *her*, she's the safest person in France. But she won't lift a finger."

Gilles studied her for a moment, taking in the sloppy male dress, the disheveled hair, the stains on a once starched collar. Then he took the cup away and replaced it with a mug of ale. Thaïs spat. "What's that? I'm not English."

"Indeed not."

"Well, then. . . ."

"But you are in my bar. Which means you drink what I give you."

"Hah." But she picked up the mug and took a deep swallow. "Tastes like washing water."

"So I've been told."

"The things I know about her. . . . I could threaten to tell the king. . . ."

Who would not listen. Sober, Thaïs would know that well enough. Gilles propped an elbow on the bar and looked at her again. A thread wound about the fingers of her right hand, tangling them. Too thin for most eyes to note, most likely. Certainly too thin for Thaïs to see, set as she was in her worldview of patronage and corruption. His brows drew down: he glanced quickly below the counter, at a tall black bottle.

She had to ask. It was better that way. All he could do was wait. She finished the beer and wiped her mouth. Then she said, "The old woman is one thing. But Madeleine. . . . She's done nothing. She doesn't even remember what happens when her mother summons the voices. The angels. She's just a silly girl." Gilles said nothing, refilling her mug. She said, "There must be something. . . ."

There was something. Gilles looked again at the bottle beneath the bar. Thaïs said, "It should be Madame, not her. Or one of those other court women. They're the ones who wanted things." She sighed, running a finger round the rim of the mug. "It should be me, I suppose. I went with Madame and I never said anything."

"What would you do if it was you?" He had to ask carefully, now. Leading was improper.

"What do you think?" Thaïs shot him a wolfish smile. "What I do anyway. Let people know what they're like, those courtiers." The smile dropped. "Madeleine doesn't know anything. But they'll put her to the question anyway. And she's such a little thing."

"Perhaps her mother will exonerate her."

She snorted, "Monsieur de La Reynie doesn't believe anyone is innocent. That's what they're saying at court, anyway. The king believes it, too. He thinks everyone wants his love and favor and will do anything to get it."

Dangerous words, those, in any other Paris bar. Not so much here, where too many of the other patrons had heavy secrets of their own.

Thaïs said, "Madame could save her. She *should* save her." And then, at last, "I would, if I had the means."

Gilles' hand closed on the bottle. He said, "I could help you."

"How?" Thaïs snorted, this time in derision. "Oh, you're big enough, but not even you could overthrow Vincennes."

"There's no need to overthrow Vincennes. But I can help you get her out."

She examined him narrowly, slowly. He could feel her gaze on his skin, weighing his reliability, his honesty, his sanity. He held still and, at the last, she dropped her gaze and nodded. "Do it, then."

He brought out the bottle and a clean drinking glass. Into it, he poured a single finger of a dark fluid. Then he set it in front of her. He said, "All you have to do is drink this, and wish. I'll tell you how."

"You get five minutes," the guard said. "No more. And I'll be watching, so don't try passing notes."

Thaïs nodded. It had cost her all she had earned for her last two satires to bribe her way this far. It would be enough, if what Gilles had promised was true. More than enough. She made herself look up and smile at the man. "Thank you, Monsieur. Your kindness means much to me."

The man shuffled his feet. "Just don't make any trouble."

They reached a turn of the stair and he turned onto a small, cramped landing. Three doors led off it, all dark and heavy. He rummaged through the keys on his belt and selected one. Then he opened the lock on the left-most door. "In here."

The door opened on a small dank cell, lit only by a thin sliver of late daylight that squeezed its way through a long slit high in the wall. The floor was scattered with greasy straw: to one side, this had been heaped up to form a makeshift bed. Madeleine huddled on it, wrapped in a thin blanket. She did not look up at the sound of the door. Pain closed a hand on Thaïs. She crossed the room in three steps and crouched down. "Madeleine. Madeleine, it's me."

Madeleine uncurled, raising a face smudged with soot and tears. Her long hair hung lank over her cheeks. She said, "You're not. It's a trick."

"It's really me." Thaïs reached out and put her hand on Madeleine's shoulder. "See."

Madeleine gulped. "Did . . . did *she* send you? She must be kind, she's so pretty."

Thaïs shook her head. Madeleine was likely to realize soon enough that Madame's pretty face did not always guarantee kindness. Then she said, "No, I came by myself. To help you."

Madeleine clutched at her hand. "How?"

"I'm going to get you out." Thaïs' heart pounded in her ears. If she did this, if she went through with it, she was signing her own death-warrant, most like. But Madeleine, sweet silly Madeleine, would go free, as the fortune-teller had wished. She glanced quickly over her shoulder at the hatch in the door, through which the guard watched them. He would take her words for comfort, for false hope. She turned back to Madeleine. "You liked my job, remember? All the pretty things?" Madeleine nodded, hanging onto her hand. "Would you like to do a job like that?"

"Yes." Madeleine's voice was a whisper.

"Well, when you leave here, that's what you'll do. You'll have to be careful, especially at first, be quiet and polite and don't make any fuss. Can you do that?"

"Yes."

"Then close your eyes, and wish hard, and it will happen. I promise. Do you believe me?"

"Yes."

"Close your eyes, then. . . ." Madeleine squeezed her eyes tight shut. For a moment, Thaïs hesitated, listening to the thud of her own heart, the quick rhythm of her breath. She looked down at her hands, thin and brown and strong. Then she leaned forward, and kissed Madeleine on the lips.

The room dipped: she gasped and fell forward. And then she opened her eyes and found herself gazing upwards from the straw bed into what used to be her own face.

THE TAVERN FIRE

D.B. Jackson

Boston, March 19, 1760

THERE was no fire when he woke. The room had gone cold and a bleak gray light seeped around the old cloth that hung over his window. He heard no wind, which was good. Tiller didn't like the wind; not this time of year. But he wanted to see gold at the window edges, and there was none.

He sighed and rolled out of bed, the ropes beneath his mattress groaning. He relieved himself and left the pot by his door, so that he wouldn't forget to empty it. He did that sometimes.

Then he dressed, donning a frock over his shirt for warmth, shrugging on his coat over that, and pulling his Monmouth cap onto his head. He stepped to the door, pausing as always at the small portrait of his mother and father. He touched his fingers to his lips and then to the drawing.

"Bye, Mama, Papa. I'll be back later."

He opened the door, emptied the pot into the yard, and, after checking to see that the key hung around his neck, pulled the door shut.

A leaden sky; still, icy air. Just as he had known.

126

He heard Crumbs before he saw him; a coarse *cawing* and the rustle of silken feathers as the crow glided down from the roof to Tiller's shoulder.

"Good morning, Crumbs," Tiller said. "Looks like we got a cold one today." He fished into his coat pocket and found a morsel of stale bread, which he fed to the bird. Crumbs ate it greedily.

"We'll find more later. I'm hungry, too."

He started toward the cart, but before he reached it, he heard a door scrape behind him.

"Thomas!"

Tiller turned, but kept his gaze fixed on the ground. "Good morning, Peter," he said quietly. "I'm sorry if we woke you."

"That's not—you didn't. It's time for rent, Thomas."

Tiller knew that. Just as Peter knew that he didn't like to be called Thomas. He hadn't been Thomas since he was a boy. But it angered Peter when Tiller reminded him, and since Peter leased him the room, Tiller tried not to make him mad. A cousin should have known what to call another cousin. Tiller should have been allowed to remind Peter of that, at least. But he rented the room and he kept his mouth shut. He had heard bad stories about the almshouse.

"Do you have the money, Thomas?"

Tiller shook his head. "Not yet. But I will."

"Today is Wednesday, Thomas. You know that, right?"

He nodded slowly. Yes, that sounded right. Wednesday.

"And rent—"

"A shilling by Friday," Tiller said. "Yes, I know."

Peter exhaled the way Papa used to. "All right then. Good day, Thomas."

"Good day, Peter."

He waited until Peter had gone back into the house and closed the door before walking to the cart and pushing it out of the yard onto Leverett's Lane. It rattled loudly on the cobbles, pots and pans swinging on their hooks and clanging together, old blades and rusted tools bouncing in their wooden compartments, the empty bottles he had carefully arranged the previous evening falling over one another like drunken sailors.

There had been seven pence in his pocket when he counted just before going to bed. He could get the other five today or tomorrow. Peter wouldn't have to put him out. That's what he told himself, anyway. But he pushed the cart down to the wharves, his eyes raking the streets, searching for anything that he might find and clean and sell. It always amazed him, the things people lost. Books, jewelry, coins sometimes. Once, a few years ago, he had found a half-crown in the North End on Charter Street. He often went back to the same spot, hoping to find money again, but so far there hadn't been any more. Still, that wouldn't keep him from checking later.

He didn't see much today, at least not right off. A scrap of metal here, another bottle there. Once he crossed over into the North End, he found a bit more: a knife with a broken blade, which might fetch a few pence; a full copy of Monday's *Gazette*—someone would pay a penny for that, if they hadn't read it yet; and a lady's linen kerchief that was almost clean. He tied that to the top of the cart beside the pans, so that people could see it. It was sure to sell.

Crumbs rode on his shoulder for a short while, but then flew down to the harbor's edge to scavenge for food. The water was still, but dark as ink. Tiller could smell salt and dead fish in the air. The wharf workers shouted at him and laughed; he wasn't sure what the men said, but he could tell that it wasn't kind, and he tried to ignore them. After a few minutes he made his way up from the docks.

He stopped first at the foundry on Foster Lane. Paul, who worked there, was always kind to him, and often bought an item or two. Tiller had started seeking out goods that would interest him, and earlier in the week he had found a small hammer, its head only slightly rusted, that he thought Paul would like.

He rummaged through the cart until he found it, and entered the smithy. He found Paul at the forge, his round face ruddy with the heat, his sleeves rolled up, revealing powerful forearms. Seeing Tiller, he raised a hand and stepped away from the fire.

"Good morning, Tiller."

"Hello, Paul." Belatedly, Tiller snatched the cap off his head.

"Where's your bird today?" Paul asked.

Tiller shrugged. "Eating somewhere," he said. "He'll find me later. I have something for you. Found it in Cornhill." He held the hammer out to the man.

The smith's forehead creased and he came forward. "This is very nice, Tiller," he said, taking the hammer from him and turning it over in his hands. "Very nice, indeed." He rubbed his thumb over a patch of rust. "A bit of polishing and this will be good as new." Paul looked up at him. "How much?"

Tiller gazed up at the ceiling, as if considering this, though he had already decided. "I dunno," he said, his gaze meeting Paul's for an instant before darting away. "Five pence maybe?"

The smith smiled. "Five pence seems more than fair."

He dug into his pocket and took out a sixpence. "I don't have it exactly. How about we settle on six and call it even?"

"I have a penny," Tiller said, reaching into his own pocket.

"It's all right, Tiller. Six is a good price."

Tiller took the coin, a grin on his face. "I found a good one, didn't I?"

"Yes, you did."

He hesitated a moment, wondering if he should say more. At last he put his cap back on. "Well, thanks, Paul. I'll see you again in a few days."

"Good day, Tiller. May the Lord keep you."

Tiller left the shop and immediately Crumbs fluttered down to his shoulder.

"Got rent, Crumbs," he said, holding up the sixpence.

The crow bent toward it, his beak open.

"No, you don't. I need that for Peter."

He slid the coin into his pocket and started pushing his cart again. He stopped at a few other shops, but didn't sell anything more. By midday, he was back in Cornhill, and he made his way to the public houses, hoping to trade for a meal. He stopped first at the Bunch of Grapes and when the innkeeper there refused to look at his wares, he went on to the Light House. That proved no more fruitful. Against his better judgment, he then made his way to the Brazen Head, on Cornhill Street.

Mary Jackson, who owned the tavern, had never liked him. She called Crumbs "that filthy bird" and insisted that the crow stay outside. And she talked to Tiller as if he were a little boy.

He knew that he wasn't as smart as some people, but he had gotten by on his own for a long time now. He didn't need Miss Jackson telling him how to take care of himself.

Occasionally, though, he had something she liked, and she gave him a free meal in exchange. He hoped that the kerchief might catch her eye.

She was at the bar when he walked in, and she greeted him with a frown. Her hair—black, streaked with silver—was drawn up in a bun, and she wore a pale blue gown with a stomacher of white linen. Tiller noticed that her stomacher matched the kerchief perfectly.

"What do you want?" Miss Jackson asked, the lines around her mouth and eyes making her appear angry. Tiller had seen her smile now and again, and each time he was surprised by how pretty a smile made her look. He thought that she should smile more. "I've told you I'm not interested in buying the rubbish you find in the streets."

"Yes, ma'am," Tiller said, stopping just inside her door and removing his cap. The tavern was crowded, and most of the people were craning their necks to see him. Tiller tried hard to ignore them. "But I have something I think you'll like." He held up the kerchief for her to see.

She stared at it briefly, wrinkling her nose. "What is that?"

"A kerchief, ma'am. A nice one. Linen it is. With a bit of cleaning—"

Miss Jackson began to laugh, and it didn't make her look pretty. She glanced back at the others and they laughed as well. "You think I want to buy someone's dirty kerchief? You're mad!"

Tiller slowly lowered the hand holding the kerchief. "I have some other. . . ." He stopped. Their laughter was only growing louder. He started to leave.

"Wait."

He faced Miss Jackson again.

"You spend some time at that other pub, don't you? The Fat Spider?"

"Yes." That was where Tiller intended to go next. It was a long walk, but Janna and Gil—who ran the tavern—they were his friends. They always fed him, even when he didn't have something on his cart that they wanted.

She beckoned him toward the bar. "Come here. Are you hungry ... Tiller, is it?"

"Yes, ma'am," he said quietly, still standing by the door.

"It's all right, Tiller." She indicated a stool with an open hand. "You can sit right here." She glanced at her barman, a tall thin man with a high forehead and long plaited hair. "Johnny, fetch some chowder and bread for Tiller, will you?"

"Yeah, sure," Johnny said, and went back to the kitchen.

Tiller crossed to the bar. Some of the others were still watching him, but they had stopped laughing. He halted by Miss Jackson, who nodded in encouragement.

"That's it. Sit down."

He sat on the stool beside her.

Miss Jackson narrowed her eyes, which were the same color as her gown. "What can you tell me about that woman at the Fat Spider? Janna, right? What can you tell me about her?"

"Um ... well ... she's very nice. She ... she gives me food sometimes and—"

"Where's she from? Do you know that?"

"An island somewhere, I think. Her skin's dark, and she speaks with an accent."

"I know that." She sounded the way Peter sometimes

did when Tiller couldn't figure things out. But then she exhaled slowly. "Tiller, have you ever seen her do strange things?"

"You mean magical things?"

Her face brightened, and she smiled at him, a pretty, friendly smile. "Yes, that's exactly what I mean. How smart you are."

"I've seen her do that," Tiller said, pleased with himself. "I've—" He stopped, his cheeks burning. He had been about to say that he had felt her magic, too. That it made the ground hum beneath his feet. But Janna had warned him about telling anyone that, and while Miss Jackson was being nice to him right now, he was smart enough to know it wouldn't last, and then he would be sorry that he had told her. He wondered if he had been wrong to say that Janna did magic. He knew that men and women were still hanged as witches in New England. He didn't think that Miss Jackson wanted to get Janna in trouble, but still he regretted saying as much as he had. "I've heard that some people do it," he said, keeping his eyes fixed on the bar. "It might not have been Janna. I don't know who it was."

"It's all right, Tiller. She won't mind that you told me. I want her to do magic for me. I'll pay her for it. She'll be glad that we had this little talk."

Tiller wasn't so sure. But before he could say anything, Johnny emerged from the kitchen with his chowder and bread.

"You want ale with that?" Johnny asked.

Tiller looked at Miss Jackson.

"Of course he does," she said. She smiled at Tiller again. "Janna doesn't like me very much, Tiller. Did you know that?"

"No," he said. A lie. Janna didn't like anyone very much. She liked Gil, and she was nice to Tiller, but he had never seen her show any sign of liking other people. And she sometimes said bad things about Miss Jackson. Like that she was a lying snake, and that she couldn't be trusted to care for her own Mama, much less anyone else.

"Well, she doesn't," Miss Jackson went on. "And so I need your help. I need you to convince her to do a little magic for me. Can you do that?"

"I don't know," Tiller said. "It might not have been Janna."

"Of course. But if it was Janna, what kind of magic did she do? Can you remember that?"

He didn't know what to say. None of this had gone the way he wanted.

"I've heard people say that she does love spells," Miss Jackson said, her voice dropping to a whisper. "Is that what you've seen?"

Tiller stared back at her, too afraid to speak.

"Do you know how much people pay her for the charms?"

When he still didn't answer, her expression turned hard. "That's my food sitting in front of you, Tiller. I want answers. Now tell me: Does she do love spells?"

Tiller nodded. "Yes, ma'am," he whispered. "I don't know how much money she gets for them."

"Do they work?" Miss Jackson asked, hunger in her eyes and in her voice. "Is the magic real?"

"I think so," he said. "I've . . . I've heard people thank her."

She smiled like someone who had just won at cards. "That's what I needed to know. Thank you, Tiller."

Johnny put a cup of ale in front of him.

Miss Jackson stood. "Make sure he gets whatever he wants," she told Johnny. "He's our guest. You understand?"

"Yes, ma'am," Johnny said.

"You go to the Fat Spider when you're done, Tiller." Miss Jackson bent toward him, forcing Tiller to look her in the eye. "You tell Janna that I'm coming, all right?"

Tiller nodded, taking a spoonful of the chowder, which was very good. "Yesh, ma'am," he said through the food.

She patted his arm and walked away. Johnny moved to the far end of the bar to talk to the men sitting there. Tiller was left alone. He didn't mind. He ate and he drank, and when he finished, he got up and left the Brazen Head. No one seemed to notice.

His cart still stood outside the tavern where he had left it, with Crumbs perched on the edge. The bird *cawed* crossly at Tiller.

"I didn't forget you," Tiller said, taking a piece of fresh bread from his pocket. "Here you go."

Crumbs took the bread and hopped to the far end of the cart. There, he began to tear at his food with his thick black beak.

Tiller pushed the cart down Cornhill and onto Marlborough, passing the lofty spire of the Old South Church and the solid brick façade of the Province House. Soon, the closely packed houses and shops of the South End gave way to more open ground—pastures and fields, country homes and rolling lawns. Still Tiller pushed the cart, sweating now, despite the cold.

The Fat Spider sat by itself on a lonely stretch of Orange Street on the Boston Neck. It didn't look like much from the outside. It was made of old, graying wood, and it seemed to lean to one side, as if too tired to stand straight. Its shingle roof sagged in the middle, and the sign out front—which showed a fat, smiling spider crawling across its web toward a fly—had been bleached of color by years of rain and snow and sun.

Inside, though, it smelled of roasted fowl and fresh bread, pipe smoke and musty ale. Aside from his own room, it smelled more like home than any place Tiller had ever been. A fire burned in the hearth, and spermaceti candles glowed in iron sconces around the great room, casting flickering shadows on the walls.

There were never many people in the tavern, and today there were fewer than usual—just a pair of old men sitting in the back, talking quietly. Tiller recognized them both; they came here often.

Crumbs flew to his usual perch over the hearth. Tiller went to the bar, his cap in hand. Janna was polishing the ancient wood with a dirty white rag, her back bent, her head tipped to the side.

"Hi, Janna," Tiller said.

Janna didn't look up. "Afternoon, Tiller. You hungry, darlin'?"

"No, I ate."

At that, she stopped and raised her head, her eyes hawklike—dark and fierce. He had seen men twice her size flinch under that gaze. She was small and bone thin, with white hair so short that you could see through it to her brown scalp. Her face was bony, wrinkled, and forbidding, even when she wasn't angry. Tiller had been afraid of her for a long time, but he wasn't anymore, now that he knew her.

Janna had been a slave once when she was a little girl. She had told him that. She and her family had worked on one of the islands. But when she sailed with her master to the colonies, their ship encountered a storm. Everyone was killed except Janna. Tiller didn't know any more. He had heard people say it was a miracle she hadn't been taken by another slave owner. Others said that she had been, but had eventually bought her freedom. Tiller didn't know which was true. He only knew that she and Gil owned the Fat Spider together, and that Janna didn't like to answer questions about her past.

"Did you sell somethin'?" she asked Tiller, starting to polish again.

"I did, but that's not how I got food."

"Who'd you sell to?"

"Paul, up in the North End," Tiller said.

"He's a good man. An' where'd you ge' th' food?"

"From Miss Jackson."

Janna scowled. "What'd she want?"

Tiller opened his mouth to answer, but then closed it again. The more he thought about what had happened back in the Brazen Head, the more he realized that he had done wrong. He didn't know how to tell Janna. Maybe he was still a little bit afraid of her after all.

Janna straightened, resting her hands on her hips. "Tiller, what'd she want?"

"She asked me questions about you," he said, speaking to her belly. "She wanted to know if you could do magic. She wants you to do a spell for her, so she told me to talk to you. She knows you don't like her."

"She's right abou' that last," Janna muttered. "An' she wanted you t' arrange it for her."

He shook his head. "Mostly she wanted to know if you really did magic. And . . . and she asked me to talk to you. I'm sorry, Janna."

"Look at me, Tiller."

Tiller raised his eyes to hers. His gaze kept sliding away, but each time it did, he forced it back.

"I ain't angry with you. You didn' do nothin' wrong. You understand me?"

He stared back at her, wanting to believe her, but still feeling that he had done a bad thing.

"Wha' kind of magic she want? She say?"

"Love spell, I think," Tiller said. "She's coming here to talk to you."

"Who is coming here?"

Janna turned. Tiller stayed utterly still. Gil stood in the rear doorway, a cask of wine resting on his shoulder, anchored there by a large, powerful hand.

"Don' worry about it, Gil," Janna said. She started polishing the bar again, but she cast a quick look Tiller's way and gave a small shake of her head.

Gil walked behind the bar and put down the cask. He extended a hand to Tiller, as he did whenever they met. Tiller gripped it, watching as Gil's hand appeared to swallow his own.

"How are you today, my friend?" Gil asked, his accent more subtle than Janna's, and harder to place. He had the dark curls of a Spaniard, the pale grayish green eyes of a Scotsman, and a black beard and mustache, with long, thin braids hanging from either side of his chin that was unlike anything Tiller had seen on any man.

"I'm fine, Gil. How are you?"

The barman frowned. "I would be better if I had an answer to the question I asked a moment ago. Someone is coming to my bar, and Janna is unhappy about it. I would like to know why."

Janna rolled her eyes. "Tiller, would you like an ale?"

"Yes, all right."

She filled a tankard and handed it to him. "Why don' you take a seat over there near th' fire."

He did as he was told, knowing why she was sending him away. He sat with his back to the bar and stared into the hearth. But he listened.

"It's Mary Jackson," Janna said, her voice low. "She sent tha' boy here t' get me t' do magic for her."

"Mary Jackson. She owns a tavern, does she not?"

"Th' Brazen Head."

"Do you know what kind of magic she wants?" Gil asked.

"Uh huh. She been chasin' tha' merchant o' hers for more than a year now. She wants me t' spell him. Make him see her different, or somethin'."

"So cast your spell, make her pay a lot of money, and send her on her way."

"Yeah, I know," Janna said. "But I don' like her usin' Tiller tha' way. He's barely more than a child."

"I'm not a child," Tiller said, loud enough for both of them to hear.

He heard Janna sigh, then heard her walk out from behind the bar.

"You weren' supposed t' be listenin'," she said, sitting down across from him, a small smile on her lips.

"I'm not a child," Tiller said.

Her expression sobered. "I know you're no'. I'm sorry for sayin' that."

"I might not be smart like you and Gil, but I get by all right."

"Yes, you do. Bu' tha' don' give her th' right t' use you as a way of talkin' t' me."

"Maybe I used her," Tiller said. "I'm the one who got free food."

Janna stared at him for a moment and then burst out laughing. "Well, tha's true enough, isn' it?" She eyed him a moment longer, shaking her head, a big grin on her face. Then she patted his arm, stood, and walked back to the bar.

Tiller sipped his ale, pleased with himself. It wasn't every day that he managed to make Janna laugh like that.

The feeling didn't last long. A few minutes after Janna left him, the door to the tavern opened, flooding the great room with silver light. Tiller twisted around in his chair and saw that Miss Jackson had come.

She stood at the entrance to the tavern for a moment, squinting in the dim light. Her gaze passed over Tiller as if he wasn't there and settled on the bar where Janna stood, a scowl on her lean face.

"There you are, Janna," Miss Jackson said, as if she and Janna were old friends. She walked to the bar, pulling off her mitts and unbuttoning her coat. "What a lovely aroma. What are you cooking?"

"Chowder," Janna said stiffly.

"Would you mind spooning me a bowl? I must try it."

Janna eyed the woman, her tongue pushing out her cheek. But then she stalked into the kitchen, returning a few seconds later with a bowl and spoon, which she placed on the bar. "Four pence," she said.

"Yes, of course," Miss Jackson said. But she didn't pull out her purse. Instead, she took up her spoon and tasted the chowder.

"Oh, that's very good. Even better than my own. And I grew up eating chowder."

Janna frowned, picked up her polishing rag, and started to make her way to the far end of the bar.

"Hold on there, Janna. I'd like to talk to you about something."

Janna stopped and faced her again. "Yes, Mary, what is it?"

A cold smile flitted across Miss Jackson's face. She glanced briefly in Tiller's direction. "There's something else I'd like you to do for me," she said, her voice dropping. "I'll pay whatever you normally charge, but I want it done today."

"Uh huh. And wha' would tha' be?"

"I think you know," Miss Jackson said, still speaking quietly.

Janna walked back to where Miss Jackson sat. "No," she said.

"You don't know?"

"I won' do it."

"Won't do what?"

"I won' be castin' a spell for you. I don' care how much money you have."

Miss Jackson glanced around quickly, like she thought that lots of people were listening. Tiller was. But the two old men in the back didn't seem to care what she said.

"You don't even know what kind of magic I want," she told Janna, whispering now.

Janna grinned, her teeth sharp and pale yellow. "You wan' a love spell. You wan' tha' man you fancy t' leave his missus and come 'roun' t'—"

Miss Jackson stood abruptly, spilling her chowder onto Janna's bar. "How dare you!"

"I don' like you usin' my friends t' ge' t' me. I don' like you comin' 'roun' my place an' pretendin' you an' me got anythin' in common." Janna crossed her arms over her chest and raised her chin. "I don' like you."

"I will not be spoken to in that way! Certainly not by a Negro! I don't hold with slavery, but I believe a lashing would do you some good!"

Janna laughed. "My Mama always though' so, too. Turns out she was wrong." She started to mop up the spilled chowder. "I think i's time you were leavin', Mary."

Miss Jackson didn't move. "I need this done."

"You'll have t' find someone else t' do it."

"Ten pounds."

Tiller's mouth fell open. Ten pounds! He couldn't remember ever seeing that much money.

Janna didn't even look up. "No."

"Fifteen."

Janna picked up the bowl and spoon, and started toward the kitchen. "Goodbye, Mary."

Miss Jackson leaned forward, her hands on the bar. "There are those in Boston who would be quite alarmed to learn that a witch lives here in the city," she said, her whisper sounding harsh, like a spitting cat.

Janna halted.

"There are clergy—men I know—who would relish the chance to hang a servant of Satan."

"You can' prove anythin'."

"I don't have to. I'm a Christian woman and you're a Negro, a former slave. My word against yours. Be smart, woman. Who do you think people will believe?"

Janna walked back to the bar and carefully put down the bowl. Gil loomed in the doorway behind her, but he hung back and kept silent.

"All I want is one spell," Miss Jackson said, whispering again. "Cast it, and you have nothing to fear from me. You can have the money, and you can keep your tavern." She surveyed the room, her lip curling. "Such as it is."

Janna took a long, weary breath. "One spell, you say?"

Miss Jackson smiled, opening her hands. "That's all."

"An' otherwise you'll tell everyone tha' I'm a witch."

"You leave me no choice."

Janna shrugged. "My answer is still no." Her expression went stony. "Now get out o' my place."

Miss Jackson looked like she had been slapped. Her eyes were wide, her cheeks pale, her mouth open in a small 'o.' At last she drew herself up and said, "Fine, then! You'll be in prison by nightfall."

She was halfway to the door when a booming voice said, "Wait!"

Miss Jackson stopped.

"I will do this magic you want," Gil said, stepping to the bar.

"Gil, no!"

"Forgive Janna," Gil said, his gaze never leaving Miss Jackson's face. "She forgets herself sometimes. Just as she forgets that I do not work for her or follow her commands."

Miss Jackson walked slowly back to the bar. "You can do magic, too?" she asked quietly.

A sly smile lifted the corners of his mouth. "I have some skill, yes." He tapped the bar with his hand. "Put your money here, and I will cast for you."

"Gil—"

"Get the tablet," he said to Janna.

She shook her head. "Don' do this. Jus' let her go."

"Get the tablet."

Tiller had never seen such fear in Janna's eyes. She walked out from behind the bar and over to the hearth. She dragged a chair over, and stood on it so that she could reach a large square slab that hung over the fireplace. Tiller had seen it on the wall before, but had never paid much attention to it. It was similar in color to the bricks used to build Faneuil Hall, and it was covered with strange lines and symbols. Given how Janna cradled it in her thin arms, Tiller guessed that it was heavy.

"Do you want me to carry that, Janna?" he asked.

She merely shook her head and carried it back to the bar.

Miss Jackson had placed several coins on the wood.

"Good," Gil said, when Janna placed the tablet before him. "Now, fill a cup with ale."

"Gil—"

"Ale, Janna."

She filled a cup. Gil reached below the bar and produced a stoppered bottle that could have been just as old as that clay tablet. The glass was clouded and stained, and the cork was as black as pitch. Gil placed the cup of ale on the tablet. Then he unstoppered the bottle and held it over the cup. Muttering to himself, he allowed three drops of clear pink liquid to drop into Miss Jackson's ale.

Tiller found that he was on his feet, straining to see what happened when the two liquids mixed. He saw nothing unusual, but he felt that same vibration in the floor that he felt when Janna cast her spells. Only stronger. Much stronger. It was as if the bar was a giant violin, and Gil had just dragged a bow across its strings.

"What now?" Miss Jackson asked, sounding a little nervous.

"Now, you drink," Gil said. "Drink it all. And when you are done, go back to your home, and wait."

"That's it?"

"That is it."

She picked up her ale, hesitated for an instant, and then drank. It took her several minutes to finish the cup, and in all that time, no one spoke. When at last she finished, she looked expectantly at Gil.

"Now he'll come to me?"

"I swear that he will," Gil said. "Go home and wait."

"Yes, all right. Thank you." Miss Jackson stood, pausing to eye Janna. Tiller thought she might say something, but in the end she merely turned away and hurried from the tavern.

"What'd you do t' her?" Janna asked, when the woman was gone.

"I sent the man to her, just as she wanted."

Janna shook her head. "Tha's no' all you did. There's always more with your magic."

"Tiller," Gil said. "I am going to roast venison tonight. Will you stay and eat with us?"

Tiller beamed. "Sure I will, Gil. Thank you."

"Good. In the meantime, have another ale."

Gil walked back to the kitchen, Janna staring after him. After a few seconds she seemed to remember that Tiller was still there.

She filled a new cup with ale, and brought it to him.

"Here you go, Tiller," she said kindly.

"I'm sorry, Janna. I shouldn't have said anything to Miss Jackson."

"Don' worry 'bout it," she said. "Gil took care of it."

Tiller drank that second ale and two more, enjoying the warmth of the fire and the feeling of having his rent in this pocket. As the day wore on, and the sky outside the tavern began to darken, the great room filled with the scent of roasting meat, so that Tiller's mouth watered and his stomach growled.

More and more people came to the Fat Spider. By the time Gil emerged from the back bearing a huge platter of food, the tavern was as crowded as Tiller had ever seen it. Somehow, men and women from all over Boston knew to come. Maybe the smell of Gil's venison had drifted through the streets. Maybe word of his feast had spread from home to home. Whatever the reason, it was a night unlike any Tiller could remember.

He ate and he drank until he'd had his fill, and then he had more. Eventually he must have dozed off at his table by the hearth. When he woke, sometime later, most of the people were gone. Gil stood beside his chair, firelight dancing across his features and gleaming in his eyes.

"I want you to stay here tonight, my friend. It is late for you to be walking home."

"But my cart. And Crumbs."

"They will be fine. You have my word." Gil smiled. "Crumbs has eaten well." He draped a blanket over Tiller and pulled over another chair so that Tiller could rest his legs. "Is there anything at your home that you need?" Gil asked. "Anything dear to you, that you must have?"

"Just the picture of my Mama and Papa."

"A painting?" Gil asked.

"A drawing."

"How big?"

Tiller held his hands a few inches apart. "Like this."

Gil nodded. He strode back to the bar and spoke in low tones with Janna. She cast a quick glance Tiller's way, but then nodded, drawing a small knife from a pocket of her dress. Tiller recognized the blade. It was the one Janna used when she drew blood from her arm for a conjuring.

Tiller saw her step back into the kitchen. Moments later, he felt another pulse of magic. It was weaker than what he had felt when Gil made Miss Jackson her drink, but still it made the tavern floor hum.

Janna reemerged from the kitchen, stepped out from behind the bar, and walked to Tiller's makeshift bed carrying the portrait.

"Here you go, darlin'," she said. "Sleep well."

"Thank you, Janna," Tiller whispered. He studied the drawing, front and back. It was his. He touched his fingers to his lips and then to the image of his parents. "Goodnight, Mama, Papa."

He propped the picture against the back of the second chair, settled back down, and was soon sleeping once more.

He woke again several hours later. The tavern smelled strongly of smoke, and he could hear Janna and Gil speaking at the doorway, their voices lowered.

"What've you done?" Janna asked him.

"I have done nothing. I granted her wish. The rest she brought to the casting herself."

"Tha's no'—"

"You said it yourself," Gil told her. "Her merchant has a wife. Did she not expect that when the man came to her, the wife would follow? Mary was foolish."

"Bu' your spell—"

"Did nothing more or less than I promised it would. Her man came to her. That he did so clumsily, making no attempt to hide his destination. . . . That is not my fault."

"His wife started th' fire?"

"I know nothing for certain."

"Sure you do," Janna said, a smile in her voice.

"If I were to guess, I would say that the fire started upstairs, in Mary's bedchamber. And that many items were thrown in anger, including a candle or two, or perhaps an oil lamp."

"You a dangerous man, Gil."

Gil said nothing, and when Janna spoke again, she sounded worried.

"It looks like th' whole city's burnin'."

"It is not. Only a portion of it."

"Still, look at it. Who knows how many're dead?"

"I know. None."

"Gil—"

"None are dead, Janna. You have my word. You also have my word on this: she will not be back, and she will not threaten you again."

"Gil?" Tiller called. "What's happened?"

"Go back to sleep, my friend."

"What time is it?"

"After midnight, but still several hours before dawn. You should be sleeping."

Tiller got up from his chair and crossed to the tavern entrance. "What's happened, Gil?"

Gil didn't answer right away. "There is a fire."

"Where?"

"Near your home. There was a great wind, and it pushed the flames all the way to the water's edge."

Tiller peered out into the night. Janna was right. It did look like the whole city was ablaze. The sky over Boston glowed a baleful inconstant orange, and dark smoke billowed over the spires and rooftops.

"I am sorry, Tiller," the barman said, looking down at him.

"That's all right, Gil." Tiller sensed that he was pardoning Gil for more than sad tidings. "Pushed them from where?"

"What?"

"Pushed the flames from where to the water?" But Tiller already knew the answer

Gil glanced at Janna, who still stared out toward the city. "From th' Brazen Head," she said quietly. "Tha's where this started."

"You say that Miss Jackson isn't dead?" Tiller asked.

"She is not," Gil told him. "I swear it."

Tiller nodded. "Good. She gives me food sometimes."

Historical Note: Early in the morning on March 20, 1760, a fire started at Boston's Brazen Head Tavern, which was owned by Mary Jackson. Driven by powerful winds, the fire consumed three hundred forty-nine buildings and homes, left more than a thousand people homeless, and destroyed more than one hundred thousand pounds worth of property. Miraculously, no one was killed. To this day, the cause of the fire is unknown.

LAST CALL

Patricia Bray

THE first time I 'met' him was in a London coffee-house, though I confess met is perhaps too strong a word for our brief encounter. Indeed I hardly noticed him at all when I stumbled inside, trembling as much from the night's events as from the bitter November cold.

It was just past dawn, but the coffeehouse was already bustling, the best seats by the fire taken up by a pair of haggling merchants. The serving boy eyed my disheveled appearance with disdain, but a flash of silver inspired him to fetch me a chocolate with due haste.

I took a sip of the dark brew, hoping the sweetness would drown out the taste of my fear, then held the cup between both hands to warm them.

It was my duty to report to my uncle at once. But I could not let him see me like this—my limbs shaking, fear-sweat soaking through my linens as my gorge rose in disgust. Archibald Harker was the greatest hunter the Order had ever known. While I was merely young George Harker, only son of his wastrel brother. An inconvenience at best, a distracting nuisance on those days he deigned to notice me.

Last night had been my first night with the hunters. I'd been told to join Tom Porter as he kept watch over Madame D'Argent. A simple enough assignment and a chance to prove myself worthy of the Harker name.

It had all gone wrong from the start. Tom had followed Madame's coachman into a public house, leaving me to watch her residence on my own. But instead of summoning her carriage, Madame had slipped out the servant's entrance. There had been no time to summon Tom. I had followed her on foot, growing deeply uneasy as she ventured into the poorer quarters, where no respectable woman would dare be seen. With each step I knew we had made a terrible mistake. Madame was not waiting for the full moon. Tonight was the night she would feed.

Still I hesitated. Waited. Hoping that Tom or one of the other hunters would find me. In the end it had been too late. Madame had found her prey, a young flower seller, clutching her empty basket in one hand as she made her way homeward.

Madame had struck swiftly, grasping the girl and dragging her into an alleyway, the better to feed undisturbed. She hadn't heard me approach, but my knife in her back had been warning enough. It had taken three blows to kill her, a bloody butchery that succeeded only because of her arrogance. If she'd been a fraction more cautious, I would have become just one more in the long line of victims.

Any triumph I might have felt had faded when the wounded girl crawled out from beneath Madame's corpse. Her eyes were wide with fear and why not? To her I was a crazed murderer.

My arm was in motion even before I could think. The

bloody spray from her severed throat splashed across the alley as she sagged down onto the dirt. The horror of what I had done should have overwhelmed me, but instead I was strangely calm, as if this were a tale that was happening to someone else.

I knelt beside the girl, waiting for the moment when she died. Then I checked Madame, ensuring that no breath of life remained within that treacherous bosom.

"I am sorry," I told the girl's corpse. "But there is no cure for the lamia's kiss."

It was only after I had left the bodies behind that the fear and self-loathing had struck. If I had killed Madame as soon as I had realized her errand, the girl would still be alive. But I had been weak. I had hesitated, consumed by doubts, where a true hunter would have had no such misgivings.

I took another sip of chocolate, remembering how the girl's golden hair had fanned out around her fallen body, the only shroud she would ever wear. Then I glanced down at the cup, and saw that my fingernails were bloody.

I turned and vomited on the floor.

Moments later I was seized by the back of my waistcoat and hauled unceremoniously to my feet. A great hulking brute dragged me to the entranceway and then heaved me onto the cobblestones outside. As I lay there, blinking, I wondered if it was possible to sink any lower.

The brute disappeared for a moment and then returned with my pack, which he tossed out beside me. From my position on the ground he appeared godlike, taller than any mortal man, his curly black hair and dark complexion lit by the rising sun. Strangely, there was sympathy rather than contempt in his light green eyes.

"Next time beer," he said.

He retreated inside, shutting the door behind him. I shook my head to clear my wits, then slowly got to my feet. It was time to face my uncle's wrath.

A decade later I was still known as Young George, though now I had a score of kills to my credit. My uncle still frowned when I came into his presence, but gradually he had given me more and more responsibility, as the ranks of the Order dwindled.

Tom Porter was dead, his throat torn out by a vampyr. Quincy Jones might as well be dead—a drooling, bedridden cripple who'd been cursed by a gorgon's dying gaze. Other men had taken their places, but few lasted more than a season. Either the work drove them mad, or they fell victim to one of the many evils we fought.

A secret war, with no medals, no recognition, nothing except the privilege of serving the Order of Sidon. For centuries the members of the Order had labored in secret, driven underground by papal persecution and a world indifferent to the evils that walked in our very midst.

It was tempting to wonder what would happen if we shrugged off the cloak of secrecy. Would governments give us soldiers to help root out the evils that lurked within their borders? Could men of science find new ways to destroy these monsters, rather than the painstaking rituals passed down from the first knights? How many men would be sacrificed before the great Archibald Harker deigned to ask for aid?

In my mind I heard my uncle's voice. "You reason as a child," he would say, as he had said countless times before. "The world is not so simple. For every dozen that would fight these monsters there is at least one Judas who would swear allegiance, and that is a risk we dare not take."

Twelve to one odds sounded fair to me, but I was merely a hunter. And my uncle's point about the traitors within mankind's midst was well taken, as my presence in Paris attested. At least two members of the infamous Monks of Medmenham had fled to Paris, bringing their sacrilegious rites with them. The villains—not content with dressing up orgies as Bacchanalian ceremonies— had plunged further and further into the dark arts until at last they'd summoned up a demon. Henri Brun, the head of the Order in Paris, had sent for help, and I'd been dispatched to assist him.

We'd tracked down and destroyed the demon, then dealt justice to those who had summoned him. But by then my interest had been piqued by the work of Doctor Mesmer, who had taken Paris by storm.

Mesmer claimed to have discovered an essential life force, that he called animal magnetism. I had read his papers and after attending a lecture by one of his colleagues I'd emerged wondering if he had indeed discovered proof of the living soul within us. Many demons fed upon humans, some on blood, but others drained their victims without leaving a single mark. Could they be feeding on this force? And if so, was it possible that we could understand it? Could we find a way to prevent demons from feeding, or perhaps even create a weapon that could be turned against them?

If Mesmer were not such a public figure, the Order would have approached him long ago. Instead we'd been reduced to indirect overtures, carefully interviewing his associates and gathering as much information as possible before making contact.

I'd spent weeks trying to get an appointment with Joseph-Ignace Guillotin, a distinguished member of the Faculty of Medicine, recently appointed to the royal commission investigating Mesmer's claims. Doctor Guillotin was far too important to waste his time on an Englishman with neither rank nor fortune to recommend him, but finally he'd agreed to a brief meeting. He'd chosen the place, a popular café near the opera houses.

In the street outside, brightly-dressed jades plied their trade, but the café was surprisingly civilized. Giving my name to the attendant at the door, I made my way to one of the small tables inside.

A few moments later a serving woman came over. "*Une bière pour vous?*" she inquired, apparently having recognized me as English by the cut of my coat.

It was surely ignorance rather than an insult, for she had no means of knowing that only uncouth laborers drank beer in the evenings.

"*Vin pour deux, s'il vous plait,*" I replied. "*Un bien port.*"

She returned a few moments later with a carafe of port and two glasses. I poured one for myself as the clock chimed the seventh hour.

Around me voices chattered away, speaking too swiftly for me to understand. But the tone was familiar even if the words were not, as the inhabitants argued, gossiped and recounted the news of the day. Looking at the dandies dressed for an evening of leisure, I could not help wondering if one of their number would fall prey to evil's dark lure. Perhaps the next would-be sorcerer was right before me. There, that man with the wine-flushed face and sober black coat. Was he simply unfashionable? Or had he chosen the color black as a sign of his evil intentions, even now fancying himself in allegiance with Satan?

I swiftly downed the glass of wine and poured myself another, disturbed by the fancies which crowded my brain. I had been away from home for too long, and saw evil everywhere.

The memories of that cellar, and the corpses Brun and I had discovered, still haunted me. Bones jumbled together; men, women, children, even animal bones mixed in as if there were no difference between them. We'd been reduced to counting skulls to try and guess the number of victims.

The irony was that the demon had been responsible for only a handful of deaths. The others had been murdered by ordinary men, as part of their profane rituals.

A second glass followed the first, as the quarter hours chimed past, and still there was no sign of Doctor Guillotin. When the carafe was finished, the servant fetched me another.

It was nearly nine o'clock when Doctor Guillotin arrived, full of apologies for his delay. Fortunately his English was quite good, so I did not have to search my wine-soaked wits for what few scraps of French remained.

I introduced myself as an instructor from King's College in London, who had been sent to inquire into Doctor Mesmer's methods. Explaining that I was a surgeon by training, I was eager to seek out advice from such an esteemed physician as Doctor Guillotin. Indeed I was as well trained as any English surgeon, having been taught by the Order how to wield a knife to both heal and harm. Guillotin, like most physicians, regarded surgeons as little more than butchers, but he seemed pleased that I recognized my limitations.

"The report must be reviewed by the committee and then presented to the king, of course," he said.

"Of course," I agreed. "But surely you must know enough by now to advise me. Is it worth the time and expense to learn Mesmer's methods and then teach them to others? Or is he deluded as some claim?"

"Mesmer is a fraud," Guillotin said, without the slightest hesitation. "A fraud of the worst sort, one who preys upon the desperate for his own enrichment."

He took a sip of his wine, while I took a gulp of my own.

"Evil," I said.

Guillotin frowned as he considered my remark. "I would not have used that word, but there is some truth in it. By convincing his patients to turn away from proper scientific treatments, he is prolonging their misery, perhaps even condemning them to madness or death. Such a man has to be stopped."

For a Frenchman, Guillotin was surprisingly insightful. Then again, he had been born in England.

"If you stop one evil, another springs up," I explained. I leaned forward, pressing both hands against the marble tabletop, which had developed an alarming tendency to wobble. Or perhaps that was me. "The only solution is to cut off its head."

Guillotin drew back. "Cut off its head?"

I nodded emphatically, then drew my right hand across my throat. "A single blow."

I thought back to my first kill. My first strike on the lamia would have been a fatal blow to a human, but it had barely slowed her down. It had been luck, not skill, that had enabled me to stay alive long enough to strike the killing blow.

"The trick is to find the monsters among us. Then death should be swift."

"Your English justice is not as ours," Guillotin said. "But even the condemned should not suffer from barbarism."

I blinked, having lost the thread of the conversation. Was he referring to Medmenham's victims? Or to something else?

Doctor Guillotin rose to his feet. "I have an engagement elsewhere," he explained. "I hope my information has been useful."

"Indeed," I said, standing up in a show of gentlemanly good manners. "I must thank you again for the courtesy of your time."

The crowded room began to blur, and I blinked my watering eyes to clear them. I caught a glimpse of a figure behind the bar—a tall, broad-shouldered man, with curly dark hair. His eyes met mine, and for a moment I thought I knew him.

Someone bumped into me from behind, and when I looked back at the bar, the man was gone.

Shrugging, I left the café and returned to my lodgings. I had lost my taste for foreign mysteries—let the French tend to their own affairs. Guillotin's evaluation of Mesmer matched the conclusions I had drawn from my own investigations. My word alone would not have been enough to convince the Order, but Guillotin's reputation was impeccable.

I spent the next few years in Scotland, dealing with a coven of hags and the nightstalkers they had unleashed. I'd completely forgotten about Guillotin and that night in the café, until news came from France of his terrible invention.

Cut off their heads, I'd suggested and indeed he'd found a way to do just that. But it was of no use to me, since unlike the ill-fated aristocrats, vampyrs couldn't be convinced to walk calmly to their doom.

Decades passed. I took an apprentice. When he was killed, I took another. Mere survival was enough to earn me a seat on the council. Later, when my uncle died of apoplexy, no one was more shocked than I to discover that he'd named me his heir.

These days the London branch of the Order consisted of men that I'd trained myself, or who had been apprenticed to one of those that I'd trained. When someone referred to The Harker, it was me that they spoke of. Which was better than my other nickname, The Old Man.

I was past sixty now, a ripe old age for any man, for all I looked barely thirty. There were days when I hated the figure that my mirror revealed, hated the unlined skin that showed no signs of what I had endured.

My wife Mary had died in childbirth decades before, and there were none left in the Order who remembered her. None to recollect the babe who had been sent to the countryside to be raised by distant cousins. The child—or rather man, for surely so he must be—had no notion of what it meant to bear the Harker name. It was the one gift I could give him.

As the years passed and my body refused to age, I withdrew more and more from the world. Members of the Order accepted what the rest of society would not. The burdens of leadership were heavy, and it was only now that I finally understood my uncle. Like him, I was obsessed with both preserving the Order, and ensuring that I found a fitting successor who could take my place.

Samuel Forsythe seemed a likely enough lad. Though lad was perhaps not quite the term, since a stranger seeing us together would presume him the elder. I had left Forsythe in charge in London, while I visited the European outposts of the Order, doing my best to renew ties that had been severed by decades of conflict.

Some of the outposts had been welcoming, others less so, wary that I would use England's recent military triumphs as an excuse for seizing control. When they discovered I had no intention of trying to exert my will, they'd gradually warmed to me. Not enough to share all of their information, of course. But enough to promise cooperation, and to share those bits that they deemed safe.

It would take years to rebuild the network of alliances, and I knew I wasn't the man for the task. It was all I could do to force myself out of bed each morning. It had been a relief to leave the chapter house in Geneva behind, and to fall back into the guise of an indolent traveler.

When a chill spring rain started falling, I stopped at the first likely inn, rather than pressing on. I was tired, with a weariness that had sunk into my very bones. I'd seen too much, lost too many good friends, and the prospect of enduring endless decades of the same inspired only dull apathy rather than the righteous fervor I had once commanded.

Yet neither could I leave the fight, not while I still had breath in my body.

My host, who spoke French with a German accent,

showed me to my quarters, a small room tucked under the eaves. He apologized, explaining that his finer rooms had been bespoken by a party of English travelers. I'd observed them in the courtyard when I'd arrived. There were two ladies accompanied by a solitary gentleman. One of the ladies was clearly with child, but it was the other that the gentleman referred to as his wife, as he asked for rooms in halting German.

In my younger days I would have gone over at once and introduced myself, marveling over the coincidence of discovering fellow Englishmen in a tiny Swiss village. But today I'd lingered off to the side, content to wait as the innkeeper attended to them, knowing that my Italian-made cloak and Prussian cavalry-style boots marked me as a Continental.

The inn's tiny common room was empty, consisting of one large table, and a smaller one next to the serving station. I rapped sharply on the door that appeared to lead to the kitchen, then sat down at the small table.

A few minutes passed, and I was about to help myself to the wine I could see behind the counter when the door swung open. The man who entered was so tall he had to duck as he came through the door. When he straightened up, I knew him at once.

"You!" I exclaimed.

"Are you ready for that beer?" he asked, as if it had been forty minutes since we last spoke, not forty years.

"Wine, the Rhenish will do," I said, pointing to the bottle that had caught my eye.

He took down the bottle and poured me a glass. After a moment's consideration he poured a second for himself, then came over. Setting the bottle on the table between us, he took a seat.

He was still a big man, though not the giant of my youthful recollections. But his appearance was unchanged, as if the years had no power to touch him.

"To long life," he said, raising his glass in toast.

Habit had me lifting my glass automatically before I realized what he had said. "Life," I repeated, feeling my lips twist in a wry grin.

We each drained our glasses.

I eyed him warily, still not quite sure what to make of him. Unnaturally long life was often the sign of a pact with the devil, but I'd never yet met such a one who retained a sense of humor.

"You look well for a man of your age," I said.

"I could say the same for you," he replied. He spoke excellent English, but no one looking at him would mistake him for an Englishman.

Five years ago I would have pestered him with questions.

Ten years ago I would have made a strategic retreat, gathering allies so I could launch an investigation.

Thirty years ago I would have tried to kill him.

He poured another glass and we drank in silence. After a few moments he rose, making his way back into the kitchen, then returning with a plate of brown bread and goat cheese.

We sat in companionable silence as the rain pounded against the shutters, sipping the pale Rhenish wine.

By my fourth glass I found my voice again.

"Unicorn vomit," I said.

He raised both eyebrows, great hairy monstrosities that briefly distracted me from my tale.

"Slipped, fell, and some must have landed in my mouth. Nasty stuff." I shuddered in remembrance.

My ribs broken, my hands burning from the hag's final spell, I'd nonetheless labored to free the unicorn from her trap. Then, after vomiting out the hag's poison, the damned beast had trotted off without so much as a backward look. Ungrateful buggers. It was no wonder that the royal herd at Balmoral was the last in the land. No one else would bother to care for such fickle creatures.

"You?" I asked.

"A curse."

Poor bastard. Most men thought of eternal life as a gift, but he had the right of it. It was a curse.

"I have seen much in my days. As have you," he said.

We traded improbable stories. Guillaume claimed to have seen the great fire that destroyed London. I told him of hunting the dancing apemen—humans who went mad as their bodies were transformed into beasts.

He topped that with an improbable story of the night a god and an emperor had strolled into his tavern.

The party of English travelers arrived for their dinner. The innkeeper summoned Guillaume to service, but one glare from Guillaume was enough to send the innkeeper scurrying to fetch his own dishes.

I sensed Guillaume would no longer be employed come morning.

Our dinner consisted of sausages fried with potatoes, again fetched by Guillaume. From what I could see, the English party was enjoying less common fare, not that I had any complaints.

As the sun had set, our stories grew darker.

"It's not the grave robbers you have to worry about," I explained, picking up the threads of an earlier tale. "The men who dig up corpses for medical students are simply greedy. Even those who are said to hasten the sick along their way—in order to provide the freshest of corpses—they are merely amoral. No, it's the ones who buy the corpses that you should fear."

"And why is that?" he asked.

"Because at least some of them are resurrectionists. They aren't studying anatomy, they are trying to create life."

I noticed that one of the women had moved her chair closer to us, so she could eavesdrop on our tales. It was the dark-haired woman, who had been introduced as Frau Shelley.

"They take bits from this corpse and bits from that, then sew them together. Trying to create an automaton—a creature without a soul, slave to their wishes. The very worst kind of abomination."

The woman's gasp of horror was everything I'd been expecting. Her husband looked up, noticing her defection, and loudly declared that it was time for them to retire.

I'd crossed a line tonight. I'd exposed the secrets of the Order to a stranger, recounted tales that had never been meant for outsiders to hear. No matter that Frau Shelley would dismiss what she'd heard as the fanciful imaginings of a drunkard. It was enough that I knew what I had done.

Worse yet, I did not care.

As silence fell over the common room, Guillaume regarded me for a long moment. At last, he nodded.

"Are you ready for that beer?" he asked.

I thought about the years behind me. The horrors that kept me awake at nights. The endless regrets, for each victim I had failed to save.

I thought of enduring this way for decades. Centuries. Waging a war that could never be won, could only be endured.

Forsythe was ready to lead. There'd be no one to miss me. Not really. The Old Man would join the ranks of heroes—legends meant to inspire those too naïve to realize the cost of their service. Better a dead legend than a living relic who would infect them with my own bitter despair.

I watched as Guillaume pulled a dusty jug out from under the counter and filled a pewter tankard. Even from here I could feel the waves of magic that rolled off it.

I wondered if this was his true curse—that he could bring ease to others but never to himself.

"Yes," I said. "I am ready."

THE ALCHEMY OF ALCOHOL

Seanan McGuire

San Francisco, California, 1899

A faint tracery of the evening light managed to bleed in through the bar's windows, tinting the air the color of good Barbados rum. It had started as light rum, trending into golden as the sun continued its descent. Now it was turning a dark-rum-red, which meant true night couldn't be far behind. "Andy, go ahead and turn the gas up. Just a quarter inch, mind, and no more."

There's an art to properly lighting a drinking establishment—an art that's dying fast in this vulgar age of electric lights and cheap gas. Too dark and no one sees what they're drinking; too bright, and everyone sees what they're drinking. Neither direction is good for business. A successful bar needs to balance mystery with secrecy, true class with shabby gentility and, most of all, obscurity with discretion. People need to feel confident that they can drink in peace, without concern that they'll be intercepted while conducting whatever assignations they can't expose to more direct light. That's why, in my bar, the windows are always covered with a carefully maintained mixture of dust, soot, and coal powder, the gas is never opened past a certain mark, and there are no electric lights outside the living spaces above and the workroom below. Perhaps the time for places like mine is ending, but until it does, the lights will stay low, the windows will stay opaque, and the house whiskey will stay cheap.

I generally ask Gil to adjust the lighting, when I can't take the time to do it myself. He has delicate hands for such a large gentleman. Sadly, I'd spent the night occupied with my studies, and he'd been forced to work the early shift behind the bar, despite having closed three nights in a row. Gil was asleep upstairs, and likely to remain so unless the building actually caught fire. That left the task to Andy, who was never the best choice for anything requiring fine attention to detail.

The few drinkers who'd arrived before sunset grumbled as Andy adjusted the lights, but subsided back into their cups once it became clear that things wouldn't be getting any brighter than they'd been before. I nodded approvingly in his direction, and went back to polishing the bar. She's a grand old girl, pure ash wood from England, older than me by a hundred years and likely to outlive me by at least a hundred more.

I was topping off a pint for one of the regulars when the door swung open, the sound familiar enough to attract no more than a flicker of interest. Whoever it was would either find a seat and wait for service or come over to demand it. Either way, I'd ruin the foam if I didn't finish the pull before letting myself get distracted.

The sound of shattering glass was more than sufficient to distract me. Old Tom, sensing that his beer was about to move beyond his reach forever, broke a cardinal rule of bar etiquette and leaned across the bar to snatch the pint from my hand. I scarcely noticed. I was already turning toward the sound, shoulders rigid with fury. Realizing that I might need a weapon, I grabbed a bottle from the back of the bar, brandishing it.

The man responsible for sweeping half a dozen glasses and a quarter-bottle of good scotch to the floor stared at me. I returned the favor, though he only held my attention for a moment, I must admit.

In my defense, the corpse was entirely unexpected.

I have been working in bars and public houses since I was sixteen, when my father got me a job as a waitress in the bar he tended. In that not-inconsiderable length of time, I've seen all manner of things displayed on bars. Gold doubloons from pirate treasure, rare artifacts from South America, rattlesnake skins, and—on one note-worthy occasion—a ship's cat and her litter of kittens. I kept one of the kittens, and she's done an excellent job at keeping the mice from the storeroom ever since. I did not think the dead woman was likely to perform the same service. Nor would I be inclined to keep her.

Fixing the corpse-bearer with a stern eye, I folded my arms—the gesture somewhat complicated by the bottle—and demanded, "What, sir, do you think you're doing? This is a public house, not a funeral parlor." As an afterthought, I added, "And you'll be paying for those glasses."

"I'm terribly sorry, miss, but this is an emergency." He straightened as he spoke, and I realized for the first time how distressingly attractive he was. His hair was the color of ripe wheat, and his skin was a deep tan entirely at odds with the cut of his coat, which bespoke a man who'd never done a day's labor in his life. Gentlemen are a rare sight in my establishment. Gentlemen carrying corpses were an entirely new experience. "I'd heard that this bar—ah." He glanced around at the regulars, all of whom were ignoring the dead body in favor of their drinks, and at Andy, who was openly gawking. Then he lowered his voice, and said, "I'd heard that the owner was an alchemist. Please, can you fetch him for me? I can pay quite well for his time."

"First you can pay for the glasses," I countered. "After that, you can get the body off my bar, and perhaps I'll let you start explaining why you brought it here."

"I—what?"

I put down the bottle and thrust my hand in his direction, palm upward. "I'm Mina Norton. This is my bar, hence the name of 'Norton's.' Now, sir, if you would like to depart here with both your bodies intact, you will pay me, and then explain yourself."

"Oh." He fumbled for his purse. "I didn't think you'd be so. . . ."

"Female?"

"Accessible." A large wad of bills was slapped into my palm. *That* attracted the attention of several regulars, who could've heard a coin clink half a mile away. I glared until they went back to their beers. Meanwhile, the blond gentleman was looking at me anxiously. "My name is James. James Holly. This is my wife, Margaret."

"I see. I would claim that it's a pleasure to meet the pair of you, but as she is dead and you have placed her on my bar, that is somewhat difficult. Did you require aid in preparing her for burial?" I allowed my attention to return to the body. Her attire was as fine as his, although I couldn't imagine any living woman allowing herself to be corseted so tightly. "I can see why you wouldn't want the undertaker to work any further. I have cosmetics that can easily cover the damage he's done." The tradition of painting bodies before burial has always struck me as ghoulish, and I'd rarely seen it taken to such an extreme. The poor girl's skin was paper-white, and her lips were the color of blood. That might not have been so bad if she'd been blonde, but her hair was black as coal. It was like having a dead fairy-tale princess decaying gently in my place of work.

"What? No!" James put a hand protectively on the dead woman's shoulder. "I'm not here so you can prepare her for burial."

"What, then?"

"I'm here so you can wake her up."

After convincing Andy to take over for me—not the easiest task, given that I employ him for his willingness to follow instructions, not his ability to think for himself—I waved James into the back storeroom. The question of what to do with his dead wife was easily resolved: he picked her up like she was made of cotton and swan's-down, carrying her easily as he followed me. The door swung shut behind us, sealing us away from prying eyes.

"You can put her on Andy's cot. He won't mind." I stepped out of the way, watching the dead woman for signs of life. There weren't any. The alchemist's art doesn't require quite as many anatomical samples as, say, necromancy, but I still pride myself on being able to tell the dead from the living. Margaret was definitely among the former. "Now, sir, I'm not sure where you learned of my craft, but I'm afraid I must disappoint you. Alchemy is the art of transfiguration and transformation. This does not give me the capacity to transform the dead into the living."

"That's where you're incorrect."

"I am reasonably sure that I know my own business better than you, sir."

"Not that. You come very highly recommended—although by one who, I admit, failed to identify your gender, probably because he was having a bit of amusement at my expense."

"Then what?"

"Margaret isn't dead."

I eyed the body. "I beg to differ."

"Well, I suppose technically, she's dead right *now*. But she isn't always."

"Most of us start as the living. It's a natural part of the human condition."

James rubbed the back of his neck with one hand. "I really am *terrible* at this part. All right: Margaret is dead right now, but she won't be dead in another three weeks or so. It's just that I need her to be awake *now*, as we're being pursued by some rather unpleasant people who want to have her buried before then."

"I see," I said, slowly. "You're insane."

"No. I'm the Summer King."

I stared at him. He nodded encouragingly. "Oh, *bollocks*."

"Funny." James smiled a little. "That's what Margaret said the first time I told her."

"And she would be ... ?"

"The Winter Queen."

I bit my tongue and counted to ten before allowing myself to answer. It wouldn't have been productive to say the first things that came to mind, which began with "get out" and promptly devolved into language even an alchemist wasn't expected to be familiar with. Finally,

I said, "Absolutely, how silly of me not to have seen it before. Can you wait here for just a moment?"

James eyed me suspiciously, smile fading. "Where are you going?"

"To get the rum. This is not something I am prepared to deal with while sober."

The tedious thing about magic is the way it insists on existing. There's far more of it than the world's assortment of magicians, alchemists, shamans, and sorcerers could ever make use of, and so it gads about manifesting in inconvenient places. Some people—like my father and myself—can learn to use magic. Others simply *are* magic, existing according to rules outside the normal boundaries of the human condition.

This includes the seasonal monarchs, once ordinary men and women who somehow, through luck, effort, or coincidence, have been chosen to live as the physical incarnations of the seasons. One human standing for Summer, one for Winter. They can live for centuries if they hold onto their thrones, and their presence prevents the seasons from getting out of balance. The world needs them to keep turning. They provide stability to an unstable system. I would have been perfectly happy to live a long and prosperous life without encountering either of them, much less both at the same time.

"And whoever heard of a Summer *King*, anyway?" I muttered, as I stalked behind a startled-looking Andy to grab a bottle of the best spiced rum in the house. As an afterthought, I also grabbed a glass. "Don't they know it's supposed to be a Summer *Queen*?"

"Ma'am?" said Andy.

I stopped. Upsetting Andy isn't nice. He's a little slow.

Not stupid—slow. Understandable, given that I crafted him from some particularly nice boulders I found beneath the Golden Gate. He does his job well, providing Gil and I don't change his instructions too quickly, and don't mind when sweeping the floor takes all day. "Don't worry, I have everything well under control. You're going to be minding the bar for a while yet. Don't let anyone into the back unless you hear screaming, all right?"

"Yes, ma'am," said Andy, nodding contentedly as he returned to wiping down the already spotless bar. Golems are easy to please. That's the nicest thing about them.

In the storeroom, James had taken a seat on the edge of the cot, holding Margaret's hand in his. Now that I was looking at him properly, it was easy to see the veracity of his claim. Fair-haired gentlemen are common enough, but how many of them actually brighten a room with the faint glow coming off their person? His eyes were the color of a midsummer sky, which seemed to me to verge ever so slightly into the kingdom of "simply too much." It even felt as if the temperature had gone up a few degrees since I left to get the rum. I fixed him with a stern eye.

"Are you bringing summer to my storeroom? I have things in here that shouldn't be heated."

James had the good grace to look faintly abashed. "I'm terribly sorry, Miss Norton. I can't help it. If it helps at all, we're near enough to harvest that I probably won't make flowers start growing from the floorboards."

"How your housekeeper must adore you." I uncorked the rum, pouring three fingers into my glass. "Now, then. If your—let's call it 'indisposed'—wife is meant to wake up in three weeks, why are you here now? Can't you simply be patient for a little while longer?"

"It's not impatience that brought us to your door. Margaret and I are quite accustomed to our . . . arrangement. It's quite soothing, actually, having a spouse who's dead for three months out of the year. Gives you time to remember why you married in the first place."

I elected not to think overly much about the implications of his statement. It seemed safer all the way around. "So what, then?"

"It's Margaret's sister, Jane. She wants to take the Winter. If she can have Margaret interred before the harvest starts the turn of seasons, then she can step up to the throne, and ascend to Winter Queen. At which point I'm in rather a lot of trouble, as Jane's husband is a huge, strapping brute, and would simply subdue me until Winter's ascension renders me powerless."

"I suppose this would be followed by his claiming Summer."

"Precisely." James gave me an earnest look. "Please, Miss Norton. I've endeavored to be a good Summer King, and a good husband. I wish neither to be deposed, nor for my wife to truly die."

I sighed before draining my rum glass in one long swallow. It didn't help much, but it made me feel a little better. "Oh, all right. Bring her along."

"Where are we going?" he asked, as he hastened to comply.

"My workroom in the basement. If I'm going to wake the dead, I'd rather not do it where it can frighten the paying customers."

There are those who insist that maintaining a business above a large hole in the earth in San Francisco is foolhardy, given the region's propensity for earthquakes. I subscribe to the school of thought which says "earthquakes are rare, explosions, less so." Through tempering and tampering, I had rendered the stone basement walls all but indestructible, which muffled the sound of any accidents I might have. The seals and sigils chiseled into the floor and ceiling blocked the room from almost all forms of magical viewing; useful, given some of the treasures it contained.

Three of the four walls were lined with shelves packed with alchemical ingredients and bottles of rare liquor—and if you don't consider well-aged scotch a treasure, you're a heathen and a fool. The fourth wall was taken up almost entirely by the twin of the upstairs bar. It was backed with a silver mirror, and held books instead of bottles. Some of those volumes were older than any tongue still spoken on the Earth. Most were alchemical in nature. Others dealt with the arcane art of bartending. They served as a personal library, and as excellent camouflage for the pride of my collection: the sacred tablet of Ninkasi, containing the original recipe for brewing beer.

"Put her on the bar," I said, as I lit the lamps. "Without destruction of property this time, if you would be so kind."

James moved to do as I instructed, positioning her in apparently perfect repose. The effect was eerie, especially with the mirror gleaming behind her.

"Snow White is not a good look for anyone," I muttered, and began taking bottles down from the shelf. "I must warn you, I've never attempted anything like this before. I can be reasonably sure I won't kill her, but I can't guarantee results."

"I understand, and will pay you for your time regardless."

"Mmm. I might like you after all." I walked over to place the bottles I'd selected on the bar next to Margaret. "Quiet, please."

James nodded, and went silent.

Mixing a potion and mixing a drink are more similar than most people would think. Both require a steady hand, a firm understanding of the ingredients, and a good idea of the desired result. Just now, this was the early resurrection of the human embodiment of winter. Not as easy as pulling a pint of ale, perhaps, but a good sight simpler than turning lead into gold and getting it to *stay* that way.

I didn't dare use mistletoe or quicksilver, for all that they were very "wintery" ingredients; Winter Queen or not, I had to work on the assumption that Margaret was still essentially human, and would look poorly on being poisoned. Bearing that in mind, I began with gin, for juniper berries and the smell of pine forests. The lady's looks influenced my next ingredient: applejack, the fruit of Snow White's downfall and a hundred harvest fairs. The resulting liquid was clear and slightly golden. I added a shot of pomegranate molasses, for Persephone's folly, which brought about the winter to begin with. "This wants ice," I said, and dropped a slice of crystallized ginger into the liquid, to add the bitter bite of winter. "Sit her up."

"What is it?" James boosted Margaret into a sitting position, leaning her against him like a full-sized rag doll.

"Either the best drink I ever mixed, or a waste of some excellent alcohol. We'll know in a moment." I uncorked the last bottle, adding a single shot—and with it, the ice. As soon as the liquids met, frost began to form, spreading up the sides of the glass to sting my hand. I gave the concoction a single stir with a silver spoon from my workbench, more for show than anything else, and offered it to James. "Here. Give her this."

He looked at the icy glass warily. "What's in it?"

"Gin, applejack, pomegranate molasses, ginger, and a shot of liquid midnight, captured on the coastline on winter solstice. If that isn't enough to bring her around, I can't help you."

"How did you bottle midnight?" James took the glass from my hand, the frost melting instantly where his fingers touched. Stirring had turned the drink from clear amber with dark red at the bottom to an overall autumn-leaf red. It smelled like snowfall, and like secrets.

"Trade secret."

"I see. Thank you, whatever the results." James inclined his head solemnly toward me, and raised the glass to Margaret's lips. It was disturbingly like watching a child playing tea party, offering drinks to stuffed rabbits and favored dolls.

Then the dead woman raised a pale, trembling hand, folding it over his, and began to drink on her own.

Her first sips were tentative ones, still mostly asleep and acting only on instinct. Then she started drinking in earnest, back straightening, head coming up as she started to support her own weight. James released the glass, and she held it on her own, still drinking. The light coming off him was getting brighter as relief overwhelmed his ability to damp down his connection to the summertime. It failed to make a bit of difference in the overall illumination, because even as the light began to pour off of him, the dark began to radiate from her. It wasn't true darkness, not exactly—I could see her as well as I ever could—but it was the opposite of light, all the same.

Ice clinked against her teeth as she upended the glass, emptying the last of its contents into her mouth. The sides were coated entirely with frost now, although the places James had touched seemed to have acquired a somewhat thinner coating. She swallowed. She took a breath. And the Winter Queen opened her eyes.

They were the color of deep glacial ice, so dark a blue they were almost physically painful to look at. She frowned in obvious bewilderment, turning her head as she made a slow study of the room, which became a slow study of my person. I flushed red, burying my hands in my apron and resisting the urge to curtsy. James alone had been odd, but not so odd as to warp the world around him. The two of them together, and her all out of season. . . .

This was not the way the world was meant to be. And it was, without a doubt, my fault.

Finally, Margaret turned to her husband, and said, "It's August. This is August."

"Yes, it is," James agreed, glowing even brighter. "You have no idea how glad I am to see you awake. Can you stand?"

"That's beside the point. It's *August*." She shook her head, bewilderment still plain. "I can't be awake yet. The harvest horns haven't sounded. I'm supposed to be waiting for the winter. Why am I awake?"

"That would be my doing," I said. I promptly regretted it, as they both turned to look in my direction. A good alchemist is ready to defend his—or her—work against an uncomprehending world, and so I cleared my throat, and said, "I mixed a tincture at your husband's request. It appears to have worked. I may write a paper. Although I can't imagine it to have terribly wide uses—"

"Miss Norton is an alchemist," James said. "I asked her to wake you because Jane and Stuart are back, and this time they've set the authorities on us. Reported me for improper storage of a corpse in a residential neighborhood—and implied that I was using it for things which were, ah, even more improper. The police were preparing to arrest me if I didn't agree to your removal."

Margaret coughed into her hand. "Are you saying that my sister was going to have you arrested for necrophilia?"

"Ah, the modern world," I said, sotto voce.

They ignored me, which was probably for the best. "That's the gist of it," said James.

Margaret sighed. "I really don't think you're equipped to spend your summers unsupervised."

"Which reminds me," I said, louder this time. The seasonal monarchs looked my way. "I've left my bar essentially unsupervised while I dealt with the two of you. If you wouldn't mind continuing your charmingly unseasonal reunion upstairs, we can discuss the matter of my payment."

"We're in a public house?" said Margaret, wonderingly. When James nodded, she began to laugh, and kept laughing as the two of them followed me up the basement stairs.

We were almost to the storeroom when the screams began.

The door to the storeroom had been blown off its hinges by impact with some large, solid object—Andy, whose body lay in shards all across the floor. I came skidding to a halt, feeling a scream of my own building in my chest. It only needed a target, which presented itself, readily, in the dark-haired, dark-eyed woman who stood in the smoking remains of the doorway. Her clothing was cut to shout "expense"; it probably cost no more than Margaret's, but proclaimed its value several times as loudly. The man next to her was attired much the same, and his hair, while also dark, had been bleached, badly, to a dead straw gold.

Margaret and James shoved up behind me, knocking me a step forward. A piece of Andy crunched underfoot. "Jane!" said Margaret. "How *dare* you?"

"How dare *I*?" Jane sneered. "I find the Winter Queen awake out of season in a den of iniquity—"

"This is a perfectly respectable establishment!" I shouted. "And even if it isn't, that does not give you leave to detonate my employees!"

"—and you want to know how dare *I*? How dare *you*, sister dear. I have had quite enough. You could have gone quietly, slipping into the death you've avoided so long, but no. You couldn't see the value of a gentle exit. And now, I'm afraid, this is going to be much harder." Jane attempted an expression of sisterly affection. I've seen more loving looks on a rattlesnake. "On all of us."

James stepped up to take my elbow, tugging me out of the direct line of fire. The light bleeding off him was so bright that standing next to him was like standing on Market Street at noontime without a parasol. "I apologize for what's about to happen, Miss Norton," he said.

I risked a glance at the other three. The dark was gathering around Margaret like the pomegranate syrup staining the gin, and as it came, so did the cold. Frost was spreading around her feet, biting and warping the floorboards. As for Jane and Stuart, they might not have had seasons to call their own, but that didn't render them defenseless. Jane's hands glittered with witchfire—horrible stuff, no magical practitioner worthy of the name would touch it—and Stuart, more distressingly, was holding a small tube of quicksilver speckled with red, which I recognized as one of the nastier weapons in the alchemical arsenal.

"You might have mentioned that she was a witch married to an alchemist," I said.

"Slipped my mind," James replied. Then Jane flung the flame in her hands at Margaret, who met it midair with a blast of frigid cold, and the fight was on.

It's true that, unprepared, I am little more use in a fight than your average bystander. I don't dare strike anyone with my unprotected fists, as my work depends upon possession of agile hands, and I have never really trained in any of the more common weapons. It's also true that, in a fight where all other combatants are either supernaturally powered or at least very well-prepared, I am likely to be overlooked. Taking that to my advantage, I began to creep around the edge of the room, only pausing to duck poorly aimed blasts of one thing or another. What failed to hit me frequently succeeded in hitting the storeroom shelves, and I kept a silent-but-steady accounting of the damages as I crept.

Andy's head had rolled to a stop beneath the workbench near the door, still almost entirely intact, if somewhat chipped. I stooped to scoop it into my skirts, and stayed stooped over as I scurried out the shattered door and into the bar proper.

The place was deserted. This was something of a relief, as it proved my customers had at least the common sense of wharf rats. The screams we'd heard must have been theirs, uttered as they fled. The damage caused by Jane and Stuart's entrance seemed confined to the storeroom door and the shelves to either side of it. That was still quite a lot of wasted liquor, but it was nowhere as bad as it could have been. Small blessings.

Pulling Andy's head from my skirt, I placed it on the bar. He opened his eyes and looked mournfully up at me.

"I'm so sorry, ma'am. I tried to stop them."

"Don't be ridiculous, Andy. Did they hurt you when you blocked their way?" He nodded. "And is that when everyone screamed and ran away?" He nodded again. "There, you see? They didn't enter the storeroom until after the screaming had started. You did exactly what I asked of you." Almost as an afterthought, I added, "And I'll construct you a new body as soon as this tedious business is concluded."

"Thank you, ma'am."

A blast of cold air poured out of the storeroom doorway, and small white flowers were beginning to sprout from the floor. I sighed. "Stay there, Andy. I'm afraid I need to stop some very silly people from leveling the place."

The fact that Andy couldn't have moved if he wanted to didn't appear to change his calm acceptance of my instructions. "Yes, ma'am."

"Very good, Andy." The majority of my supplies were in the basement, but I would be a poor alchemist—and an even poorer bartender—if I didn't possess at least a small talent for improvisation. Taking a bottle of rum from the shelf, I grabbed a pitcher and began to pour.

And that would be the point at which the fight, not content to leave me to work in peace, spilled out of the storeroom and into the front of the bar.

James was the first out of the storeroom—largely, I believe, because he was flying through the air, propelled by a blast of dirty orange witchfire. He slammed into an antique table that originated in a tavern in Barbados, reducing it to splinters. I said a word even my father would have been shocked to learn that I knew, snatching Andy's head off the bar and shoving it behind a stack of pint glasses. Crafting a new body was one thing. Crafting a new brain was something else entirely, and would be substantially more work.

Another blast of witchfire emanated from the storeroom, followed by Jane, who had her hands raised in preparation for another blast. She didn't have time to deliver it.

"Get away from my husband!" shouted Margaret, the ambient temperature dropping by several degrees as she came barreling into the room.

Jane stopped to look back at her sister, providing an opportunity for James to hit her in the back with a chair.

"At least they're keeping each other busy," I muttered, remaining crouched behind the bar as I reached up and opened the register drawer. Luckily, I'm accustomed to working in the dark, and was able to find what I needed by feel.

Bottles smashed against the wall as I worked, sending debris raining down on me. Several chunks of glass grazed my arms and cheeks, and I had to stop more than once, scuttling to different points behind the bar. I didn't like to consider how much damage they were doing. The changes in temperature alone—one moment midsummer swelter, the next midwinter freeze—were enough to guarantee that I'd be needing new windows several years ahead of schedule.

The fight was still going strong when I finished assembling a drink that would, I hoped, convey the appropriate message. A bottle of rum came flying over the bar. I grabbed it from the air and pulled the cork with my teeth, taking one swig for courage, and a second swig as a prayer to any God of Bartenders that might be listening. Thus fortified, I picked up the fruit of my labors, and stood.

The Winter Queen was backed into the corner near the window by Stuart, whose entire body was burning with a lambent white flame that seemed to be countering the effects of her frost. The Summer King, meanwhile, had his hands full dodging the fireballs Jane was flinging in his direction. More of those white flowers carpeted the floor, and mistletoe was beginning to drip down from the ceiling. I cleared my throat.

"Ex-*cuse* me," I said, in my most authoritative tone. "If this nonsense does not cease this instant, I am afraid I shall have to put a stop to it myself."

Jane laughed. "Good lord, you little slattern. Count yourself lucky that we're willing to let you go, and run before we change our minds." She flung another fireball at James as she spoke. He dodged to the side, looking increasingly winded. It was August. His powers were in their natural decline, and Margaret wasn't even supposed to be awake yet. This was the time of year when they were both as close to the human norm as it was possible for them to get.

That was good. It meant they were highly likely to

survive. "Lucky?" I demanded, letting my temper off its reins. "You're demolishing my bar! You broke my assistant! Do you have any idea how *difficult* it is to construct a golem that can pass that well for human? Weeks of work, shattered!" All four of them hesitated, floored by the sight of a seemingly ordinary woman trying to shout a battle for supernatural dominion to a stand-still.

Which is when I threw the contents of my pitcher onto the lot of them.

Jane shrieked with indignation as the liquid hit her, and the fire around her hands went out. She didn't seem to notice. She spun in my direction, hands raised to fling a fireball at me. Nothing happened. I watched her calmly. She blinked, and repeated the gesture. Nothing continued to happen. It made a pleasant change.

Stuart, meanwhile, had noticed that he was no longer on fire, and did not seem entirely pleased by this development. Lifting a hand, he tasted the liquid dripping from his fingers. His eyes widened, and he turned to stare in my direction as he said, wonderingly, "Why, you little bitch. . . ."

I smiled. "Salt, spiced rum, three iron pennies, and a shot of the holy water Father Andrews brings me every Sunday. Oh, come now," I said, shaking my head at Jane's shocked expression. "Didn't the presence of a golem behind the bar tell you I was the better alchemist? Using quicksilver as a base for your explosives, I mean, *really*."

Jane and Stuart continued to stare at me. That was fine. It meant they weren't paying attention when Margaret and James rose up behind them—the one clutching a bottle of port, the other, Andy's left arm—and clocked them squarely in their respective heads.

                              *   *   *

In the end, we decided that the best approach with Jane and Stuart was the simplest. I fetched a memory tincture from the basement and poured liberal quantities down their throats, while James hailed a carriage to take them to the Ferry Building. They would wake miles from the bar, with no recollection of where they'd been or what they'd been doing there—and no powers, either, unless they had the foresight to jump immediately into the bath. The potion I'd mixed would continue to work until they scrubbed the last of it from their persons.

"I truly *am* sorry to have brought such trouble to your door," said James, for at least the tenth time. Margaret placed a hand on his arm, smiling ruefully, before returning her attention to the enchantingly unusual experience of drinking a cup of tea without it attempting to ice over.

"As long as all damages are covered as a part of my bill, I really see no reason to be put out," I said, continuing to collect bits of Andy from the floor. "It was quite educational, and I'd been wanting an excuse to renovate— especially with someone else supplying the funds."

"And you say this . . . disconnection . . . will last until we wash it off?" asked James.

"Yes. Longer, if you drank the stuff, but I don't recommend it. No telling what it might do to the seasons if you decided to disappear for more than a few hours."

"It's never happened," said Margaret. "Let's not test it."

"My thought precisely." I placed one of Andy's feet on the bar, adding it to the heap of rubble I had already created. "I always did have a reputation for brewing stronger drinks than was strictly necessary."

"Well, Miss Norton," said James, gravely, "after to-night, I don't suppose anyone will say it's undeserved."

"No, I suppose not." I looked thoughtfully at Margaret, who showed no signs of going back to sleep. "So, out of curiosity—what will the two of you do with these three extra weeks?"

Margaret smiled. That was, in its way, quite enough.

Margaret and James left shortly after midnight. I waved them out and locked the doors securely before picking up Andy's head, walking through the storeroom, and descending the stairs to the basement. He looked around with interest, apparently enjoying the new perspective that being carried under my arm was affording him. I set him gently on the duplicate bar. "Comfortable?"

"Yes, ma'am."

"Good." I turned to survey the shelves. "I'll have to start with rum, I think. . . ."

"Ma'am?"

I cast a quick smile back in Andy's direction. "If I've woken one, it stands to reason that I'd best be prepared to wake the other. In case of the inevitable emergency, you understand."

"No, ma'am."

"That's all right, Andy. That's just fine."

In the end, the mixing took most of the night, and several medicinal shots of rum, to get precisely right. Ah, the sacrifices I make for my art. If only every sacrifice could taste so terribly sweet.

COCKTAILS

To Wake the Winter Queen

1 part midwinter midnight (or, failing that, 1 part vodka)
2 parts gin
1 part applejack
1 splash pomegranate molasses or cordial
Garnish with a slice of fresh or crystallized ginger

Mix gin and applejack in a highball tumbler. Add pomegranate molasses and stir. Pour a shot of midwinter (or vodka) on the top. Ice to taste, garnish with ginger. A sweet, tart taste of winter, smelling of apples and pine.

To Wake the Winter King

1 part summer noon (or, failing that, 1 part blackberry
*   brandy)*
1 part light rum
1 part golden rum
1 part dark rum
2 parts rose mead
Garnish with candied orange or lemon peel

Crust the rim of a pint glass with sugar. Mix the rums and the mead in the glass. Top off with summer (or blackberry brandy), and garnish with candied orange or lemon peel. A sweet and syrupy glass of summer, smelling of sugar and harvest berries.

Thanks to Elizabeth Bear for her alcohol assistance

THE GRAND TOUR

Juliet E. McKenna

n. esp. *hist.* a cultural tour of Europe, made for educational purposes.

Concise Oxford English Dictionary

"HAVE you any idea where we are?" Hal demanded.

"Not since you took that turn I said not to," retorted Eustace. "We should have stayed on the main road to Vienna."

He peered at the map in the gathering dusk, struggling to pick out routes and writing alike. Snatching a glance ahead, he was relieved to see a small town nestled at the bottom of the valley. "We must find someone to ask."

"If we stop, I don't rate our chances of starting again." Irate, Hal thumped the steering wheel. "Your Aunt Verity's chap swore this bally motor was fit for the trip."

The Lanchester coughed spitefully one last time before falling silent. The only sound was its wire-spoked wheels rumbling down the road.

"Hal!" Eustace exclaimed, alarmed.

"Show some backbone, Ferrars!" Though Hal sounded none too calm as the automobile gathered speed on the steep slope.

Eustace gripped the top of his shallow door with one

hand, the other clinging to the front of his seat. "Over there!" He didn't dare let go to point. "A fuel pump outside that blacksmithy!"

"Right you are." Setting his jaw, Hal wrestled with the steering wheel.

The Lanchester wobbled perilously as they swept into the market square. Eustace's heart was in his mouth until more level ground prevailed and the vehicle slowed to a halt.

His relief was short-lived. There was no sign of life in the blacksmith's workshop; no lamps lit or any breath of a fire within.

"Try the starter," Hal ordered.

Eustace swallowed a curt rejoinder as he opened his door. Going to the front of the vehicle, he bent to crank the obdurate engine's handle. He tried, once, twice, a third time. All his efforts went unrewarded.

"The rotten thing's dead." Standing up, he rubbed his aching wrist.

"Then we had better find that blacksmith and see if he knows anything about motor cars. If he does, all well and good. If not—"

Hal paused to take stock of their situation. The market place boasted some splendid dwellings crowned with bulbous turrets, their windows festooned with swags of carved garlands. Though the cobbled expanse was entirely deserted at this dinner hour.

"We find somewhere to stay for the night," Eustace decided. "I'll cable Aunt Verity in the morning. If there are no Royal Automobile Club patrolmen, she can at least send her beau to explain himself and get us back on the road."

Unless the motor was completely crocked. Pa would get in the most fearful bate.

"Try—"

Whatever Hal might have suggested was lost as a group of youths entered the market square. One hailed them.

"What did he say?" Hal asked quickly.

"I don't know," protested Eustace.

Hal shook his head, exasperated. "I thought you were the linguist."

"When they're speaking Latin or Greek, I'll parse the conversation," Eustace offered, sarcastic.

"It didn't occur to you to learn the lingo, when you knew we were coming to Austria?" But Hal's heart wasn't in the rebuke.

The approaching youths paused to contemplate them from a distance. One stepped forward.

"Good evening. What appears to be the trouble?"

"You speak English?" Eustace broke off, confused by unseemly laughter among the fellows, followed by a scornful flurry of German.

"Get back in the motor car, Eustace," Hal said quietly.

But the English-speaker was approaching, a tall youth with an athlete's build.

"I have learned your language among several others." He smiled, supercilious. "At Heidelberg." He turned his head this way and that, to display the neat scars on his chiseled cheekbones.

"Good evening." Eustace offered his hand. "We're Oxford men ourselves. At least, we will be this Michaelmas." He smiled hopefully.

Hands still in his pockets, the Heidelberger inclined his head in a curt bow. "My condolences."

"I'm sorry?" Challenge sharpened Hal's tone.

"On the recent death of your king," the Heidelberger said smoothly.

That's not what he'd meant at all. Eustace was convinced of it, as the rest of the gang sniggered.

"May I offer my congratulations on your King George's accession?" the tall blond youth continued. "And his lovely qveen. Let us hope good German blood will strengthen your so-called royal line."

Eustace couldn't believe he'd heard the bounder correctly. "I beg your pardon?"

"Forgive me, but Great Britain is ruled by mere Hanoverian Electors." The Heidelberger didn't sound in the least contrite. "You must admit that's barely a monarchy compared to the Imperial powers of Europe."

"What about India?" Eustace demanded. "Africa? Canada? Australia? That's the British Empire, you know!"

The Heidelberger didn't reply, addressing Hal instead. "Do you suppose your new king can save England from all these anarchists and socialists running riot in London?"

"That's enough of your infernal cheek," Hal said wrathfully.

The Heidelberger spread innocent hands. "There have not been anarchist outrages? What of that Tottenham incident last year, when that poor policeman was shot?"

Hal's lip curled. "Piccadilly's gutters are hardly running with blood."

"My pa says this new Home Secretary will put an end to such nonsense," Eustace said stoutly. "Quite the coming man, Winston Churchill, so my pa says."

But the Heidelberger threw back his blonde head with a raucous laugh. "Churchill? Horsewhipped by some suffragette whore last month? How can such a man command anyone's respect?"

Eustace saw Hal redden with anger as he flung open the Lanchester's door. He was all the more furious himself because he could hardly deny that the lunatic woman had tried to give Churchill a thrashing.

"We've had enough of your jaw." Stepping over the running board onto the cobbles, Hal squared up to the Heidelberger. "I'll take an apology, if you please."

"An apology?" The tall youth feigned surprise. "When you English owe the whole German people your apology? You English with your arrogance, who deny us our rightful place in the sun? You boast of your British Empire, when you have kept the German Empire from the overseas possessions that are our due? While your British Navy builds mighty Dreadnoughts to forbid free passage of the seas to every other nation?"

The Heidelberger punctuated each challenge with a shove to Hal's chest, forcing him away from the car. Anxious, Eustace moved to follow, only to find his path barred by the youths who'd originally accompanied the Heidelberger.

"What right have you two fools to be in Austria?" the young German demanded. "Are you spies? We know how England conspires with the Russians and the French against the Hapsburgs. We know your government has divided up Persia with the Tsar, so the Romanovs can hem in all of central Europe with their railways."

"That's utter rot," Hal said hotly.

"You are welcome to your Triple Entente," the Heidelberger sneered. "Germany has science and industry.

While your English aristocrats bleat about being bled white by taxes, Kaiser Wilhelm oversees triumphs like Graf von Zeppelin's airships. Britannia might think she rules the waves, but Germany will claim the skies."

Eustace thought, just for a moment, that the youth had satisfactorily vented his spleen. Perhaps he intended to spit on the cobbles, not on Hal's shoe. But as the repellent spittle landed, Eustace saw his friend's fists clench and that was that.

Hal swung with all the pugilistic science of an English boarding school education. The punch connected with the ruffian's scarred cheekbone to send him spiraling away. As he fell, he knocked several of his fellows flying.

Eustace braced himself as the closest ill-shaven brute aimed a brutal blow at his stomach. Tensed muscles kept his wind intact. Two more yahoos rushed him, fists milling wildly. Eustace landed solid body blows on each and followed up with a right hook and an uppercut.

But he couldn't fend them all off. Vicious fists landed thick and fast. Insults rang in his ears, incomprehensible yet unmistakable. He couldn't see what was happening to Hal over on the other side of the car.

An agonizing stamp on his ankle and Eustace dropped to one knee. His enemies seized their chance. As their brutal jostling floored him, he could only curl into a ball. One hand clenched over his groin, he buried his face in the crook of his other arm. Boots and fists pummeled him, merciless, bruising his back and his thighs, his shins and his shoulders.

Until they broke away. For no apparent reason their attackers scattered, tossing a last barrage of insults as they fled. Eustace lay dazed, hardly able to believe the torment was over.

But what about Hal? Eustace blinked away blood and tears, trying to focus on a dark shape slumped beyond the motor car. He cautiously raised himself up on his elbow. He grimaced. How could such a beating leave him in such agony and yet numb? He didn't think his legs could support him. Eustace forced himself to his knees. After a moment's concentrated effort, he managed to stand, albeit doubled over. Step by excruciating step, he staggered towards the huddled shape.

For a heart-stopping instant, he truly thought that Hal was dead. He lay limp as a discarded rag doll, his face an ashen mask smeared with filth. Then he drew a shuddering breath and Eustace's relief momentarily overwhelmed his own sufferings. Until he saw Hal cough up a mouthful of blood and groan with heart-rending agony.

"I'm here, Hal." Eustace knelt, ignoring the pains that cost him. "Come on, old chap. Upsy-daisy!"

As he tried to lift his friend, Hal yelped. Worse, he was wracked by a ferocious coughing fit. Fresh blood trickled down his chin.

Eustace was terrified. But what to do? He dared not leave Hal alone. There was no knowing if those roughs would return. They had to find somewhere safe, some chance of summoning a doctor, of sending a telegram back to Salzburg.

"You have to get up!" Steeling himself, Eustace hauled Hal to his feet.

He draped Hal's left arm over his shoulder, gripping his hand mercilessly. Shoving his right shoulder into Hal's armpit helped him bear as much of his friend's weight as possible. He wrapped his arm around Hal's waist and grabbed a handful of tweed. "Come on, old chap!"

"Just—" Hal gasped in pain. "Let me get my breath."

"How badly are you hurt?" Eustace had to ask.

"A broken rib, I think," Hal took a labored breath. "Dash it all, I've had worse playing rugger. Let me get my hands on that blighter. I'll make him sorry."

"You and the Brigade of Guards?" Eustace snapped. "Don't be an ass—"

He broke off as heavy boots echoed somewhere between the houses set around the square. Hal stiffened with an inarticulate whimper.

"Let's try that way." Eustace nodded towards a lane bounded by garden walls topped with leafy trees.

But as they toiled through the gloaming, closed gates and shuttered windows offered them no succor. Eustace pressed doggedly onwards. They soon reached humble streets very different from the baroque elegance of the market place.

The lane grew steeper. They found a flight of stone steps, treacherously dished by the tread of countless centuries. Eustace forced himself upwards, jaw clenched. Hal's breath hissed painfully through his nose.

After what felt like an eternity, they reached the top of the steps to find a small square. On the far side lamplit windows glowed golden in the darkness. One illuminated a swinging sign. The White Rose.

Eustace managed a faint laugh. "We've made it all the way to Yorkshire!"

Hal's only response was a pitiful moan.

Eustace summoned up the last of his strength to carry them both to the tavern's door. He had to let go of Hal's hand to reach for the handle. That was a dreadful mistake. Hal slumped senseless on the threshold. Unable to rouse him, Eustace could only batter the nail-studded wood with feeble bloody knuckles.

A broad-shouldered man, aproned over shirt and trousers, opened the door.

"Please—"

Before Eustace could continue, the man stooped to scoop Hal up into his arms. He turned to carry him inside.

"He's hurt. He needs a doctor." Eustace ignored his own agonies. "*Doktor.*" That was one German word that he knew.

The barman carried Hal to an alcove tucked beside a black-leaded stove mercifully unlit for the summer. He slid him on to the padded bench by the table.

Hal's head lolled against the oak-paneled wall, his eyes glazed. Eustace's heart twisted in his chest.

"He needs a doctor!" Overwrought, he grabbed the sturdy barman's sleeve, shaking his arm like a terrier.

Only then did he wonder what he was doing. The man topped him by more than a head, solidly muscled with curling black hair and a handsome beard.

"Don't worry, my friend." Though accented, the man's English was fluent. "We will look after you both." His grey-green eyes were calm and reassuring. "Please, sit."

Astonished as well as exhausted, Eustace did as he was told. What else could he do?

He searched Hal's white face for any sign of his wits returning. Nothing. Sick at heart, he turned away, only to realize that the other patrons of this out-of-the-way inn were staring at them. Some were avid with curiosity. Others looked indignant, even outraged at such rude interruption to their peaceable evening.

What must the two of them look like? While his tweeds had endured their rough treatment surprisingly well, Eustace could see that his shirt was an utter disgrace, his collar half torn from its studs.

He looked up, as if to study the carved beams supporting the creamy plastered roof. Countless knick-knacks crowded the high shelves that ringed the room. Pewter-lidded tankards jostled dusty flagons with faded labels and all manner of trinkets from fat-sailed ships in bottles to a gunmetal model of the Eiffel Tower. Lamplight burnished Mediterranean pots for all the world like the ones in the British Museum. Greek athletes cavorted on red-glazed curves. Propped in a far corner, a slab of ancient terracotta was checkered with incomprehensible symbols.

As he managed to blink away the last of his treacherous tears, their host returned with an anonymous bottle and two small glasses. "Drink this."

Eustace looked doubtfully at the clear liquor. Pa had warned him never to drink from an unlabelled bottle. But the man was cradling Hal's head with one broad hand, easing the rim of the glass between his nerveless lips. Hal coughed and opened his eyes.

Faint with relief, Eustace reached blindly for his own glass. Even Pa wouldn't deny him a stiffener in this dire emergency.

The liquor filled his mouth with subtle warmth. He smelled mingled perfumes of summer fruit, sweet without being sickly. As he swallowed, he could swear the warmth spread from his stomach to the tips of his fingers and toes, soothing every ache and bruise along the way. He still knew he'd been in a fight but he no longer feared he might pass out.

As the man released him, Hal sat upright. He coughed again, pressing a hand to his mouth. Eustace was inexpressibly relieved to see no fresh blood on his lips and a healthier color return to his cheeks.

"Thank you." He set his own glass down. "Please, forgive this intrusion. Eustace Ferrars, at your service." He braced himself for the strong man's grip, only to discover this chap felt no need to grind another man's knuckles to prove himself.

Even more disheveled and bloodstained, Hal offered the barman his hand. "Harold Brandon," he said, stiff with embarrassment. "So sorry to have troubled you."

The barman simply smiled, teeth white against his black beard. "I am Gil, to my friends. Are you Harry to yours?"

"Hal, as it happens." He managed a crooked grin, only to wince as a split in his lip oozed.

"'Cry God for Harry, England and Saint George'?" The barman's smile widened. "Let me guess. If you had half a crown for everyone who says that, you would dine at the Savoy Grill every night?"

"Something like that."

Eustace was relieved to see Hal was too intrigued to be as annoyed as he usually was by that blasted quotation.

"Do you know London well?"

"I travel." The man waved an airy hand around the cluttered shelves. "But you two are far from home."

"We're travelling for the summer," began Eustace.

"We go up to Oxford next term. Corpus," Hal nodded at Eustace, "and Christ Church for me."

"We're travelling with my aunt," Eustace interjected, "and her fiancé. All quite above board," he added. Or at least it had been—

Hal waved an impatient hand. "They're in Salzburg

but we wanted to see Vienna. So they said we could take a couple of days to make the trip while they stayed behind."

And wouldn't Pa cut up rough about that, when he learned what had happened? Eustace sighed, his head drooping.

"What misfortune befell you?" the barman Gil enquired.

"We had trouble with our motor. We would have been fine until that stiff-necked, sauerkraut-munching Prussian turned up," Hal glowered at the thought of their erstwhile foe. "Arrogant brutes, every man jack of them. Just as my Pa says."

"Is that so?" Their host sounded amused.

"You're not—" Eustace looked up, aghast.

"Prussian?" The barman's grey-green eyes held his, penetrating, as though he could read every thought inside Eustace's head. "Would it make any difference if I was?"

Before Eustace could answer, the man stood, gathering up bottle and glasses. "Excuse me, please."

As their savior departed Eustace glared at Hal. "Will you hold your tongue?"

"What—" He fell silent as an old lady bustled up, full skirts dark beneath her snowy blouse and embroidered bodice.

Her sympathetic tone needed no translation, even if her heavy dialect defeated Eustace's rudimentary knowledge of German.

She set a tray on the table and handed them each a glass tumbler and spoon. Then she placed a dish of eggs and a smaller one of butter between them. As the young Englishmen exchanged a puzzled glance, she clicked her tongue in toothless exasperation.

"*Eier im glas!*"

Still mute as schoolboys, they watched her take an egg from the dish and tap it all over with a spoon.

"It's boiled," Eustace realized.

The old woman's gnarled fingers stripped the soft whiteness of every fragment of shell and dropped the naked egg in the tumbler. Just as quickly she peeled a second and added a slice of butter.

"*So?*" She handed the glass to Eustace, looking at him expectantly.

Realizing he was utterly famished, he dug the spoon into the egg's golden heart. His mouth full an instant later, he nodded as he swallowed. "Good. *Sehr gut*," he essayed sheepishly.

The old woman smiled as Hal followed Eustace's lead, talking all the while. Now her tone rang with incomprehensible indignation, though Eustace didn't think it was directed at them.

"You feel better for something to eat?" Gil returned, bearing two tankards of foaming beer.

"My oath, I do." Eustace sucked the last trace of yolk from his spoon. "Beg pardon, but what is she saying?"

"She's so sorry you were attacked by gypsies." The barman broke off to speak briefly to the old woman. Satisfied she nodded and headed back to her kitchen.

Hal was puzzled. "Why on earth would she think that?"

Gil shrugged. "Gypsies are responsible for every evil that strikes a traveler, according to her. They are cursed by God, ever since they cast the Golden Calf for Moses' brother. They even forged the nails for the crucifixion."

"That's not something I've ever heard," Eustace said cautiously.

Granted, some of the gypsies that came and went

around his father's estate weren't above poaching pheasants. But plenty helped with the fruit picking and the potato harvest and they worked hard for their day's pay.

Hal was more forthright. "That's superstitious tosh. Anyway, gypsies had nothing to do with it."

"You won't persuade her of that." Gil placed the tankards on the table. "Any sooner than your Pa would give a Prussian the benefit of the doubt." His eyes glinted vivid green in some trick of the light.

Eustace saw Hal redden but before he could say anything foolish, a gentleman arrived at their table. He was wearing a gray and green loden jacket, buckskin knee breeches and polished brogues. They had seen several men in such garb, as they'd driven along without a care in the world.

"Good evening." With a punctilious bow of his head, he removed his black-cockaded hat. While his English was far more heavily accented than the barman's, it was perfectly comprehensible. "May I present my card?" He hesitated, not knowing where to offer the pasteboard.

"Please," Eustace invited with instinctive politeness. "Join us."

The gentleman pressed the card into his palm, though he didn't sit. "Konrad von Ledebur, at your service. Please, this dreadful business—" Distress momentarily overwhelmed his English. "By the time the alarm was raised, no one knew where to find you—"

Gil broke in with swift reassurance and Eustace was relieved to see the gentleman nod, mollified.

"I understand you have trouble with your automobile?" He cleared his throat. "Perhaps my own chauffeur could be of assistance? He is the most competent engineer."

"That would be marvelous." Eustace looked helplessly at Hal.

"The Lanchester is in the market place," Hal said stiffly.

Eustace couldn't tell if he was still suffering an excess of pain or smarting from the barman's rebuke.

"*Also,*" Herr von Ledebur said in the German style. "I drive a Daimler. I bought it in London last year."

"You've visited England?" Why wouldn't the chap? Eustace silently rebuked himself.

"Many times. Also, Ireland." Their new benefactor smiled tentatively. "I very much like to hunt the fox in your beautiful country."

"You ride to hounds?" That instantly won Hal's attention. "Whereabouts?"

"Northamptonshire and Leicestershire," Herr von Ledebur explained with careful precision. "In Ireland, in the Qveen's County."

"We live in Devon." Hal instinctively reached for his pocket book and visiting cards. "We have some very fine coverts—oh, lord!"

Aghast, he withdrew his hand from his inner pocket. Ink stained his fingers. "Those blighters broke my fountain pen!"

Eustace might have been amused, if he hadn't seen sudden tears glisten in Hal's eyes.

"*Also.*" Herr von Ledebur hastily clicked his heels while donning his hat. "If you will excuse me, I shall see what I can discover of your *auto*. And of these blackguards who assaulted you." He said something scathing in his native tongue.

"Thank you, sir, you're very kind."

As Herr von Ledebur departed, Eustace's eyes resolutely followed him to the door, to give Hal a chance to get his emotions in hand.

Hal scrubbed his face with his ink-free hand. "Mater gave me that pen for passing Common Entrance," he said gruffly.

Much as Eustace wanted to offer his sympathies, he searched desperately for a change of subject. He nodded at their untouched tankards. "Have a drink, old chap."

He was as glad as Hal to drown the sorrows of this horrible day in the fragrant ale.

"Gosh!" Hal exclaimed after a deep draught. "That's the finest brew I've tasted yet."

"I'll say so," Eustace agreed. They'd enjoyed some excellent beer on their journey through Bavaria but this outclassed everything.

Though getting pie-eyed wouldn't improve their situation. What should they do now?

He looked around the tavern again. While some patrons were now intent on their own conversations, others were stealing glances at their table. As sympathetic smiles caught his eye, he nodded self-conscious acknowledgement.

There was a fine variety of ages and complexions among them, he noted belatedly. An elderly man with ferocious whiskers was deep in conversation with a younger, darker-skinned man. A few tables away, two mild-faced scholarly types were intent on the chessboard between them. One wore a skull cap so was clearly a Jew. No one was giving him a second look though. Eustace couldn't imagine that in an English country inn, where dubious glances would warn off anyone with a touch of the tar-brush.

"Do you think this place has rooms for the night?" he

wondered. "Even if our new friend's chap can mend the motor, it's surely too late to set off."

"You want to stay?" Hal looked at him dubiously. "After our welcome in the square?"

"What about our welcome here?" Eustace countered.

Hal looked obstinate. "We don't know these people."

"They don't know us," Eustace retorted, "and a right pair of hooligans we must look, all muck and blood. But they're helping us and that chap von Ledebur is a gentleman without question."

He waved to catch the barman's eye. The tall man was talking to a purple-bonneted lady. Gil came over, bringing her with him.

"Excuse me, but do you have rooms for the night?" Eustace began.

Gill nodded. "We do and Magdalena is making them ready. Frau Bauer will fetch some of her sons' outgrown shirts—"

"Oh, I say," Hal protested.

"Don't you be silly, my lad." The purple-bonneted woman wagged an admonishing finger. "You can't go on your way in rags."

"Madam." Her Kentish accents propelled Hal instinctively to his feet before words failed him.

The comfortably plump woman patted his hand. "You and yours would do the same, if my boys washed up on your doorstep."

"Then—thank you, Madam." Hal bowed, rigid with mortification.

"Frau Bauer met her husband when he served in the *Kriegsmarine*," Gil explained.

"We met in Malta when I was visiting my sister. Her husband was Royal Navy." A saucy smile dimpled her cheeks. "Two of us girls all the way from Chatham. Just fancy."

"You are a long way from home." For the life of him, Eustace couldn't think of anything else to say.

"Aren't we all?" The purple-bonneted lady glanced around the inn before nodding to Gil. "I'll just step out and fetch that linen."

"We really are most grateful." Eustace called after her. "To all of you," he added hurriedly to Gil.

The barman chuckled deep in his barrel of a chest. "You are very welcome."

"Thank you." Sitting down again, Hal studied the foam on his beer. "And I'm sorry. I was talking through my hat earlier."

Eustace was quite knocked off his stride. He couldn't recall when he'd ever heard Hal offer such a heartfelt apology.

He cast around for some fresh topic of conversation. "We're not the only travelers here, from what that lady was saying?"

Gil regarded him for a moment before replying. Eustace found his intensity rather unnerving, until the big man smiled.

"Your British Empire may span the globe but you're too used to life among your own kind, in your own islands. Here we have Slav, Magyar, Czech, Rumanian, Istrian."

He indicated different men and women round the room, beginning with the elderly man with the fine whiskers. "The margrave rode with the Austrian Imperial Cavalry in his younger days. His nephew is visiting from Zagreb." He nodded towards the chess players. "Dr. Aslan Bey is a Mohammedan scholar from Bosnia. Herr Schneider's family lives in Prague."

The barman picked up Herr von Ledebur's card from the table and tapped the smaller writing below the name. "*Kaiserlich und königlich*. Imperial and Royal. Do you know that the Austrian Empire encompasses three kingdoms, two archduchies and countless lesser fiefdoms, alongside the Hungarian Kingdom of St. Stephen? There are almost as many languages spoken within these borders as there are across the rest of Europe. Catholics live alongside Orthodox Christians and Lutherans have Calvinists for neighbors."

His gaze encompassed the room. "Naturally there are tensions and misunderstandings, old hatreds and feuds still cause trouble from time to time. But when people stop to share a meal and a drink and have the leisure to talk, they discover they're not so different."

"It takes a broad field to make a horse race." Eustace recalled his Pa saying that more than once.

Gil smiled, enigmatic behind his beard. He gestured towards the stairs. "Once you've eaten your dinner, I imagine you would welcome a hot bath."

"That sounds wonderful." Eustace reached for his pocket book. "What do we owe you?"

He froze, appalled. His inside pocket was empty. Somehow in the fracas, their money had been lost or stolen. What on earth would they do now?

His throat closed with panic. This was all too much, after such a long and fraught day.

"Keep your money." Where Gil's eyes had glinted green, now they were mysterious gray. "Repay me by remembering this night, every detail, the good and the bad. Both of you," he emphasized. "Remember who was so quick to accuse without reason and who was so quick to take offense with as little justification."

"Right-ho," Hal said nervously.

Eustace looked down at his grazed knuckles. But they hadn't actually told the barman how the fight started. Had Herr von Ledebur? But he hadn't been in the market square to hear the quarrel.

Eustace raised his tankard and drank deep. At least this splendid beer was straight-forward.

Rain lashed the tall windows. Todd glanced up at the gray sky outside. Nope, no trip to the beach today. But, hey, Patti loved visiting these grand old houses.

What had Morgan said, when they'd told the guys they were going on vacation to England? "Europe's where history comes from!" Pretty cute, for a third grader.

All the same, he was keeping a close eye on the boys. All these antiques and paintings and vases were so tempting, and a few velvet ropes weren't much of a barrier.

For now, they were both behaving. Morgan was studying some kind of square piano just the other side of the rope. Eliot stood, mouth open, staring up at the awesome painted ceiling.

"Honey, can you see one of those cards?" Over by a dresser loaded with photos, Patti was looking around. She'd caught on real quick how much information was available in these places, if you only knew where to look for it.

"Here you are, my dear." A little grey-haired old lady rose from her seat in the corner, a plastic-laminated sheet in her hand.

The British sure had a different approach to security guards. At least this one in her tweed skirt and cashmere sweater didn't glare at the kids like they were here to steal the silver.

"Is that the Queen?" Patti was pointing at one of the pictures.

"That's right, my dear," the old lady said warmly. "With Sir Harold, Sir Andrew's grandfather."

"He's the current owner?" Patti nodded as the old lady handed her the guide to the pictures. "Hey, Todd, there are army photos. My husband's grandpa spent some time over here before the D-Day landings," she explained.

"He sure did." Todd went to look, while keeping one eye on the boys.

"That's Sir Harold in the Great War." The old lady used the aerial of her walkie-talkie to point. "Enlisted in 1914 with the 5th Dragoon Guards. He was in some of the British Army's last cavalry charges."

As she shook her head, Todd shared her wonderment. Horsemen riding against tanks?

"After France, he served in Egypt," the old lady went on, "then India and Palestine."

"Who's that?" Patti pointed at a different photo, where Sir Harold stood beside another young man.

"Sir Eustace Ferrars. Lifelong friends, right from school." The old lady smiled. "That's Sir Harold as best man at his wedding."

"What a beautiful bride." Patti glanced at Todd and he could see the memory of their own wedding in her eyes. What a great day that had been.

"Beatrice Dashwood was the prettiest deb of her year," the old lady said fondly.

Patti nodded, though Todd guessed that meant as little to her as it did to him.

The old lady didn't seem to notice. "Sir Eustace served in the trenches through the first war. He won the Military Medal. Then he went into the Diplomatic, working on the Treaty of Versailles."

"Hey, is that Hitler?" Todd bent close to the velvet rope to get a better look.

The old lady was unperturbed. "1936 Olympics. Sir Harold had friends in the equestrian events. Him and Sir Eustace, they both saw the writing on the wall in Germany. They always said we'd live to regret Versailles. Not that either of them had any time for Chamberlain," she added swiftly. "Or appeasement."

"What did they do in World War II?" Todd searched the massed ranks of pictures for any uniforms he might recognize from film or TV. Wow. That was Churchill!

"Sir Eustace was in Intelligence so that's all classified. Sir Harold worked with the Special Operations Executive—?" The old lady broke off to look at them both.

Todd nodded. "Secret agents."

Satisfied, the old lady continued. "He organized Free French goings-on in Occupied France and after D-Day."

Patti had moved on. "That's some family photo. Oh, wait." She looked confused.

"That's Sir Harold's first wedding to Lady Imogen Bertram. She died in the Plymouth Blitz, 1941." The old lady pointed to a second picture. "He married again in 1951. Carlotta Leibowitz, her ladyship was. Italian, from Rome."

"How many children did they have?" Patti wondered at the crowd in a later photo.

"Five daughters, eleven grandchildren. That's Miss Winifred's wedding to David Ferrars, Sir Eustace's third son." The old woman was as proud as if they were her own kin. "They went all over the world, Sir Eustace and his family. In Germany first of all, helping with the

Marshall Plan and reconstruction. After that he worked with the colonies when they wanted independence. That's him in Ghana. He always said there was no call for trouble, not with goodwill on both sides." The old girl surprised Todd with an impish grin. "You Americans taught us that, he used to say."

"Right." Todd couldn't help smiling back.

"What about Sir Harold?" Patti was looking at a long photo of rows of children.

"When he wasn't in London, he was here in Devon." The old girl nodded at the photo. "Always supported the Scouts and the Girl Guides. Youngsters from all over Europe came to camps on the estate after the war. He got involved in town twinning too, to promote understanding and friendship." She pointed to a picture of the old boy on a platform under some banner. "Even campaigned for the EEC in 1975, in his eighties."

Whatever that was. Todd could see Patti was intrigued but he didn't think they had time to find out.

"Uh, honey, I think the guys are ready to get going."

The ceiling had lost its fascination for Eliot. He was heading for his brother, already hovering in the doorway to the next room. No way was Todd letting them out of his sight.

"Thank you so much." Patti said apologetically at the old lady. "That was really interesting."

"You're welcome." The old lady smiled and returned to her seat.

"Remind me to get a guidebook from the gift shop," Patti said as they hurried after the kids. "I want to find out more about the family. Hey, guys! Wait up!"

PARIS 24

Laura Anne Gilman

THE streets were damp with the afternoon rain still, the air warm and filled with softer noises than he was accustomed to. Foreign noises, strange and distracting. Montparnasse, Richard thought, was chaos and confusion: people everywhere, ornate streetlamps casting electric light that framed the scene alternately into brightness and shadows. The cafes were filled with people, some slumped over their hands even this early in the evening as though sleeping off a hard night of drinking, no one paying them the slightest mind but talking over their heads, arms moving as they argued and laughed. Men, wearing everything from formal evening wear to the sweaters and bags of students and the smocks of artists, mingling together without any seeming regard for class. And women, too, dressed in the smart modern fashion that still raised eyebrows and shocked whispers back home, laughing and smoking and drinking in public.

It was heady stuff, making his head spin. The sights, the sounds, even the smells were richer, more exotic, the blend of fresh breads and rabbit and beer and sweat mixing in the damp air like a perfume. He wanted to linger, to sniff the passing bodies, to run his hands over the colorful murals painted on walls and the stylized metal bands around the doors, to look in the darkened windows of storefronts and the brighter-lit facades of cafes and bars—out in the open, unlike back home—but his companions dragged him forward, men on a mission.

"Bonjour, m'sieur. Vous m' payez un verre?" a woman called, catching his eye and smiling at him.

"Keep walking, Dicky," George said, laughing, slinging an arm around his neck. "You couldn't afford her."

They were halfway down the block before Richard finally translated what the woman had said, and his ears flushed bright red. He was the youngest of the team, barely eighteen, and they never let him forget it.

The entire team had arrived in France two days before, in a tumble of trunks and shouted orders, loaded into conveyances and taken to their destination with barely time to breathe, overwhelmed with the rush of excitement on seeing the great flags of every nation flying over the cottages they had been assigned to, just beyond the stadium. Three weeks crossing the Atlantic, anticipation growing more intense every day, and then suddenly: there.

Richard had thought they would spend the time practicing and resting for opening ceremonies, but once they assured themselves that all their equipment had arrived and was properly stored, had made sure that everyone was where they were supposed to be, none missing or mislaid, the close lure of Paris, that terrible center of sin and desire, was too great to resist.

George and Henry, who had appointed themselves his caretakers, were leading the way, bypassing one café

and bistro after another, leading them somewhere—
somewhere special, they promised him. Someplace like
you'll never see back home.

Richard kept his laughter within his own chest, so
the others would not ask him what he found so amusing. There wasn't anything like this back home. This
was *Paris*. But he let his teammates tow him through
the stone-cut steps of the *arrondissement,* turning this
way and that through crooked streets and down what
seemed scarcely alleyways, until they finally fetched up
in front of a building, two stories high, built of yellow-
gray stone. Glossy brown wooden panels fronted the
door, with its polished brass handle, and there was one
window, frosted over so that you could not see in, with
one word painted on it: *Gil's*.

"Doesn't sound very French," George said, suddenly
dubious.

"Everyone says this is the place to go," Henry re-
sponded, already reaching for the door. "Before your
first bout, not after."

"Why?" Richard asked, curious.

"I have no idea." Henry was gloriously unconcerned,
the way he was unconcerned about all else, touched with
the assurance that the world would move for him as he
desired. "Good luck, maybe?"

"Bad luck, if the coach finds out we're out carousing?" He couldn't, he wouldn't, do anything to jeopar-
dize his chances, not this close to the prize.

"It's not illegal here, Dicky," George scoffed, the five
years between them suddenly a chasm. "Lighten up!"

They were speaking English, but nobody gave them a
second look; on George's advice they had left their iden-
tifying badges behind, dressed in what they had hoped

were casually smart flannels and coats that now seemed almost conservative amid the flash and chaos of Paris.

"Nobody ever gets caught at Gil's," Henry said confidently, as though he had done this a hundred times before, and went through the doorway, assuming the others would follow him.

They did. They always did.

Inside, it was as though the dampness and noise of the city faded away, the space larger than it seemed from the front; the center dominated by a horseshoe-shaped bar topped with a gleaming marble top, glassware racked and glittering overhead. Scattered on either side were dozens of round tables, large enough for two or three to sit at, but most crowded with four or five, save the occasional table where a single soul sat crouched over his drink, like a cat guarding its mouse. The walls were lined with brown leather banquettes, people lounging against the whitewashed walls as though they were in the comfort of their own homes.

The door closed behind them, and Richard was tugged further into the bar itself, George's grip not allowing him time to gawp.

Although Gil's was not as crowded as the artier, more open-air cafes they had passed, there were already men two deep at the bar, with that elegant slouch Frenchmen somehow perfected, elbows down and shoulders back, looking as though they could spend all day just where they were.

Henry managed to find a way through, the way Henry always did, and those already drinking obligingly made room for them.

"*Bon soir.*" The bartender was a slender, almost short man with polished brown skin who could have slipped into their team without a moment of doubt; whipcord strong and probably just as fast. He took another look at them, and then switched into English. "Good evening. What may I fetch you?"

"Trois 'Sidecars,' s'il vous plait," Henry said. He was the only one who knew much French at all, beyond what they drilled into them before leaving the States—and of course the terms of the sport, but somehow Richard didn't think "*en garde*" was going to get him anything to drink.

"I've got this," George said, reaching for his money clip. Richard hoped he wasn't going to haul out the wad of bills he had seen George shove in there before they left: George's clip was bright silver and set with a stone that glittered enough to catch even the most honest eye.

Thankfully, George knew enough to keep it in his pocket, pulling out a few crumpled francs and counting them twice, to make sure he knew how many he had.

"What do you think of the Italian team?" Richard asked, uncomfortably aware of the stranger at his back, the hum of a foreign language being spoken around him. In the Village they were housed in there were a dozen or more languages around them, but it had seemed less confusing, somehow.

"They're Italian," Henry said, as though that was all that needed to be said.

"I think they're overrated." George sounded more like he was wishing that was true, rather than believing it. Their coach was worried; that was reason enough for them to take the other team seriously. "You should worry about Hungary. Their boy, the captain, is damn good."

Richard bit back a smirk. They were better than the Hungarians.

George paid for the drinks, and then nudged Henry with his elbow, indicating where a small table against the far wall had become available. It was only slightly less crowded than at the bar, but they'd be able to sit down and drink comfortably.

Gil saw them the moment they came in. He saw everyone; the quick pass of a gaze that had once sized up potential opponents, and now merely gauged, in an instant, if the newcomer was of interest or not. All too often the answer was 'not.'

Even here, in this city filled with men—and some women—aching to make their mark on history, to achieve a fame and glory he once chased himself, he found little of interest walked through the doors. The usual assortment of sad drinkers and happy drinkers, hopeful drinkers and those who were resigned to there being nothing more than a momentary pause at the bottom of a glass; that was what came through his door.

Something made him hesitate when the three children came in.

Americans, from the language. Not part or parcel of the scribblers and scrawlers and social parasites who had overrun the city in recent years; these three were too healthy, practically alight with youth and vigor. Olympiads. Skinny but strong; not runners, the wrong build for that, and not swimmers . . . swordsmen. Fencers.

An elegant sport, removed from its bloody origins but not so far as to make it bloodless. Gil approved. Men still died at the edge of a blade, even in mock-combat, and all the protection and training in the world did not remove that risk. Fencers knew what they held when they picked up their blades, even blunted and capped.

But why these three? Of all the would-be champions in Paris this summer, why these three to catch his eye, to pique his age-weary attention? He put down the glass he had been polishing, and drifted toward the front of the bar, even as they placed their order, the tallest of them speaking in execrable French.

Like any good bartender, Gil could read his patrons. Over the millennia he had been trapped within the confines of this bar, he had honed that skill until it was almost uncanny, knowing what they desired, what they feared, what they needed.

Most of the time it was merely a pause: for refreshment, for drowning their sorrows or speaking them, before they went back out into the world again. Gil's served them what they needed, and let them go. Sometimes they needed a fight, to get the blood moving and the spark of life relit within themselves. Gil himself obliged them, holding back his own considerable strength so that they felt they had a chance against the burly owner.

Sometimes, not often, they needed more. Sometimes they had *earned* more, merely by being more than their fellows, having some spark of fire their fellows lacked, banked or slow-burning, waiting only the gift to make it bloom into open flame.

Was one of these three such a man?

Gil watched as they moved to a smaller table, leaning their elbows against the zinc countertop with the nonchalance of men who were utterly comfortable with their bodies, but not to the point of vanity. Three men, but one sparked with more fire than the others, the faint halo of potential glory that had been given to Gil to see.

See . . . and act upon. If he chose.

*   *   *

"Did you hear about Ignacio? Already threatening to fight a duel with everyone who looks at him sideways"

"It's the women." The Olympic Committee had allowed females to compete in foil this year; an experiment. The United States had two women on their own team, although the males didn't have much to do with them, separated by chaperones and the knowledge that a single infraction could endanger the entire team. "Having them around distracts him," George went on. "Good for us, I say. Bastard's too good when he's focused, we can use all the help we can get."

They laughed, an arrogant sound of men who know that the only help they needed was within their own abilities.

"Enough fencing," Richard decided. "I'm bored of talking about nothing but fencing." It was all they had discussed on the voyage over, endless hours at sea filled with practice and theory, discussing their possible opponents, and wondering who they would face.

"What would you prefer we talk about? Women?" Henry shook that idea off. "I haven't been near one since we were picked for the team, and I know that you haven't either. And I don't think that's going to change tonight, even for George. Finance? Politics? No thanks. Time enough for that when I am back home, facing nothing but meetings and ledgers." Henry was the son of a banker, and it was understood that he would follow his father into the industry, once the Games were done.

"You love it." George said, his eye caught on a lively bird who was, sadly, on the arm of another man. George's father was a well-to-do businessman as well, but George had claimed no desire to take his turn as a Captain of Industry. Fencing was everything to him;

he lived and breathed it—except when he was chasing after women, anyway. The others called him Casanova, not without some envy.

"I do," Henry admitted ruefully, smiling. "It's almost like fencing, the move and countermove, touch and point. Only when you win, you earn potloads of money, in addition to a shiny medal."

The woman passed by them, and gave George a sly smile, then was gone before he had a chance to make a fool out of himself.

"I'm not bailing you out if you get your hat handed to you over another woman," Richard said, not entirely joking. "That will be harder to explain, come morning, than a simple headache from overindulgences."

"You don't know what you're missing, old man," George said, but let the woman disappear into the crowd, and raised his glass to the others in toast. Richard smiled, and raised his as well, clinking the rim lightly against theirs before taking the first sip. The concoction was a pale orange, and tangy-sweet with a bitter kick at the back of the throat, and he could feel the alcohol start to work swiftly, bringing him a sort of calmness that had been rare ever since he was selected for the team, and the fuss had begun.

Henry was right. There wasn't anything except fencing to talk about. That was all that mattered, while they were here. The rest of the world would wait, while they claimed their gold.

"I'm not going into my old man's business," George said suddenly, his drink halfway gone already. "I'm going into the Army."

"What?" That was new, and unexpected.

The other man shrugged, trying to make his admission into a minor thing. "Makes as much sense as going into business. There's going to be another war. Everyone knows it. If I join now, I'll be in a position to give orders, not take them by the time action starts. Not for me, foxholes and gas masks for breakfast."

Richard looked around, cautiously, to see if anyone had overheard, or taken offense. Americans had suffered in the Great War, but the Continent had seen far worse. Paris might seem filled with life and laughter now—but it had not been that long ago that all Europe felt the shadow of the Huns and their allies. The thought that it could come again. . . .

His cousin had been in the Army, and not come home. Another war, it might well be him.

Richard took another sip of his drink, as though to wash away that thought. "The silver won't get you far," he joked, instead. "You'll need to show them the gold, to jump over other officers."

"Damn straight," Henry said. "I'm not here to bring home silver or, God help us, bronze." He raised his glass again. "To glory—in sport, in war, and in the almighty dollar!"

They clinked again, and drank. This time the booze went down cool and smooth, without any bitterness at all. Richard thought that he could get to like this Frenchy drink, whatever it was called. Maybe they could bring it back to New York, make it a sensation.

A man at the table next to them overheard them speaking. "*Vous êtes aux Olympias, non?*"

"*Oui, nous sommes,*" Henry said. "*Suis Americain.* We are here to compete in the Fencing events. *Épée.*"

"Ah," the stranger said, seemingly delighted. He was their own age, but heavyset, with a hooked nose and slicked-back hair, dressed casually in an open-necked shirt, with a thin brown cigarette held carelessly between two stained fingers, emitting a strong, almost fruit-like smell. "American! Many Americans in Paris these days." His English was heavily accented, but understandable. "Perhaps you too will stay, after you lose in horrible defeat to the French team."

"Bah," Henry treated that suggestion with the scorn it deserved. "We will trounce your team, and leave them crying for the bronze."

The man laughed, and offered his hand. "I am Jacques."

"Henry, George, and that's Richard," their captain said, taking the offered hand and shaking it firmly.

Suddenly they had gone from being three alone to part of a larger group, the bar opening up somehow and voices surrounding them in raucous good humor, a constant stream in two different languages. All men; none of the bright, flirtatious women they had seen at the other bars, but a rougher, more familiar camaraderie.

George and Henry took it all in stride, accepting offers of drinks, exchanging toasts and letting the locals practice their English—so much better than the Americans' French—on them. Only Richard felt adrift, the calm of earlier fading away, even as his glass was taken away and refilled. The boasting, taunting tone of the conversation began to chafe him, making him impatient rather than amused.

He rose, excusing himself, and headed for the toilet. When he returned, his place at the table had been taken by someone else, who was finishing his drink.

There was a flush of annoyance; that was *his!* Then, shaking his head, amused despite himself, Richard went toward the bar to order another.

Halfway there, he noticed that the bartender who had served them the first time was gone, replaced by a much larger man, broad-shouldered and tall, with black curls and a close-trimmed beard covering a square chin. Richard read him quickly, the way he would an opponent, and decided to go with English rather than French to avoid any possibility of offending the man with a poorly-chosen word.

Before he could say anything, a scuffle erupted from the depths of the bar.

"T'as une cervelle d'un mammouth congelé!" The deep-throated shout rose through the hum of the crowd, and Richard felt his reflexes kick in, dropping into a defensive posture even as he tried to find where the angry shout had come from, just in time to see two men in dark pullovers stagger at each other, clearly intoxicated.

"Et toi, t'as des couilles d'un lapin," the man on Richard's left spat, holding up his fists in a classic pugilistic move, obviously challenging the other man to follow his words with action.

Queensbury rules were clearly not in order, here. A sloppy roundhouse punch from one actually, through some miracle of God, managed to land on the other's jaw, and he staggered back into the crowd, who shoved him back toward his opponent. Neither man looked to be under forty, but they were still well-muscled, and determined to do damage.

"Assez!"

The shout came from the bar behind Richard, a deep, booming voice, and it was as though the voice of God Himself had come down on the two. Their arms dropped, and they stared at each other with the blinking, slightly dazed look of men who had just been doused with cold water.

And as quickly as it began, the fight was over, the two men grinning stupidly at each other, the crowd going back to its previous discussions, leaving a careful bit of space around the two in case they decided to start up again, but otherwise ignoring them.

Richard found himself shaken as much from the abrupt end to the fight as the suddenness and close violence of it. The bar had settled back into the same low buzz as before, once the offenders had been settled, and when Richard craned his neck to see over the crowd, even Henry and George seemed to forget about it entirely, talking happily with their new companions. Richard tried to make his muscles relax, to imitate their seeming nonchalance. It had only been a scuffle, nothing he hadn't seen before—hell, he'd been involved in one or two himself, in college. Somehow, in this place, it seemed so much more . . . brutal.

He shook his head, and turned away, intent on getting another drink.

The new bartender watched him approach, his gaze unnervingly intent, enough that Richard felt the urge to look behind him, to see who this man was staring at.

"Bon soir. What can I get you?"

Something about the man's voice, his expression, made Richard suspect it was a loaded question, something being asked beneath the words that he wasn't swift enough to hear.

"Bon soir. I would like, ah. . . ." What were they called, again? "A sidecar?"

The bartender nodded, reaching overhead for a clean glass. "You are American."

"Yes." He felt the urge to apologize. "Is my accent that terrible?"

"It could use some work," the man said, and his face eased a little, no longer holding such a still intensity. "The trick is to relax. And have another drink. We are all multilingual when we are in our cups."

"You ... aren't French?" The other man sounded British, there, or German, but that was unlikely, even years after the end of the Great War.

"No," the barkeep admitted, leaning forward, a confiding pose, one old friend to another. "My home is nowhere you would ever have heard of. But I have traveled. . . ."

In fact, Gil had not left the confines of the bar—was not able to leave the confines of the bar—in too many centuries to count. All he knew of the world was what came through these doors, carried by voices and newspapers. But he knew a great deal about men, and dreams. And hunger.

The boy handled himself well, when startled by the fight, when accosted by strangers. Dark haired, dark-eyed, younger than the other two he had come in with, although it might be less years and more a lack of experience. He was not hard yet, for all his toughness.

In that moment, Gil decided.

The new bartender fussed with the bottles, and then poured him another drink, not the sidecar he had ordered but something different, mixing it with a flourish, like a magician. Richard thought about protesting, but didn't trust his French, or the bartender's mood, enough to risk it. The bartender pushed the drink across the bar, accepting the coins Richard pushed back at him with smooth motions that reminded Richard of the second crossing of blades, where you think you have your opponent's measure, but want to make sure before you ventured anything tricky

"I've never gone anywhere," Richard admitted, not sure why he was telling this man anything except . . . that was what you did with bartenders? He took a sip of the drink, and nodded in approval. It was much better than the sidecar. "I mean, I've traveled across the States, of course. I'm from Chicago, in the Midwest, and I've been to Boston and New York, and Pittsburgh, and. . . ." The names of the cities were only that to the bartender, he realized, somewhat taken aback. 'American' was all he knew, and all he saw. "But well, that's all home. We speak the same language, mostly, except for slang and such."

"But among your fellows, these Olympiads, there is . . . fraternity?"

Richard considered the question, taking another sip of his drink to give himself time. It was much stronger than the first one, too, or maybe he was feeling it, suddenly. "Yes," he said. "*Oui*, there is . . . fraternity." He liked the word, the more he thought of it. "We are all here for the same purpose; we've been working for years to reach this point, and even though there is competition, there is also a bond in knowing that we want the same thing."

"Do you?"

The bartender's eyes were an odd shade, a green that was closer to seawater than grass or stone, stormy and changeable and oddly compelling.

"Of course." Richard let out a laugh, fiddling with his cuff a little, to avoid that gaze. "We all want the gold."

"Ah, *oui,* all want to win." The bartender nodded as though that were self-evident, and Richard in fact felt foolish for having said it, like the greenie the others teased him for being, younger and less sophisticated. Of course they all wanted to win.

"Why?"

Why? The question was like the roundhouse punch, throwing Richard into blinking silence for an instant. "Winning . . . it means that you are the best. Proving yourself against the rest of the best. It's a thing to bring home, to hang on the mantle, or on an office wall, to show that you've proven yourself. 'Ah, Dicky, he's been with us for ten years, since he took the gold for the States, you must remember. . . .'" Richard managed to do a credible imitation of Henry imitating his father the banker, although there was no way the bartender could know that.

"Ah. Glory, to build the reputation, make others fear you, respect your ability . . . that is a fine goal for a man."

It sounded grand, when the bartender said it, not silly at all. Richard turned the glass around, watching the condensation on the bartop fade and dry up, only to be replaced by new rings as he moved the glass. His mouth was dry, and he took another sip.

"Hey, Dick!" George was calling to him, and he turned, waving a hand to indicate that he would return soon. The stranger was still in his seat, however, and an odd bitterness rose in his throat.

"Glory. Fame. Fraternity. It's all fleeting, isn't it?" Even a name on a medal was fleeting; eventually people would stop looking at it. Someone else would win another, the way someone had taken his chair.

"All life is fleeting," the bartender said, but there was a weight to his words that made Richard frown again, aware that he'd missed something unsaid. This second drink was much stronger than the first; his head felt muzzy and his eyesight seemed almost blurred, as though he'd been drinking all night, and not just this brief time.

"There has to be something in life that lasts, that matters," he protested, not quite sure why—or what—he was arguing. "And not the way the pastor claims, glory in the hereafter, either."

"Bah. There is nothing." The man to his left had terribly accented English, but he seemed to understand enough to have followed their discussion. "We are born, we sweat, we are for the worms."

The bartender held Richard's gaze, and the American could not look away. "*Jacques, arrêter de causer, t'es un vieux fou.* You make despair a religion, you."

"Bah." But the old man went back to his own thoughts, his weathered, whiskered face scowling down into his drink.

"At least, in feeding worms, we live again?" Richard said, attempting to smile, unsure why the words had shaken him so. The bartender—the owner, Richard suddenly realized—scowled at the old man, as though he would take up the argument again, with Richard, were they alone.

"Dicky!" George came over, a little unsteady on his feet, and slung his arm across Richard's shoulders, startling him from any further rejoinder he might have made. "You're being anti-social again, chum. What's eating at you?"

George had an edge to his voice, and Richard wondered if he looked or sounded as half-under as his teammate. How long had they been there? It seemed as though they'd just arrived, and yet he felt as though he had been talking to the bartender for hours. The occasional gin taken in a speakeasy never had this effect on him—what had the bartender put in this drink? Or was it the air in here, the pungent smell of the butts these Frenchies smoked, harsher and more aromatic than cigarettes sold back home, until the air was practically blue with it? Richard shook his head, as much to clear his thoughts as to answer them. But George took it the wrong way.

"Come on, old man. You need a keeper, get you home safe so the coach doesn't have a strip of hide off us in the morning. Don't drink alone, it's not good for you."

It was easier to give in, go back and rejoin the group. They would make room for him, shove the interloper out of his seat or find him another one. He was just letting nerves nibble on him, was all. Once things got started he'd have his focus back, his eye on the gold, and everything would make sense again.

That was what they'd worked for, why they'd come here. To go home known as the best, the very best. Anything less was unthinkable.

"Knowing what you want," the bartender said, speaking, it seemed, only to Richard, his shagged-curled head leaning in close, his voice pitched to carry through the endless murmur of noise. "Being very sure of what you want. *C'est ce qui compte.* That's the trick."

"Trick to what?" His tongue felt thick, his skin feverish.

"To getting it. To living with it, once you have it."

It seemed as thought the bartender was waiting for him to respond. What did he want? He wanted to win the gold, of course. He would accept silver, or even bronze, but it was important to bring home a medal, to show everyone back home what they could do, to represent the United States against the other nations. . . .

But what did he truly want? After the bouts were done and the excitement and strangeness of it all faded away ... what did he want then? It seemed impossible to think that far. The moment was now, the now was the moment. After that would come war, George was right; even though nobody talked about it, everyone knew it.

Glory. Honor. Pride. A shiny gold medal hung on the wall in some office, or over the mantle, and the memory of soldiers just come home from war, their faces gaunt, butts held in shaking hands as they told stories that didn't tell the real story. Eyes that were too intent on something you couldn't quite see, or looked at nothing at all, even when they looked right at you. Richard had seen the soldiers come home, not the generals or the heroes, but the boys who'd gone and bled and made it home not entirely whole. His friends could talk about being officers, but there was something in Richard that shied away from the thought of giving orders that sent men to such a fate.

Given a choice, he would choose to sleep at night, to wake anticipating the day, not dreading it.

"So be it," the bartender said, softly, sounding almost pleased. Then, louder: "Drink up, young Olympiad. Drink up, and face your destiny!"

There was no gold for the team that year. No silver or bronze. The Games ended, Richard went home, and hung his favorite *épée* on the wall. He went to war, and came home and got married. Taught high school, and raised two daughters. Saw them grow up and get married, and held his grandchildren when they were born. All those years, the *épée* hung on the wall, and he would touch it, every now and then, as he passed by. And when his wife died at the age of 79, two months after he had been diagnosed with lung cancer the doctors could do nothing about, he held her hand as she breathed her last, remembered the despairing words of a drunk old man in a bar in Paris of 1924, and his expression was one not of bitterness or regret, but content.

STEADY HANDS AND A HEART OF OAK

Ian Tregillis

IN November of 1940, the average life expectancy of a sapper in His Majesty's Royal Engineers was six weeks. Reggie Brooks had been on the job eight weeks and three days when the Jerries lobbed a 1500-pounder onto Guy's Hospital in Southwark, in the shadow of London Bridge.

The bomb had crashed through three floors before coming to rest beneath the foundation, where it lay quiet and malignant as cancer. From his vantage point wedged beside the iron eggshell of unexploded ordnance, Reg glimpsed a patch of sky far overhead. An azure circle shone through the clean round hole punched neat-as-you-please by the bomb's passage through the hospital.

He lay on a tarpaulin over a pile of broken timbers, legs wrapped around the nose of the bomb. It had come to rest at an angle, leaving just enough room for Reg and his kit. A stabilization fin dug into his shoulder. The bomb case still retained a bit of warmth left over from atmospheric friction, but not enough to thaw the sheen of hoarfrost over the pit in Reg's stomach.

Was this the one? Would he snuff it on his last job? Would this crater become his grave?

It would be a closed-casket service, of course.

He caressed the bomb with trembling fingertips, tracing the curve of the shell like the small of a woman's back. But instead of the buttons and latch-hooks on Sybil's dress, he fumbled for the sharp corners of steel bolts, harder and smaller than a schoolgirl's nipples, that would give him access to the bomb's deepest intimacies. He counted eight bolts arranged like the crosses on the Union Jack. Felt a rough weld along one seam.

Reg whispered into a glass funnel affixed to a length of garden hose. "Looks like a Dietrich," he said.

The hose snaked from the crater, through the wreckage, past red and white barricades (DANGER: UN-EXPLODED BOMB) to the other sappers waiting anxiously outside the blast radius thirty yards away. Every model had a nickname; this was a Dietrich, after Marlene, because the bomb, just like the bint, could seduce you, make you think she was easy.

Ease could be a trap. God knew Sybil had been easy enough.

"That's good news, Reg," said Captain Hollister. Holly led the 246 Field Company, Royal Engineers, Third Division.

"Right," Reg said. "Got my number three spanner, taking it to the aft-most bolt." Somewhere up top one of his mates recorded this, documenting each step in the procedure. A formality in the case of a Dietrich, but still absolutely necessary.

Sappers learned the ins and outs of each model by trial and error. Hence the shortened life expectancy. Sometimes a bomb didn't go off because it was a rum

fish—a dud. But sometimes a bomb didn't go off because it was booby-trapped: based on a familiar model,
but designed to blow when some poor bastard tried to
disarm it. This was a good method for killing sappers.
Also, sprinkling unexploded bombs around the city dis-
rupted civilian life long after the all-clear sounded. The
UXB was a tool for spreading terror. Bloody Jerries.

Quivering hands caused Reg's spanner to jitter
around the bolt, rapping and tapping against the bomb
like bursts of Morse, telegraphing his fear to the outside
world. He took a slow deep breath to settle his nerves.
And realized the smell was off. Mud, yes. Shattered brick
and plaster dust, yes. The sharp odor of sweat trickling
from his armpits, yes. But there was something else.

Reg took another whiff. It left his head spinning and
his vision blurred. But there, beneath the stink of his
own terror: the cloying scent of diethyl ether.

In an instant, he realized what had happened. The Dietrich had smashed through a surgical theater on its way
down, shattering the cabinet where the nurses stored vials of anesthetic. Invisible ether fumes, heavier than air,
were cascading into the crater. He lay in a cloud of it.

Marlene, you backstabbing bitch.

He had to work quickly, before the fumes overwhelmed him. Reg pressed the funnel to his mouth and
sucked down a lungful of relatively clean air from up
above. It tasted of tobacco; Holly always smoked when
he had a man down-hole. The hose stuck to Reg's fingers. Ether had a nasty tendency to break down rubber
and plastic. Those same corrosive tendrils would soon
work their way inside the bomb casing and play merry
hob with the wiring.

He relayed the problem up top. In moments he heard

the crackle of glass beneath work boots as a few mates quickly located and cleared away the chemicals. Nothing they could do about the fumes in the crater, though.

Bolts one, two, three, and four came out easy. Five and six were a bit stubborn. Seven fought back. And number eight wouldn't budge.

And wasn't that just like a bint. Sometimes a girl started out easy at first, but refused to let go. Why couldn't Sybil take a hint and shove off? If he kept having it off with girls on the side, that only served her right.

She said they needed to have a talk, but he knew what that was about. He wouldn't let himself get cornered. His mum had done that to his dad, and look how that turned out.

Reg sucked on the hose again, held his breath, gave the bolt another tug. Nothing. A dent in the access plate had pulled the bolt out of true.

He fought off a dizzy spell, and struggled to clear his mind. Reg pressed his forehead against the bomb. He imagined his awareness expanding through the casing, and tried to picture the state of affairs. The Dietrich's dark innards took shape in his mind's eye, like the pieces of an elaborate puzzle. If he loosened the last bolt, the release of tension in the dented plate would tip it inward about half an inch. Just far enough to brush the altimeter cable. The ether fumes had been working on that same cable for several minutes now; the insulation would be wearing thin. Reg looked deeper. . . . No, the battery hadn't been dislodged by the hard landing. . . . The cable was live. Contact with the plate would cause a short. And that would trigger the detonators.

Severing that cable would render the bomb inert. Only problem, the Dietrich was a mess of wires. Hit the wrong one and . . . closed casket. Reg fished out his pock-etknife. The exertion left him light-headed. The patch of blue sky above swirled and sparkled like a kaleidoscope.

"Plate's stuck," he wheezed, tasting rubber and ciga-rettes. His lips tingled. "Gotta cut. The altimeter."

Urgent murmuring on the other end. Then Peter's voice echoed down the hose: "Reg! Stop! You're not thinking clearly. That's not how you do a Dietrich!"

Reg pushed his knife blade into the gap. Gently. Met resistance. Pictured it: no, not there. Slid it backward. Deeper now. Nice and easy, just like Sybil's first time. There, something caught. That had to be it. In his mind's eye, the blade rested square on the offending cable.

He thought a quick prayer. *Lord, I'll never cheat on Sybil again.* But he knew he couldn't keep that promise. *I'll give Sybil what she wants. I'll buy her a ring. I'll take care of her. Don't let me die here.*

His hand had gone numb. Reg had to reach around and hold the knife with two hands. They were both numb.

He counted. One. Two—

The severed cable twanged apart.

Like a dented access plate, the tension came out of Reg in one go. A moist chill dampened his shirt through-and-through. He took up the hose again, fumbled it with sweat-slick fingers. The tingle spread from his lips to his face, neck, chest, arms. The crater started to spin. He could barely hold the hose.

"'Sclear," he mumbled.

The last thing he did before passing out was try to check his boilersuit for a damp stain. No self-respecting shop girl would bed a fellow who pissed himself. But the anesthetic overwhelmed him before he could find out.

He awoke in a part of Guy's that hadn't taken a Luft-waffe calling card through the ceiling. Pain had brought him round; his shoulders felt as though they'd been pulled within a wire's width of dislocation. A cool draft tickled him, and he realized his shirt was torn under the arms. Felt like he had some rope burn there, too. The other men of the 246 must have hauled him out on a harness.

"Terrific work, Reg." Holly's voice.

Reg tried to sit up. Wobbled. Heaved. His breakfast—reconstituted egg and the last pieces of his week's bacon ration—became a puddle between his feet.

"That's the ether wearing off," said Holly. "Quacks should be around in a few."

The room teetered to a halt, more or less. Reg chanced a gentle shake of his head. "They get it? The Dietrich?"

As if to demonstrate the foolishness of his question, a hoist creaked and a chain rattled somewhere down the corridor. Peter yelled, "Ho! Easy, lads!"

Reg hopped to his feet. Holly caught him when he stumbled. They went outside to where the other engineers of 246 Company had just finished transferring the Dietrich from a gurney to a flatbed lorry. They'd done the final bolt and pulled out the access panel. A mess of wires and cables spilled out like a drawn man's entrails. The thickest one, deep in the rats' nest, was cut clean in two. It was exactly what Reg had pictured.

Doyle stood to the side, staring at the defanged bomb. He'd been transferred from another field company where he'd spent the first part of the war on a comfort-able stint building citadels and bunkers for Whitehall and the Admiralty. Poor sod. He was too new to be useful, so the others had brushed him aside while they loaded the bomb. He was also too new to hide the way he kept well away from the Dietrich, and to hide the expression on his face when he saw its tangled innards.

He walked over to Reg, lifted his helmet, ran a hand through the black bristles on his scalp. His breath steamed in the cold sunlight.

Doyle swallowed. He tried to sound nonchalant, but his voice broke when he asked, "How'd you know it was a ringer?"

"I got lucky." A lie, but Reg was feeling smug. What a way to go out. His final job was already the stuff of sapper lore. Not bad for a kid who left home at fourteen.

"Reg has the Sight," said Peter. He lashed a tarpaulin, the same one Reg had lain upon, over the bomb. He jumped down and pounded his fist on a side panel. The lorry lurched into gear, leaving them coughing in a cloud of diesel exhaust. It pulled past the other sappers already at work dismantling the barricades. The crowd of onlookers gave a small cheer before beginning to disperse.

"The Sight?" Doyle asked. "What's that?"

"It's why you should stick close to Reg," said Peter. "Do that and you'll be right as rain."

Reg said to him, "Why don't you shut it?"

Peter wasn't far off. Reg didn't think of it in such mystical terms, but the fact of the matter was he did have a knack for seeing how things worked. If he could see something, or lay his hands on something, sooner or later he'd get a picture of how it went together. How it worked.

Until the war, Reg had only used it to talk women horizontal. After all, that was just another puzzle wanting a solution. You just had to see how all the pieces fit together: your words and her desires, her body language and your interests. The proper sequence of events led to an inevitable result, like chemical reactions within a fuse.

Sometimes he was too good at it. But maybe Sybil would give up if she caught him in the act with another girl. Marry her? He'd rather die.

The first time he'd gone down hole, during a cold September rain to grapple with a Lynn that had cratered West Ferry Road near the docks, Reg realized the same knack he had for knowing how to undress a bird could also save his life. Thing of it was, he never knew until it was all said and done. The Sight had a limited scope. A few feet, a few minutes.

But Peter needed to keep his mouth shut. However the Sight worked, it was Reg's gift. His alone.

The captain didn't miss a trick. He heard the edge in Reg's voice. "I'd buy you a pint," he said, clapping Reg on the shoulder. "But the quacks said you should go easy."

"I can handle a pint if it's free," said Reg.

He was finished risking his life. He'd put in his time, and now he was done with the dangerous work. Time to move up the ladder a bit. He reckoned that's why Captain Hollister wanted to have a chat.

"You lot," Holly called, "finish that Dietrich. Meet us at the Bull when it's locked down."

Reg rode with the captain. Holly used his own car on the job because many sapper units still didn't have their own vehicles. At least now they had a lorry; most sappers had to catch rides with civilians. Reg didn't mind. Month back or so, on his way to a job, he'd met a nice bird whose husband worked on a merchant ship in the North Atlantic. Poor sod was gone for weeks at a time.

246 Company worked out of Bermondsey, which, thanks to the docks and warehouses, had suffered worse than many neighborhoods under the Luftwaffe's affections. The city had become a patchwork of order and chaos. Some streets looked perfectly normal, as though there wasn't a war on. Other places were nothing but piles of rubble. Spots where the shattered brick and timbers had been cleared away left gaps in the city as conspicuous as a broken incisor on a pageant queen's smile. Here and there, a lone chimney or part of a wall towered over the wreckage, etched with curlicues of dust and soot.

"Doyle's looking a bit green," said Holly.

"Can't say I noticed," Reg lied.

"He isn't ready."

"Either he'll get ready, or the Jerries will take him off your hands quick enough."

Holly parked in front of a chemist's shop, just up the street from 246 Company HQ. He said, "And how many others along with him?"

"That's why we evacuate."

Holly pounded his fist on the fascia. "Enough, Reg. I'm not sending him in yet. That means we're short and I'm begging you to stay on."

"Like hell I will. Sapper teams are *always* down a man or two."

Holly stepped from the car. Reg followed. Long streamers of spongy cloth had been strewn across the road. Reg recognized the tattered shreds of a barrage balloon.

Nobody Reg knew could remember seeing or hearing of the Sword and Bull prior to a few months ago. Yet the pub was clearly old, as evidenced by the weathered oak sign swinging above the door. The carving depicted a bull cracking the earth beneath its hooves, a sword thrust between its shoulders. The paint had long ago flaked away except where it covered the horns and hooves of the rampant bull. They glittered like gold in the late autumn sunlight.

The two men studied the pub with the same quiet deliberation they gave a fresh bomb crater. Somebody had chalked a note on the front door: *Plenty of beer, bottle and draught.*

Holly nodded at the pub. "Let's give it a try."

"I still want that pint," said Reg.

When Holly opened the door, Reg might have sworn he caught a whiff of something humid, like a river. But they were a solid mile from the Thames, and it never smelled that clean. He shook his head, tried to clear the last remnants of ether playing with his senses. The pub itself was dark compared to the unusually bright winter day outside. It took a moment for Reg's eyes to adjust.

He took an immediate dislike to the place: it had no snug. Reg preferred a bit of privacy once he got serious about chatting up a bird. And the hearth had no fire, only cold ashes. As public houses went, it wasn't impressive.

The barkeep was a bloody giant. Easily twenty stone if he weighed a pound, yet tall enough to wear it well. He wore his long, coal-black beard in braids, and his skin was dusky bronze. His eyes, lighter than the surrounding shadows, glimmered in the half light like twinned opals.

Holly said, "Two pints of your best bitters!"

The mountain behind the bar said, "The best is also my only bitters."

His voice rumbled like a dormant volcano tossing in its sleep. And it carried an odd lilt, like the faint suggestion of foreign lands. Reg couldn't place it.

"That'll do."

When the barkeep turned his back to fetch a pair of glasses, Holly gestured at his bare chin. "Reckon he's a Celt?" he asked, *sotto voce*.

Reg shrugged. "I reckon he's a tough bastard."

The captain introduced himself and Reg.

"Gil," said the barkeep. He put two pint glasses on the bar. As he filled the second, he said, "Little early in the day for men in uniform."

"Oh, we've already been hard at work," said Reg. By now the life-and-death rush of adrenaline had evaporated, leaving him hollow and windblown. He'd come damn close to snuffing it, and the realization had transmuted his terror to giddiness. He downed a hefty portion of his pint.

Gil took a towel from the brass rail behind the bar, flipped it over his shoulder, and set to work rinsing glasses under a water tap. "What work is that?"

Reg wiped the back of his hand across his mouth. "Me? I work miracles, mate."

"I've seen miracles."

Holly clasped Reg by the shoulder. To Gil, he said, "Reg here is a bloody magician, he is."

"I've seen that, too," said Gil. He almost sounded serious. A very strange fellow.

"Best goddamned sapper there ever was," said Holly.

Gil cocked an eyebrow. "Sapper?" He said it without letting his attention stray from the glass in his hands, as though merely making conversation in the centuries-old tradition of barkeeps everywhere.

Holly said, "Yeah, sappers. Royal Engineers, mate." Gil let the silence speak for him. Didn't even shake his head. "Unexploded ordnance?" More silence. "The *Blitz*?"

"Ah. That." Gil gave the glass one final pass with the towel before stowing it under the bar. He pulled out another, inspected it in the half light. "Seen wars, too."

Giddiness and ale together became a witch's potion that left Reg feeling indignant. Sapper crews would be talking for years to come about what he'd accomplished today. He wouldn't tolerate some outsider shrugging it off.

"Hey!" He leaned across the bar to grab Gil by the arm. "We're fighting a war! Pikers like you need to pay attention to what's happening out there."

Gil looked at the hand on his forearm, and then slowly looked up to stare at Reg. Again, he didn't say anything. But his eyes, those gray-green opals, bored into him. It didn't take the Sight to see there was no winning a fight with Gil. Reg yanked his hand away.

"I meant it about you being the best," said Holly. "Which is why I'm begging you to stay on. Just a bit longer before I put you in for promotion. Please."

"I've already stayed on for you. I've done my bit, and now you owe me."

"Does Britain owe you, too? The king?"

Reg could tell from the way Gil assiduously avoided them that he was taking in every word. He might have looked bored by it all, but the tosser was listening. Reg hated arguing in front of the barman. But argue they did, through their first pints, and their second.

Holly wouldn't ease up. He kept dogging Reg until finally Reg said, "Sod off! I've done my bit, and that's final. Promotion or none, I'm not going down hole again."

He left Holly at the bar, and took up a game of darts. *Thock.* Who the hell did Holly think he was, anyway? Who did he think Reg was? *Thock.* Selfish git,

treating Reg like that. *Clack*. The next dart missed its
mark, bounced off the wall, and skittered across the
floorboards.

The afternoon wore on. More folks wandered into
the pub on their way home from work. The after-work
crowd kept Gil busy; he ran the place by himself. The
men from 246 Company arrived about an hour before
sundown, their catch from the hospital safely disassem-
bled. Doyle tried again to ask Reg how he'd known what
to do, but Reg was too busy describing his exploits to a
pair of tittering shop girls.

Holly kept to the bar, looking hurt. Peter joined
him. They seemed to get on well enough with Gil. Reg
caught bits and pieces of their conversation, and at one
point thought he heard Peter carrying on about the
Sight again, but by that point Reg had the shop girls in
his thrall and thus was more concerned with choosing
between them for a cozy overnight than with Peter's
rumormongering.

At sundown, Peter helped Gil pull curtains over the
windows. The barkeep might not have paid the war much
heed, but at least he obeyed the blackout regulations.

The evening crowd brought the pub to life. Doyle and
Holly played darts. Their hoots and calls melded with
the din of laughter and conversation, and the occasional
rattle of the flue as a gust of wind eddied down the chimney. Knowing their services would likely be needed in
the morning, the sappers cleared out early. They waved
goodbye to Reg. All but Holly.

Reg was returning to the bar to fetch two more pints,
and had just decided that he'd take the ginger-haired
girl home rather than the brunette, when Gil cleared his
throat and nodded at the door. Reg turned.

Sybil stood in the doorway. She'd come straight from work and still wore her frumpy Wren uniform. It wasn't flattering. She scanned the room while unwrapping her muffler. Her horsey face cracked into a wide, desperate smile when she glimpsed Reg. He sighed.

She crossed the pub and flung herself on him. Her kiss clicked their teeth together. Reg's ribs creaked under the ferocity of her embrace. The shop girls saw everything.

"Hi, Syb," he managed.

"Oh, Reggie," she said, still clinging to him. "I went down to the 246 and they said you were here. They told me what happened today. Thank God you weren't hurt. I don't know what I'd do."

She kissed him again. Then Sybil finally withdrew her claws and relinquished a generous half inch of personal space. But the damage was already done. The shop girls moved their chairs to put their backs to Reg.

Reg groaned inwardly. The ginger girl had freckles. He loved freckles.

While Gil poured a drink for Sybil, she slipped her arm around Reg's elbow, deftly as a trout fisherman setting the hook. "My Reggie is a true hero. Did you know that?"

"Is that so?" Gil's stare bored through him for the second time that afternoon. Reg couldn't decipher the strange look on his face. "Haven't met many of those."

"He's got more courage than anybody," said Sybil.

An uncomfortable moment passed among the three of them. Reg couldn't bear to look at Gil. He couldn't stand to make eye contact with Sybil, and though he couldn't understand why, he also felt compelled to avoid his own reflection in the mirror behind the bar. Conversation ebbed and flowed around them. Nobody noticed

the trio standing in their awkward little tide pool. Even
Sybil seemed oblivious to it.

Reg was ready to turn on his heels and leave, and
Sybil be damned, when Gil broke the painful silence.
"In that case," he said in that tooth-rattling rumble of a
voice, "he deserves a drink on the house."

"I think that's wonderful," said Sybil. She squeezed
Reg's arm, grinned at him. He flinched away.

Gil fished a key ring from a pocket in his apron. He
knelt behind the bar. A lock *clunked* open. Gil stood
again, one hand wrapped around the neck of an earthenware bottle, the other cupping a shot glass. The bottle
had no label. A thick layer of dust turned the bright
terra cotta a dull gray.

What kind of spirits would a man keep in a clay
bottle? Reg couldn't guess. But this was clearly special,
wasn't it, and he damn well deserved special recognition.

Gil wrenched out the cork. Reg caught another whiff of
the phantom river, distant and clean. He expected something dark, like red wine or even a port, but Gil dispensed
a finger of clear liquid. The shot glass warmed Reg's fingertips. He took another sniff, but smelled nothing.

He nodded at Gil. Reg touched the warm glass to his
lips and tossed the drink back in one go. It tasted like
time, the ticking and tocking of millennia, and it burned
like frostbite all the way down.

Gil's mystery drink was a damn sight stronger than it
looked. It turned Reg outside-in, twisted things about,
made it feel as though he were standing outside his own
head, looking in. Like déjà vu without the pleasant bits.

Reg sat heavily on a bar stool. Sybil frowned. From
somewhere far away she said, "Reggie?"

But he couldn't speak. Words carried too much

weight. Every utterance he might have made became a cog in some vast machine, or one piece of an immense puzzle. Each choice of wording carried effects that rippled out like waves on a pond. It was as though the Sight had gone crazy, triggered by the slightest thought.

The banshee wail of air-raid sirens saved him from trying to answer. Reg never imagined he'd feel so grateful to the Luftwaffe.

The other patrons abandoned their drinks and their darts. They knew what to do; they'd endured dozens of raids since the Blitz had begun. Gil ushered everybody down a narrow flight of stairs to a cellar. Reg and Sybil went last. She had to help him down; he was too dizzy to walk on his own. The stairs shook underfoot in time to the *crump-crump-crump* of a nearby antiaircraft battery.

They huddled in the cold and damp, alongside barrels of beer and shelves piled with sacks of onions, bunches of carrots, and tins of meat. A cast iron wood stove from the previous century huddled in the center of the cellar; wood had been stacked neatly along one wall. Which explained why the hearth up top had been empty.

The thunder of a distant explosion rattled the shelves. A coal scuttle in the corner gave off a faint latrine stink; it wasn't unusual to use such as makeshift privies during long raids. Reg glimpsed the corner of a clay tablet peeking from beneath a burlap potato sack. The tablet shared the same color and texture as Gil's bottle.

It almost made sense.... Everything Reg saw, smelled, felt, heard, and tasted was just one piece of the vast, ticking machine called London.

Gil built a fire. A handful of patrons sat in a semicircle around the stove, soaking up its heat. Reg kept to the corner, and the chill.

Sybil shivered. He pulled a blanket from a shelf. The scratchy wool smelled of mildew and onions.

She whispered, "Reggie?"

"What, Syb?"

"I need to tell you something," she said.

—Sybil in her grandmother's wedding dress. A church. Peter as best man—

Another explosion shook the earth and knocked him from his reverie. A tin of meat crashed to the floor and rolled toward the ginger shop girl.

Reg sighed. "Can't it wait, Syb?"

—Put it off, the dress doesn't fit—

"I suppose." Her voice cracked.

The bombing got worse as the night dragged on. Reg wondered if there would be anything left of the pub by morning. Or 246 HQ, for that matter.

—Reg commands his own group of sappers. . . . He doesn't mention the Sight. . . . Men die, trying to emulate him. . . . Sybil comes around, pushing a stroller—

Reg flinched.

Sybil snored with her head on his shoulder. He wanted to shrug her off, but the thought triggered the Sight again: *Sybil wakes. . . . Can't avoid it. . . . Long talk. . . . Wedding dress. . . . A baby cries. . . .*

He waited until the all-clear before waking Sybil. She peered up at him. Relief softened the weariness in her eyes. The skin beneath her eyes was dark and puffy, which made her look twice her age. She kissed him on the cheek with too-cool lips. He realized she'd chosen to sit beside him in the cold, damp corner all night long, rather than join the others by the stove.

Guilt? What the hell was wrong with him?

—Sybil wears him down until he relents. . . . A baby traps them into a long miserable marriage—

No. Reg wouldn't get trapped. Why should he? *His* father had been gone for months at a time, but Reg still turned out perfectly well.

Sybil asked, "Time?"

"Early morning," Reg said.

She shifted. Stretched. Nudged something with her foot. An onion rolled away. Scattered tins and vegetables littered the floor. Sybil shuddered at the sight of the toppled shelves.

Reg stood. "I'll take you home." He took her hand and pulled her to her feet.

They went upstairs, to where the day had dawned under a leaden-gray sky. They found Gil sweeping up broken glass. A bomb—big one, by the look of it—had ripped through the chemist's across the road. The impact had broken Gil's windows and knocked pint glasses from the bar. But the bomb must have been a rum fish. Otherwise, they'd still be waiting for rescue men to dig them out of the pub cellar.

Captain Hollister studied the crater. Doyle strode into the wreckage with a ladder over his shoulder while Peter unfurled a coil of garden hose. They hadn't come to collect him; that meant the captain was honoring Reg's promotion. Reg wondered who Holly would send down.

He felt Gil's stare piercing the back of his skull. "Come on," he said, and tugged at Sybil's hand. They picked a path through the rubble.

Peter saw them. He'd lost a bit of color. "Hi, Syb." He nodded toward the cratered chemist's shop, and spoke a bit too quickly. Must have been his turn to go down hole. "I guess your promotion came through just in time, Reg."

Sybil squeezed Reg's hand. A flash of relief broke through the fear and weariness on her face. "That's brilliant! Why didn't you tell me? I'm so proud of you."

Holly retreated from the crater with Doyle in tow. Doyle asked, "A Piaf? Is that good?"

Peter flinched as though he'd been stricken. He glared at Reg while he answered. The disapproval in his eyes reminded Reg of Gil. "No. It's not good."

The Piaf, named after Édith, was one of the Luftwaffe's worst. Every living sapper knew its reputation. Some speculated that it had multiple independent detonator mechanisms. But nobody knew for certain, because nobody had successfully—

—Three bolts, pry open the hatch, cut one wire, then two more bolts. Then take a horseshoe magnet. . . .

Reg could see the bomb laid open at his feet. It was so obvious.

Preposterous. He'd never even seen a Piaf, much less laid his hands on one. His gift didn't work that way.

—Solve the Piaf. Become a legend among the sappers. Get trapped with Sybil and a screaming baby—

Yet another scenario with that damnable baby.

Reg reeled while his newly expanded Sight shuffled the pieces of his life into new sequences of events. New inevitabilities.

Sybil hugged the blanket around herself. "Let's go, Reggie. I haven't had a bite to eat since yesterday and I'll faint if I don't eat before I'm due back at work."

She still wore her Wren uniform. She'd stayed at his side all night. She loved him. He would never love her.

—Drive Sybil away. Solve the Piaf, become a hero.

Live to hear about poor, tragic Sybil from time to time. . . .
Years after the war, a boy starts coming around. . . .

There he was again. Sybil's boy.

Oh, bugger. No wonder she was so desperate to have a talk. She was carrying his son.

The realization became a stray spark that ignited a flare of rage. How could she have been so careless? How could *he* have been so careless?

—Leave now, right now, leave Sybil behind. . . . Others find out about the baby, about Sybil struggling to make ends meet. . . . They won't leave him alone. . . . His place in sapper lore is ruined. . . .

No. He worked a bloody miracle at Guy's Hospital. He deserved recognition for it. But Sybil's efforts to raise the baby on her own were rubbish. Why did she have to be so useless? The boy deserved better.

—Stay with Sybil. A long marriage, filled with resentment, hard words. . . . Hard fists. . . . It's really the boy's fault. . . .

Reg flinched again, feeling ill. No. He would never become that man. He'd made that vow years ago.

—Let Peter struggle with the Piaf. His children grow up without a father. . . . But his widow gets a pension, and it keeps them afloat while Sybil has nothing. . . .

The thing growing in Sybil's womb was a cancer. It killed every version of the happy life Reg sought for himself. If he left her, his reputation would be destroyed. No matter how he tried to move on, to build a new life, the boy always came around to crater it. The sappers would never speak with hushed reverence about the miracles Reggie Brooks had performed; only the son he'd abandoned. But staying with Sybil meant years of misery. Meant becoming something worse than an absent father.

Every single path led to a life he hated. He couldn't escape it. But there was a solution. Reg could feel it.

—Give the other sappers just enough, and they'll know what to do with the next Piaf. Lead by example. Trial and error. Sybil can't raise the boy, sticks him in an orphanage. She never recovers. Two lives ruined. . . .

Almost. But not quite. Unless:

Widow's pension. Just enough to make ends meet. . . .

Yes. That one worked.

He put his arms around Sybil. He held her tight, kissed her cold lips.

"I love you, Syb." He didn't, but it was the right thing to say. Tears traced rivulets of joy down her cheeks. He kissed the salt away. "I'm making plans for the future," he said, and it was true.

Reg couldn't marry her. There wasn't time, not while a Piaf lurked nearby. But he could propose.

And Holly really would owe him, if he went down hole one last time. Reg would extract a bloody great promise in return. He'd have Peter and Gil witness it. Reg had a feeling nobody broke his word to Gil.

Captain Hollister and the other sappers could jigger things so that Sybil got her widow's pension.

Sybil and the boy have stability. He grows up hearing stories about his father, a legend among the sappers. Reg isn't twisted by decades of resentment. With one act he becomes a better father than he'd ever had. And he goes out on top.

Eight weeks and four days was a damn good run. Almost legendary.

FORBIDDEN

Avery Shade

IT'S time to admit it. I'm an addict.

My gaze drifts around the packed bar, sucking in the riot of sensory experiences like a newly processed youngling at the nutritional dispenser. Three nights running I've been drawn to this place. The first night had been pure chaos. For someone used to silence and order, assimilating all that went on within the confines of these four paneled walls had been a challenge. The overpowering din of a dozen or more conversations coupled with a television program about a bar with some sort of happy name—Cheery or something—had immediately set my ears to ringing. Conversely, each clatter of glass and clinking of ice cubes had made me all but jump out of my skin.

I'd almost bolted, would have if I hadn't become so mesmerized by the competent way the man behind the bar was shaking the frothy drink—amaretto sour, he'd said, then asked if I'd wanted one. Um, no. Better not. Soda for me.

So much to take in. So much to experience. This time is full of firsts for me. Three nights ago it was my first soda. Yesterday my first hair-raising cab ride—delivered by a Ukrainian immigrant who'd driven me to the Bronx Zoo. And earlier this evening I'd attended my first concert.

I close my eyes, remembering the throbbing beat of the drums, the playful trill of the flute, the eerie straining of the violin.

I shouldn't have gone. I am a geneticist, sent back to collect and analyze the genomes of a variety of species that are extinct from when I come from. Things like the Polar Bears, Gray Bats, and Muscle Men. Turns out the world needs them after all.

An elbow bumps me. I instinctively glance up to see who has entered my personal space at the same time that I get another one of those giddy thrills. My personal space has been compromised. Another first.

"Sorry," the man says, flashing me a blinding white smile. It is 1987 my research says that in-store remedies aren't available yet so he's either genetically lucky or has paid a lot of credits for that smile. Probably the latter. I'm finding that this decade is full of pomp and flash.

"That's all right I. . . ." I drift off. My gaze has moved beyond the bleached teeth and given me a real eyeful of the invader. There it is: temptation personified. At least six-two, blond-haired and blue-eyed, he wears a suit like the cover model of that magazine I picked up from the street vendor. All charming smiles and persuasive reasoning; another part of the great American popularity contest.

It's men like this who brought our civilization low. Them and the media, that is. The hand feeding the mouth. The slick men in their slick suits slid their way onto the big screen, dictating policy through looks and popularity. We call it the media wars. Their height marked by a stagnated government and polarized parties that spent more time landing prime-time commercial spots than on policy making. With the gridlock on Capitol Hill, nobody could get anything done. Media stopped being a source of news but a propaganda machine for lobbyists-R-us. It didn't matter how smart you were, or how experienced, it was who you were, how you looked. A politician could spout out garbage and if their face was pretty enough, their name popular enough, it was taken as gospel.

My gaze drifts upward, settling over his shoulder on the television with its muted blond-haired, big-breasted anchor woman and the ticker drifting across the bottom of the screen.

Point made.

"Can I buy you a drink?" Mr. Popularity asks, leaning against the bar beside me. I drag my eyes back to his face and that killer smile that seems even more potent now that he is close and I can smell his cologne. He's also close enough that I can tell there is substance under that suit. Probably pumps iron during lunch so he can show off his physique later. I decide his tactics are effective—in a visceral kind of way—yet I find it decidedly unnerving, too. Men don't look like him where I come from. Not that they are ugly; far from it. It's just that in my time everyone is perfectly normal, perfectly average. All perfectly the same.

"I'm all set, thanks." I lift my soda, hands clammy on the cold glass. Appreciating his smile is one thing, but the thought of actually engaging in a conversation leaves my heart skittering somewhere north of nervous.

He sighs. "Too bad. But if you change your mind. . . ." He taps the bar in front of me, then moves back across the room to where his buddies are waiting.

I stare down at the little rectangular piece of paper he's left. Gerard and Bon Associates. Below the elegant script is another name, then a series of numbers. A business card: my brain downloads this information from my implant. That's all it supplies, not what the numbers mean or who Gerard and Bon might be. If I were back home in my time, all that would have been available with a quick uplink. But they don't have personal implants in this era. They have to rely on clunky desk-top computers, faxes, and paper for the exchange of information.

A phone number. That's what the numbers are. So you can "call" and talk to someone—if they are home.

I lift the card up from the bar, reverently running my finger over the raised script. Fascinating. It is as I am studying the numbers, trying to figure out whether I like or dislike this sense of being . . . disconnected, that my scalp begins to tingle, as if I'm being watched—or someone is trying to tap into my implant. Alarmed, I raise my head. Meet up with the gaze of the barkeeper. He is meticulously drying a glass with his calloused hands as he stares at me.

"He's a player." The barkeeper nods over to the table where the suit has hooked up with his jeans and high-tops friends. "Picks up a different woman practically every night."

I glance at the man who'd left the card. He, too, is watching me, and when our gazes meet, he winks. Heat rises in my cheeks and I look away, imagining just what he might do with these women he "picks up" almost every night. I could be one of them. I could experience something that no one of my generation has ever experienced. And—as long as I get my sample—I could justify it all in the name of science, too.

But can you live with yourself afterwards?

I frown, looking back down at the card then up at the barkeeper who is still watching me. "Every night?"

"Practically."

I sigh. Mr. Tall and Handsome is exactly what I've pegged him as: a conscienceless disease in the fabric of the 20th century. Everyman doesn't need DNA like that. I'll keep the card though, as a souvenir of what could have been.

I look back at the barkeeper. He is even taller than Mr. Popularity and just as muscular, though his are from hard work rather than the local gym. He is definitely prime. Too bad about the eye color. Linked with the dominant dark hair, those vibrant blue-greens might be hard to splice out. Besides, I get no tingly sensations from him. Just a comfortable settledness. I have a feeling he can don and slough off roles at his whim and wear each shoe well. I don't know why, but I have this uncontrollable urge to keep conversing with him. Which is weird. Where I came from, we don't talk just to talk.

"How 'bout a real drink? On me," he says, shelving the glass with the rest of its clean counterparts.

"Sure. Why not?" If I'm not going to experience what real copulation is like tonight, I can at least go out on a limb and experience an alcohol high.

"What's your poison?"

"Poison?"

"Your preference? What do you like?"

"Something clear." I don't feel so much the criminal with a "clear" drink. Those frothy pink, smooth oranges, icy yellows, and crystalline greens he's been passing out all evening are just plain sinful. At least to look at. Color. Another thing this generation seems obsessed with.

"All right. Clear it is." He looks back at the rows of bottles behind him, a hand absently stroking the scruffy looking stubble on his chin as he studies the choices. "Sweet, sour, or dry?"

Both sweet and sour sound too much like a sensory cocktail. I don't understand how a liquid drink can be dry, but.... "Um, not sweet. Dry sounds good."

"Martini?"

I shake my head, not knowing what a Martini is.

"Yeah, I didn't think so." He reaches up for a blue-glass bottle on the top shelf. I glance at the label as he sets it down to fill a tall tumbler with ice cubes and am still at a loss as to what it is, other than it comes from Bombay and was named after a gemstone. Deftly he twists off the top then pours the clear liquid into the glass, concurrently punching a button on his "soda machine" so that some more clear liquid tumbles and mixes in with the alcohol.

I frown, thinking of the 7-Up I've been sipping. That had been sweet, and bubbly. I really liked the bubbles, not so much the sweet. Seems there is nothing in this time frame that doesn't involve an overload of sensory input.

"Lime?" he asks, picking up a wedge of green fruit.

I give a slight nod. Fresh fruit is acceptable for consumption.

He gives the lime a quick squeeze, impaling a second slice on the rim of the glass, then slides the drink in front of me with a smile. "There you go."

I tentatively take a sip—bubbly for sure—then an-

other. Not sweet. Dry seems an apt description. I like
the lime and the hint of, well, I don't know what.

"What do you think?"

"Fresh, crisp." I lick my lips, savoring the aftertaste of
the lime. "I like this Sapphire and Soda drink."

"Sapphire and Soda." He chuckles. "That's cute. I
think I'll list it as a special."

I don't say anything. I'm trying to figure out what I've
said that is funny. Maybe they call the drink after the
place, Bombay and the addition of the soda. . . . Bombay
Bubbly, perhaps? My confusion must have shown on my
face because the barkeeper's smile fades, the twinkle in
his blue-green eyes switching to studious interest.

"What?" I ask, resisting the urge to squirm on my
seat. This century must be really getting to me. How to
be still and composed are things Everyman children are
taught at a young age.

He takes out a white cloth, rubbing up a ring of
condensation from the polished bar. "So, what's your
name?"

"My name?" G5S36. But I can't tell him that. Instead I spout off the one on the fake ID in my pocket.
"Rebecca."

He flips the cloth over his shoulder, folding his body
down so he is low enough to lean on the bar with his
elbows. His head is still taller than mine. "So, Rebecca,"
he draws out the name, as if it is foreign . . . or he knows
it's not mine, "you got a story?"

"A story?" I chuckle, though even to my ears the
sound is off-key, forced. "I don't have a story."

That at least is the truth. Where I come from, there
are no individual stories. We all work together as part
of the system. Our singularity but a small gear in the

working matrix of Everyman. It's not fancy or exciting, but it's a life. One that I never questioned past the age of five—or until three days ago.

Stop that. You were content in that life. And you will be again once you go back.

I clear my throat, pushing away the drink. Self-indulgent addict. This is why Everyman came about in the first place, to eradicate such dangerous egocentricity. "Why do you ask?"

I don't like how he's watching me, as if he can see right through me and read my mind. Which is a fallacy, of course. He'd need an implant, and then my individual access codes to link up.

He shrugs, massive shoulders lifting and falling. He really is a big man—like a Roman gladiator or a Greek Hercules. Even this century doesn't make many like him. "Everyone has a story. It's in the eyes. And yours are saying that you'd like to leave it behind."

I jerk back on my stool, almost toppling off. Leave it behind? Why in the world would he suggest that? I am G5S36. Geneticist number five in sector thirty-six. I have a purpose. A reason for existing. Here I would be . . . I'd be. . . .

Different. You'd be an individual. You'd be Rebecca.

I give a quick shake of my head. I'm going to have to have my implant checked when I get back. It seems to have picked up a virus. The barkeeper is still watching me so I volley back his own question, "Everyone has a story? So what's yours?"

His scruffy cheeks twitch, the corner of his mouth lifting. "Mine? It's too long for one sitting. And you wouldn't believe it even if I told you."

I purse my lips. If a person's story can be read in their

eyes, then I believed that his is a long one, but given my own strange tale—that I'm a geneticist sent back in time to collect a random sampling of genes in order to rejuvenate our gene pool before we all become extinct—yes, well, there isn't much I wouldn't believe.

"Want to talk about it?" he asks. I realize he's still on the story thing. He's asking if I want to share, take a load off my chest, as they say in this century.

I shake my head, tracing the wood grain of the bar. "Not really. Besides, I'm thinking of writing a new one."

My hand starts to shake on the bar. Am I really? Would I really risk my secure life for a future here and now in this sensory depraved time?

No. That's crazy. That's the addict talking.

Laughter spikes through the general roar of conversation. I twist my head around to see a woman leaning forward, her hand linked with her date's over the polished table and her teased mane of hair obscuring their faces. Kissing. In public, too.

Two booths over the pack of men, including Mr. Popularity, are in a heated discussion over the sports scores being flashed on the television. I tilt my head to the side, gnawing on my lip as I watch them throw mock growls and verbal abuses at each other before the "fight" breaks up with a couple of razzed insults and a shake of the head.

Odd. Where I come from there is only one view. One opinion. The one you're supposed to have. Differ from that and you're . . . removed from the system.

And that's why I don't want to go back. Sometimes I don't share in Everyman's view. Like the concert. I just don't understand how something so beautiful and moving can be bad. Perhaps it's because it is moving, pulling from the self an emotional response. Emotions, and their baggage, good or bad, are a complication to things running smoothly.

Yet everyone here seems so happy. Even the two old men sitting at the end of the bar, quietly drinking their beers, hold a companionable sort of silence between them. The only one who seems as alone as I am is the bartender himself.

He comes back over to me, carrying another drink. He sets it down in front of me with a wink. "Here. This will hit the spot."

"I shouldn't," I say, glancing at the clock. 11:15. If I leave now I can be across town with time to spare.

A hand appears in front of my eyes. Large and calloused. The barkeeper. "I'm Gil, by the way. Gilgamesh, actually."

"Gilgamesh. That's nice." I tentatively reach out.

He gives a firm pump of my hand, then grunts, nodding his head as he releases me. "Now I really want to know that story."

I take my hand back, rubbing it where the bones feel crushed. How does he not break the glasses? "I told you, there is no story."

"Come on. You didn't even comment on the name. Everyone comments on the name."

I input a search into my implant but it comes back blank. Guess the files I'd downloaded weren't extensive enough. "I'm sorry, I don't—"

"Gilgamesh isn't exactly a common name in the here and now. Most people want to know how I came by it. And the nickname, Gil. Well, there still are Gilligan's Island reruns on TV, so. . . ."

I must have a blank expression on my face because

he frowns, narrowing his eyes. With a quick scan to first one side, then the other, he leans in close. "You don't have someone after you, do you?"

I swallow hard, wiping the clammy sweat on my torn denim. No, not yet. But if I don't make it to the extraction coordinates by midnight I probably will. "No, not exactly."

"But someone's got you on a tight leash, don't they."

Too close, fear has me snapping at him. "I don't see how that is any of your b—"

He stands up, holding up his hands. "You're right. None of my business. But. . . ." He glances around, then moves over to the end of the bar. Folding his body like an accordion, he bends down, pulling a key from his back pocket which he stuffs into a keyhole in the cabinet. I try to glimpse inside but see only what looks like a large slab of a reddish looking stone and the ever popular rolodex that seems to be the "thing" to replace personal identity codes in my century. After a moment he sits back on his heels, closes the cabinet, and pulls the key out. Then he's walking back toward me, another one of those business cards in hand.

"Take this," he says, sliding it across the counter toward me. "This guy, he's great at helping people write new stories."

I stare at the card as if it is a viper—an angry one.

He taps the counter, gaining my attention. "Take the card. Don't have to use it. But it doesn't hurt to have it."

I nod.

"And drink the drink. I made it especially for you. I'll be insulted if you don't."

I nod again.

With a last measuring look he turns away, going down

to the end of the bar to chat with the two elderly men. Their faces liven when he comes near and the balder of the two launches into what is obviously a humorous story. I watch them for a while, my hands twisting the cup around and around as I pointedly avoid looking at the card.

The change in programming from local news to a late night show brings my attention back to the clock.

11:32. Maybe if I catch a cab.

I start to shift off the stool, but as I do, my gaze passes over the card. It's laying there, white, innocuous even, against the dark stained wood. I sit back down. Pick up the drink. Set it down and pick up the card instead. There isn't much there, just an address under a name: John Doe. That one pings in my implant as a placeholder name for a male party whose true identity is unknown.

My finger flicks the thin cardboard, nerves and possibilities bubbling up in my stomach. If I don't show up they will send someone after me. But in this time, this place . . . if I can buy myself another identity. . . .

I gnaw on my lip. I still have to deal with the implant. I know enough that I can probably change my access codes so they can't track me. Better yet would be to find a hacker and get him to whip me up a virus I can upload to deactivate the chip. My gaze falls back to the card, the name. Maybe this John Doe will know of one.

Someone yells out a departure. The bartender, Gil, raises his hand and calls out a "Later, Norman," which receives a bunch of laughs. A couple minutes later the two men at the end of the bar stand up and shuffle out. They, too, are waved off with a personal farewell.

A bar, where everyone knows your name. Where everyone *has* a name.

People are leaving. It must be getting late. 11:42 to be

exact. Unless I manage to land the cabby from hell the moment I hit the curb, I'll never get to the extraction point in time.

By the Founder, what have I done? I'm stranded here without anything but a couple hundred dollars in my pocket. Alone in a strange world.

Sweat glazes my skin, my breath coming in short, shallow gasps. I feel like a fish out of water. Reverse drowning. I grab up the cup in front of me, gulping the cool liquid. It burns going down my throat and I choke, sputtering.

"What is this?" I demand of Gil who is at the end of the counter frowning as he tallies up a bill.

He glances up. "Fancy Free." Then goes back to his scowling.

Free. I tap the cup. I've always been alone. But until now, I've never been free.

Gil finishes his complex addition and moves over to a bell behind the bar, giving the rope a good yank. The resounding bong echoes through the room, patrons quiet. "Last call."

I stay where I am, watching as Gil makes brisk work of the last few orders. I'm not sure he loves what he does, but he seems settled. Like he fits. I want that. A job I pick. A place that is mine. A chance at. . . .

Well, I'll think about that when I get there. Right now the chance is enough.

"You need me to call a cab?" Gil comes over to stand in front of me, hands on his hips as he studies me intently.

I glance over at the clock: 12:07. A glance around shows everyone else is gone. I hadn't even noticed the time had come and past.

"No. I'm good. I'm just headed to the hotel on the corner." I slide off the stool, my high-heel boots hitting the scuffed floor as I simultaneously shrug on my leather coat. When I came in it was chilly, by now it will be cold. I suppose I can try and find John Doe, but somehow I think it's better to wait until after sunrise.

"How much do I owe you?" I ask, contemplating my meager supply of cash. I wonder how much this John Doe's services are going to cost.

Gil tips his head to the side.

"For the drink," I explain, gesturing toward the empty cup. I can't remember finishing it, but I guess I must have at some point, probably during those last fifteen minutes I'd been daydreaming.

He shakes his head, waving me off. "Nothing. It's on the house."

I smile in thanks and start toward door, hesitant but with mounting determination. This is not just an adventure, it's my life now. My hand closes over the handle and freezes. Ice running through my veins, anchoring me to the floor. I don't know how long I stand there, every synonym for foolish running through my mind, just that I can't do this.

"Best of luck with your story."

Gil's rumbling voice shakes me free. I do a half-turn, one hand still on the door as I look over my shoulder at him. He's drying another cup, but his attention is focused completely on me.

It's in the eyes. What I see there is confidence. Knowledge. As if he can actually see how everything is going to turn out.

Foolish indeed. That's just wishful thinking. Still. I can't help but hope he's right.

"Thanks," I say, and push open the door to my new future.

WHERE WE ARE IS HELL

Jackie Kessler

TRACY Summers used to think that Hell was auditioning for roles she knew she'd never get—not tall enough, not pretty enough, not *anything* enough. But now she knows better.

Hell is an endless corridor full of doors.

Tracy opens a door and steps through. It closes behind her, sealing her inside blackness so complete that it swallows the sound of the door locking. Once, she had been afraid of the dark. But that was a long, long time ago. Now she is far too resigned to be frightened. At times, hope scratches through her resignation, winking like an evening star searching for someone to make a wish upon it. This is not one of those times. Tracy lets out a sigh, and that, too, is eaten by the darkness.

Holding one hand before her and the other to her right, she begins to walk.

There is nothing but darkness and doors. This is how it's always been, how she dreads it always will be: Tracy, alone in the dark, alone with the doors.

She thinks she had a life before this; sometimes, she sees pictures of her past flash in her mind, the colors vibrant, even gaudy. Those rare memories—or, possibly, daydreams—are the only colors left to her. Even the doors are strangely colorless, as if they are merely the suggestions of doors, outlines to possibilities of other places. She cannot actively remember her life, if she ever did have a life before the doors. Whenever she tries, images blur and fade to nothing, leaving her blank. So she clings to the few memories that have visited her: she had been a dancer, trying to get her first big break; she had been in love with a man who had been far too good for her; she had once done something that had been very, very bad.

Sometimes, as Tracy is walking in the dark, she wonders what that very bad thing had been. Murder, perhaps, driven by insatiable greed? Callous indifference? Something worse? She doesn't know. And the longer she walks and opens doors that lead her to corridors filled with more doors, she doesn't think it matters. She is here, in the dark, reduced to a bare handful of memories. She can open doors; she can walk; she can do nothing until she is bored or desperate enough to walk and open doors.

That is the sum of her existence.

Tracy stands before yet another door. She places her hand on the panel, leans in close, and inhales deeply.

Once, she had performed this ritual with a sense of urgency; she used to hope it would indicate whether something, anything, waited for her on the other side. But time and again, there had been nothing—no sounds, no smells, no hint of anything other than patient darkness. Tracy no longer hopes for anything during the ritual; it has become as meaningless as opening doors in an endless corridor.

But this time, as she presses her ear close to the door, she thinks she can hear a voice—*his* voice. Her true love. Muffled, yes, because of the door, but she knows that it's him speaking on the other side. She listens, strains to hear his voice, his laughter. And a smile blooms on her face.

This time, it's the right door. This time, he'll be there, waiting for her, holding his hand out to her, ready to wrap his arms around her and love her.

Tracy takes a breath she doesn't need and opens the door.

And again, there's nothing but darkness.

She doesn't feel the tears meander down her cheeks as the door closes silently behind her. With a bitter sigh, she puts one hand out in front of her and one hand out to her right side and she begins to walk.

It's a bad moment, one where hope is nothing but ashes adrift in a desert wind. She knows she has a name: Tracy Summers. That remains, even with the other memories reduced once more to daydreams of a life long gone, of a life that never was.

Numb, Tracy follows her ritual before she opens a new door—and even though she presses her ear against the panel, she doesn't hear any sound coming from within. Expecting nothing other than darkness, she opens the door.

And everything changes.

Before anything else, the pungent smells of alcohol and citrus and smoke, all mixed together into a heady aroma that makes her nose tingle and her mouth water from re-membered appetites. Next, the tinny sounds of conversation and laughter and background noise, slightly off as if hearing them from the other end of a tunnel. And then, the colors—rich mahoganies, vibrant greens, startling whites, slowly resolving themselves into a picture of a bar with lamps hanging overhead, their shades like spring grass and the lights within dazzling white. Bottles and glasses glitter in tidy rows, lined up like star soldiers. There's a man looming behind the counter—he's almost godlike, with his black curly hair and braided beard, his imposing eyes flashing like heat lightning. That he's wiping down the countertop does nothing to reduce the sheer presence of this man, this god.

Tracy steps forward, one shaking hand over her mouth. Is this real? A dream? Will she see *him* here, whoever he is?

The door slams shut, and Tracy jumps, startled. Darting a glance over her shoulder, she's not surprised to see no hint of a door; it's as if she has appeared in the room by magic.

She turns slowly, gawking. She's in the middle of a tavern, complete with stylized wooden booths and tables. The walls are brick face, with scattered plaques and neon signs and—she blinks—bottle-cap art depicting what looks like a cross between Egyptian and Greek images of warriors battling lion-like beasts. Tucked near the bar is another plaque, this one made of reddish stone and looking like a combination of hieroglyphs and dominoes.

Around her, people are sitting at the tables, chatting and drinking, and yet their forms are blurred, almost faint, and their voices are oddly distorted. No one notices her, or reacts to her appearing out of nowhere. Frowning, Tracy stares at a couple seated near her, and even though she is close enough to touch them, they are smudged and indistinct, their banter nothing but a garble of sounds.

As grateful as she is to be out of the dark, the pantomime of conversation makes her stomach pitch. It's as if she's surrounded by ghosts. Or memories.

Has she been here before? She cannot remember. Biting her lip, she looks once more at the bottle-cap art decorating the walls, at the odd reddish plaque with its strange markings. Nothing feels familiar, but then, she can barely remember her name. For all she knows, she used to work here.

Her gaze returns to the large man behind the bar— and she flinches as he stares at her. It's not that he can see her when the other people at the tavern cannot; it's the expression on his face, a mixture of condescension and boredom, that makes her feel dizzy. He's tall— basketball-player tall—and his loose black shirt doesn't mask the strength emanating from him. He could snap her in two as easily as look at her. He completely terrifies her.

She flits her gaze around the room, looking for an exit. There, to the left: a door leading outside. Something in her chest flutters—not hope, exactly; more like anticipation, or possibly dread. She hurries over to the new door, the latest door, the one that will take her away from this strange pub with its distorted patrons and menacing bartender. Tracy reaches out to turn the doorknob—

—and her hand is slapped away, as if by an electric shock.

Eyes wide, she rubs the sting out of her palm as she

stares at the door. Biting her lip once more, she reaches out again, and this time she can feel the build-up of energy just before her fingers would have grazed the metal handle. She jerks her hand back with a gasp.

There has to be another way out. A fire exit, a back entrance. Something.

But a circuit around the large room reveals only a bathroom door—which, Tracy learns, she can't touch without getting shocked—and a curtained-off area behind the bar. The only way to the curtain is to go past the bartender, who's looking at her as if she were a bug with too many legs . . . which he'd be happy to remedy.

She allows herself a moment of panic. She desperately wishes *he* were here—her nameless true love, the man who means everything to her. But wishes are wasteful; they do nothing other than make her hope for something out of her control.

And she is tired of having no control.

Tracy clenches her fists. She has not endured the darkness and its never-ending doors only to be trapped in a strange tavern with no way out. So what if the huge man in black intimidates her? What's the worst he could do, when she's already in Hell?

Chin held high, she walks over to the bar and takes a seat.

The bartender continues wiping down the countertop. Without looking up, he asks, "Help you?" His voice carries a faint accent, one Tracy cannot place.

She opens her mouth, then closes it, uncertain of what to say. She wants his help, yes. But to do what? Escape? And go where?

All right—she has a starting point. She clears her throat and says, "Could you, ah, tell me where we are?"

"You're in my bar."

Helpful, that. "Yes," she agrees, "but . . . where is your bar?"

"Here."

He's probably a demon, sent to torment her, to give her a taste of freedom before casting her back into darkness. Tracy sighs, forlorn. "This is still Hell, isn't it?"

The bartender lifts his head and casts her a gimlet eye. "You call this Hell, little ghost? Why?"

The question almost makes her laugh, it's so absurd. "I've been trapped in Hell for as long as I can remember."

"Ah." Something gleams in his green-gray eyes—understanding, perhaps. Or maybe just polite interest. He's a bartender, after all. "And what do you know of Hell?"

"Doors." Suddenly cold, she wraps her arms around herself. "Whenever I open a door, I find other doors. But the last door brought me here."

He arches a dark brow. "Why do you think that is?"

Pinned by his gaze, she replies, "I don't know." Her voice is small, childlike. "For the longest time, it was just me in the dark, with the doors. And now I'm here, in your bar."

"Indeed."

A pause, as Tracy waits for him to say more. But all he does is peer at her, as if he could read her soul. What could he possibly find there?

Uncomfortable from his attention, she changes the subject. "The others here," she says, turning to motion at the people seated in the booths around the room. "What's wrong with them?"

"With them?" The bartender lets out a laugh. It's a

rusty sound, as if it's been a long time since he's found anything particularly amusing. "Nothing, other than the usual. Daily stress. Daily dreams. Life brings its own set of expectations, and sometimes we bow under the pressure. So they come to drink in the company of others, and that eases their burdens for a time."

Tracy frowns as she stares at the blurred customers. "But why do they look so odd? And sound so . . . off?"

Another chuckle, easier this time, as if he's warming to the notion of mirth. "You don't exist on the same level as they do, little ghost. You've moved past them."

"But I can see you. I can talk to you," she says, turning back to face him. A notion strikes her, and the question rushes out of her mouth: "Are you trapped with me?"

"Trapped?" He throws back his head and chortles—a full-belly laugh, the sound deep and resonant, like summer thunder. Soon his laughter slows to stray hiccoughs. He shakes his head and sheds the last bits of humor. When he finally speaks, his voice is solemn. "It's my job to serve my patrons. All of them, from wherever they come. So here I am, serving you."

"I don't understand," she says, her brow furrowing. "Please . . . am I still in Hell?"

Rather than answer her, he stares deeply into her eyes. Something passes over his face, a flash and then gone: a decision made. "You look so lost, little ghost. But you don't have to be. Where did you come from?"

Fumbling, she says, "I told you, the doors. . . ."

"No. Before that. Before this. When you were the same as them." His turn, now, to gesture to the others in the tavern. "Who were you?"

She notices the past tense, but she ignores it. "Tracy. I'm Tracy Summers."

"Welcome, Tracy Summers. You may call me Gil." He offers her a meat-platter hand, one that completely swallows her own. "Who were you, before you opened doors?"

For a long moment, she says nothing as she tries once again to summon memories of her life. Nothing comes, other than once, she had been in love. "I don't remember," she admits, her voice faint.

The bartender—Gil—nods. "Not completely unexpected. Well, I'm guessing you have no money on your person, given your condition. But that matters little to me. In my time, barter made the world go 'round." He grins, his teeth sharply white in contrast to the black of his moustache and beard. "I'll give you a drink to help clear the dust away, and in return, you'll tell me whatever you remember about who you were. What's your poison, girl?"

Tracy suddenly remembers the taste of semi-dry Riesling on her tongue; the smell of amber beer, tickling her nose; the warmth of blackberry brandy hitting her belly. She and her love would go out to the local pub on Friday nights, sometimes with friends, sometimes just the two of them, and they'd drink and laugh and listen to the local band going through the motions of budding rock stars. She remembers all of that with the abruptness of a gunshot.

"Water, please," she says, her voice cracking. "No ice."

Gil gives her an appraising look before he fills a large glass for her. He slides the drink to her, careful not to brush his fingers against hers. "Here," he says. "No ice, as requested."

She thanks him and lifts the glass. It feels wonderfully *real* in her hand, solid in a way that all of those doorknobs never had. She takes a moment to simply marvel over the weight of the glass, and then she brings it to her mouth and takes a sip.

The cool—not cold, no, she's always hated it when drinks were too cold—liquid slides down her throat, tasteless and yet filled with something stronger than mere taste. She swallows, and swallows more, and as she slakes a thirst she had not known was there, she remembers *his* lips on hers for the first time—hesitant, nervous, a gentle press that slowly blooms into something more passionate. She drinks, and when she finishes, she can still feel him on her lips.

Paul. His name is Paul.

More images flash, and she gets the barest glimpses of her life in auditions, of Paul's hand in hers.

Hints of the very bad thing, all reds and oranges, fury given form.

"Now then, Tracy Summers," says Gil. "Tell me the story of your life."

The words come slowly at first, hesitantly, as she tries to summon stubborn memories. She soon gives up trying and instead just talks, the sentences in free form, ideas scattered amidst bits of dialogue. Tracy talks, and Gil listens.

She's always wanted to be a dancer, ever since her parents took her to New York City to see the Rockettes. Bright costumes and painted faces made just as strong an impression as lines of dancers kicking high in their fishnets and heels. She took dance classes in school and at camp, but when it came time for college, her parents insisted she stay local and major in something that could actually land her a job. She became a philosophy major to spite them.

College wasn't so bad. That was where she met Paul, the boy who would later become her fiancé. He was huge and she was small; whenever he'd hug her, she'd feel him holding back a little, as if he thought she would break. They started as friends sharing notes in freshman poli sci, and by sophomore year they were dating. By junior year they were exclusive. By senior year, Tracy couldn't imagine her life without him.

But he never knew about the bad thing she had done once, long ago.

"What bad thing?" Gil asks.

The memory is there, just beneath the surface, but she can't reach it. She has impressions of fire licking along the walls, charring the patterns of roses and poppies, but more than that, she just can't say. She thinks there might have been a girl—no, a baby. A baby in a crib. A baby, a fire. Yes. Tracy did something, or didn't do something, and it had to do with a baby and a fire.

Oh God.

Sweat beads on her brow as she tries to force herself to remember, to discover whether she did something horrific, something unforgivable. But just as she thinks she can touch it, the memory slips away. She hears a soft keening, or maybe a baby cooing, and she whimpers.

"So this thing you did or didn't do, this bad thing," says Gil. "It's been with you your entire life. With you enough that when you died, it shaped your circumstances."

Died?

Gil must see the question in her eyes. "Don't you remember dying, little ghost?"

She shakes her head violently—denial, refusal. Desperation.

"Of course you do," he says.

And she does.

She'd lounged in bed, even after Paul had left for work. It had been a lazy morning for her, and she'd taken her time getting ready for her morning run. The sun was tearing through the clouds; she remembers the way streamers of light pierced through the otherwise overcast sky. She remembers straining to feel that sunlight dapple her cheeks as she jogged easily down a side street, warming up before she'd get to the park where she'd do her run. She caught a sunbeam and she closed her eyes, basking.

She remembers something slamming into her and lifting her into the air, even as she heard a thump of contact. A moment of flying, soaring—then surprise gave way to pain so intense that words have yet to be invented to describe it. She crashed to the ground, and her body rolled like a piece of trash caught in the wind.

She remembers the sound of the car's tires squealing as the driver sped away.

She remembers thinking of him, her love, her Paul, wishing she could tell him goodbye.

And then she remembers waking up in the dark, propping herself up in front of a door.

She's shaking now, and she rubs her arms as she sits at Gil's bar, her empty glass in front of her. Bits of memory cling to her mind—distorted pictures of Paul, of dance shoes, of something that could be a crib or a coffin.

"Hit and run," Gil says with a *tsk*. "Some people will do anything to escape consequences." He pauses, then adds gently: "And others will make sure they're bound by the same."

Tracy shivers.

"Little ghost," says the bartender, his voice no longer

gentle. "You told me you thought this was Hell. You're wrong. You haven't been in Hell. Not properly, at any rate. You were walking in the Endless Caverns."

The darkness that went on forever, the infinite number of doors—that wasn't Hell? Tracy's stomach lurches.

"Despite what many think," Gil says, once again wiping down the countertop, "Heaven and Hell aren't in a competition. It's all very orderly. Paperwork and whatnot. Every person is judged by his or her actions. The good are claimed by Heaven. The evil are claimed by Hell. And those in between, well. Those are the tricky ones."

Tracy swallows thickly.

"Those unclaimed spirits go to the Endless Caverns until, after much examination and deliberation and other such things, a claim is filed by one side or the other." Gil shrugs, his massive shoulders rolling beneath his black shirt. "Not as simple as stepping on a scale and being weighed against a feather, but there you go."

"How. . . ." Her voice breaks on a sob. Through the sting of sudden tears, she asks, "How do you know this?"

"It's my business to know things. I know religion and mythology and belief the way that others know the sun rises in the east. And I know you have one more door to open." He motions past her, to the far left corner of the bar. Tracy follows his gaze and spies the same door that had shocked her before.

"I couldn't open it," she says softly.

"You weren't ready then. Your memories had faded, nearly all of them. But now you have some of your life back—enough, at least, to understand the judgment that will be delivered. One more door, Tracy Summers, and then you'll finally arrive at your destination."

One more door. The last door.

Tracy bites her lip as she stares at the exit. It's back-lit, as if something waits beyond it other than darkness. "Where . . . where will it lead?"

"Either Heaven or Hell," Gil says, clearly indifferent. "You'll find out when you go through."

The possibility of being someplace worse than the darkness with its infinite doors makes her dizzy with ter-ror. Horrified, she whispers, "No."

After a long moment, Gil says idly, "There is another option."

She turns to face him, tears streaming down her cheeks.

"Stay here," says Gil. At first, Tracy thinks he is offer-ing her sanctuary, but then Gil continues. "You would be the new owner. This bar would be yours, forever. You'd be human once more, and immortal. And that would spare you from ever meeting your end."

As his words sink in, her eyes widen with hope, or fear, or some combination of the two.

"Think of it, Tracy Summers." Gil's eyes are shining with a passion she'd seen before, many times, in Paul's eyes. "You would hold any role here you wish: bartender, hostess, manager." Gil grins, a knife-like flash of humor. "Bouncer. Whatever you want, it would be yours. But only here, in the bar, in whatever guise it assumes."

She considers his words. Here, forever. Safe.

She can feel the door beckoning to her, begging to be opened.

"Take over my duties," says Gil, "and you never need worry about doors again."

Tracy knows there's more he's not telling her—that bit about the bar assuming guises hadn't escaped her—

but even so, the offer is compelling. She'd been trapped in what she'd believed to be Hell for a long, long time. The last thing she wants is to be trapped somewhere even worse . . . because in her heart, she knows that the bad thing she'd done so long ago has tainted her soul.

Some people will do anything to escape consequences, Gil said. *And others will make sure they're bound by the same.*

Gil's words spark an idea, one that quickly catches hold. Maybe . . . maybe she's wrong about the bad thing. She'd been young when she'd done—or hadn't done—whatever it was. That much, she's sure of. Maybe she had misremembered the event from the start.

Or not.

She could still wind up in Hell. She knows this.

But there's a chance—a slim one, maybe, but still a chance—that she could go to Heaven.

And assuredly, when his time came, Paul would join her there.

She worries her lip, and she understands that if she stays here in Gil's bar, she would never see Paul again, other than in her dreams.

And like that, she makes her choice. It's a long shot; in her heart, she doesn't think she's worthy of Heaven. But if there's even the slightest possibility that she and Paul could be together again one day. . . .

"Thank you," she says quickly, before she can change her mind, "but I'll open the door."

The look on Gil's face tells her he's not surprised. In his own way, he's as resigned as she had been in the dark. "Go on, then," he says, all business. He grabs her empty glass and wipes down the spot where it had rested. "Your fate awaits."

She wishes she had some money to tip him, but as Gil had guessed before, she has nothing on her; she barely has a solid form. "Thank you," she says, meaning it. He'd helped her remember parts of a life that had been cast in shadow. He'd given her Paul's name, his face, the memory of his kiss. He'd given her the hope that one day, she and Paul would be together once more.

For all of that, she is grateful.

Perhaps Gil hears that in her words, for he looks up at her. He doesn't smile; he is once again the intimidating presence behind the bar that she had first glimpsed when she'd arrived. But he meets her gaze and says, "Good luck, little ghost."

She stands up and weaves her way past the clusters of wooden booths filled with distorted patrons, heading toward the door. With every step, the chatter around her becomes less audible until there is only silence; the distinctive odors of the tavern fade to nothing. The colors, too, wash away, until she is once again in darkness.

Tracy Summers stands before the Door of Judgment, and she is unafraid. A taste lingers on her lips—the memory of a drink, the whisper of a kiss. With that taste comes a name, his name: her true love, her Paul, whom she misses and longs for and hopes to one day see again.

Hell may wait for her, yes. But Heaven, too, may be waiting.

This time, it's the right door. The last door. And hopefully one day, she'll be there, waiting for him, holding her hand out to him, ready to wrap her arms around him and love him.

Tracy Summers takes a breath she doesn't need, opens the door, and steps through with a smile.

IZDU-BAR

Anton Strout

THE near constant buzz from the outer doors shot into Bouncer Billy's brain like the heavy drill of a hangover, which was a goddamned shame because the big guy was nursing one already. From his stool sitting at the bar, he prayed it would stop on its own, hoping one of those plague monstrosities had triggered it by accident as they wandered in from the Wastes. Billy ignored it for a few more seconds, tugging at his scraggly beard and long unkempt hair in frustration, but it didn't stop. The damned walking dead weren't known for their fine motor skills so it was clearly a problem that he'd have to get his ass up to deal with.

Billy hefted his considerable frame off his stool, adjusting his gut where the leather of his belt had been digging in before heading off toward the elaborate door system at the front of the establishment. Whoever was laying on the buzzer tonight was going to catch shit once Billy got them to stop . . . and they stood a fat chance in hell of gaining entrance into the bar at this time of night, not after lockdown.

The inner wooden doors of the bar were easy enough

to unlock but the heft of them had Billy opening only one just far enough to squeeze his girth through. A small vestibule opened up past them with a set of thicker steel doors blocking his path beyond that. Billy slammed the wooden doors closed behind him and locked them again using the electronic plate set into them. The empty space between the doors echoed even louder with the sound of the incessant buzzing. Billy swore under his breath and pulled back the metal plate of the peephole in the outer door, first making sure to step back from it. One-Eyed Steve had made that mistake once, and, well . . . that's why Billy called him One-Eyed Steve now, wasn't it? Bouncer Billy was more than happy to keep his own nickname as it was, thank-you-very-much. It spoke of nothing born of mutilation and that was alright in his book.

Once the plate was open, the ringing blissfully stopped. He peered out the slit into the descending dusk of the Wastes, the floodlights high up on the exterior of the bar already kicking in, lighting up the land nearby. A sky of dark clouds threatened to open up over the vast plain stretching into the horizon. Huddled against the door was a lone figure with straw blonde hair, pale blue eyes and a hefty pack of worldly possessions strapped across his back.

"Sorry," Billy said, reaching for the pull on the steel shutter. "Full up."

"Hey!" the stranger said. "Wait!"

Billy laughed, relishing the cruelty in his voice. "Should have thought of that before riding the buzzer like you did, pal."

"Are you serious?" the stranger asked, his eyes widening in disbelief. "It's dangerous out here tonight. The brain munchers are out in full force. Just let me in."

Brain munchers, Billy thought. He liked that. Almost made those monstrosities seem like something he'd want to meet. "Full up," Billy repeated and started to slide the plate shut.

"Hold on," the stranger said, agitated. His hand flew up to the long slit of the peephole, his fingers jamming into the space, preventing Billy from closing it all the way.

Billy grabbed up a cleaver that hung on a length of steel chain just to the side of the steel door, raising it up for the stranger to see. "Move 'em or lose 'em," he said, brandishing the blade. "I'm going to be right pissed off to get blood on my biker leathers, but I'll do it, I swear."

The stranger pounded on the door with his other hand. "You are not going to leave me out here, man, are you?" the stranger asked. "I've avoided those monsters all day. If you leave me out here now, after sundown, I'm as good as dead."

Billy shrugged. "Not my problem," he said. Billy raised the cleaver, taking aim at the stranger's hand. One clean swipe and the stranger's little piggies would come off clean right at the second knuckle. Laughter erupted in Billy's throat as "*This Little Piggy*" went running through his head. Billy brought the cleaver down in a powerful arc.

The stranger cried out and turned away, exposing his back. A long wrapped object poked up out of the man's pack. Billy paused his swing and looked at the fingers still holding on to the edge of the peephole. The tips of them poked out of the stranger's half-glove. The nails were trimmed and the fingers callused, but only at the very tips of them. Billy looked back out the peephole at the stranger and his pack.

A familiar itch rose at the back of his brain. It was the visceral itch of opportunity presenting itself, one that Billy had felt before, and it was one that Billy had learned not to ignore ... not since the world had changed, anyway.

"Is that a guitar on your back?" Billy asked.

The stranger smiled. "You noticed it, eh?" he asked. "You play?"

Billy shook his head. "Me? Nah, but I *do* know the value of an intact one these days. You got strings on that thing?"

"A fair question," the stranger said. "I got lucky. I found an assload of stock at an abandoned Guitar Center just outside Albany a few weeks back. You let me in these doors, and I'll play. I'll play for the whole damn bar if it gets me off the Wastes." Thunder rolled out on the plain and the stranger turned his head. Off in the distance, lightning filled the sky. "If I don't get this guitar inside before this storm hits, the neck is gonna warp and a scarcity of strings won't be the issue any longer, mister. I don't have any money on me, but I can play something fierce."

Billy felt the itch at the back of his brain increase. A musician at the door after lockdown. Billy's pulse quickened. "Alright," he said. Gil might not like letting him in this time of night, but screw the boss. Music means more money for the bar. He unlocked the outer door and smiled with his incomplete set of yellowed teeth before waving him in. "Looks like your lucky night, mister."

"Guess so," the stranger said, hurrying into the vestibule. "Thanks."

Billy stared down at the stranger, nearly a head taller than the wiry blond, and then set about relocking the outer door without another word. When he finished with it, Billy checked it twice, then turned to the stranger.

"Now, lissen," he said. "You performing here is going to be between you and Gil, and if you do, you're gonna get some tips from the crowd. Understand right now that half of that is going to go to me, got it?"

"What?" the stranger said. "I thought the days of cover charges were over."

"There's no cover charge," Billy said, "but if you want me to let you in from the Wastes, that's the price." The stranger looked distraught, which only made Billy's blood rise. "Look. I *was* ready to cut your fingers off a second ago. You think I give a crap about leaving you out there?"

"I'm not going to make it to another way station to-night," the stranger said, and then sighed. "Fine."

"And let's keep this between you and me," Billy added. "Let's consider it the cost of me risking the boss's wrath even letting you in after lockdown. Unless you want me to send you out with those goddamned zombie bastards again?"

The stranger looked pissed, but Billy just kept staring him down until the guy finally managed to calm himself.

"I'm Wade," the stranger said, offering his hand. Billy took it, and shook it. The guy had a strong grip, good for a guitarist.

Billy turned and punched the combination into the inner door keypad. He waited for the light to go from red to green, then pushed open the double wooden doors, giving the stranger his first view of the interior. "Welcome to Izdu-Bar," Billy said.

The bouncer watched the stranger closely as he stepped into the bar. The disappointment on the man's face was almost pleasing to him, although truth be told, Billy thought the place looked even more dingy than it had just a few minutes ago despite how crowded it was. And when the hell did Gil find one of those ancient and well-worn Ms. Pac-Man machines sitting off on the left? Billy certainly didn't recall there being an entire row of dartboards along another wall, either. As he tried to remember, the guy gave a low whistle.

"Well, I've played worse," the stranger said. "But not much worse."

"I could let you back out," Billy offered. "Speak now before I lock it down."

It looked to Billy like the guy might actually be contemplating heading back out into the Wastes, which would ruin Billy's plans. If the guy left, there would be no way to roll him for that guitar of his later.

"No," he said, after a moment's consideration. "I'll stay."

Billy slammed the wooden doors shut behind him, checking the lock once he heard it all click into place. "How lucky for us," he said, pushing past the guy. "Come with me."

Billy walked the stranger over to the bar along the front right corner of the room where he knew Gil would be. The stranger followed Billy, dragging his feet as he looked around at the quiet, miserable crowd that already seemed hard at work drowning their sorrows. Billy approached his curly dark-haired boss who was busy stroking his well-trimmed beard and looking out over the crowd with concern before his eyes settled on the two of them.

"Good evening, William," he said.

William. Billy shuddered. The utterance of his proper

name was enough to make him uncomfortable. If the boss wasn't the first guy to not fire him in a long time, Billy would have punched him in the face for sounding so fruity. He suppressed the urge and focused on the itch at the back of his brain again. "You in a good mood or not, Gil?"

Gil gave the stranger a wary glance, and then narrowed his gray-green eyes at Billy. It was enough to make the bouncer look away in discomfort. "Why do I think that's going to depend on what you're going to ask me, William?"

"Just checking, boss," he said. "If you're in a good mood that usually means the crowd's in a good mood, too."

Billy didn't dare bring up what happened around the bar when Gil was in a bad mood. When the boss was miserable, the place seemed little more than a working class swill hole and that always brought everyone in the place down. Those nights became unbearable and finding the comforting of a good woman—or at least a good *drunk* woman—was near impossible, especially if he couldn't earn the money for her, thanks to a slow night.

"Am I in a good mood?" Gil asked, looking out over the crowd assembled in the great room of the bar. His face didn't brighten. "I'm not sure. We've got a full house. But then again, we've had a full house every night since the walking dead took over the nighttime world out there. Can't say it's going to be a thrilling night for folks in here. Don't suspect I'll be pulling too much from the taps, unless these fine people are looking to deepen their depression a little more." Gil picked up a rag from underneath the bar and wiped the top of it, bringing the old wood to a fine polish.

Billy's heart rose. The taste of opportunity practically filled his mouth.

"Got a little something for you then, boss. I know we're full up, but I just let this guy in—"

Gil looked up at Billy. His boss looked pissed, a dark fire in his eyes. "You know the rules," Gil said, his voice sharp. "We lock down for the night. No one comes in, no one goes out, at least not until sunrise when they can see those damn monstrosities coming."

"But—"

"No exceptions," Gil said.

The stranger held up his hand. "Can I ask why?"

"As William mentioned, we're full up," the barkeep said, going back to cleaning the bar. "I have rules to keep order around here and if there's one thing this modern world needs, it is order. It keeps the people in here safe."

"What do you want me to do, boss?" Billy asked. "Throw the guy back out there?" Billy felt the itch at the back of his brain slowly fading, but he refused to give up. "You'll like him, I swear. This guy's a *musician*."

Gil paused mid-polish and looked up at the stranger, and then to Billy. A wry smile crossed his face. "Playing on my weak spot, I see."

"I know what you like, boss," Billy said, laying it on thick.

Gil gave Billy a stern look. "This wouldn't have anything to do with you hoping to pull down a little extra money . . . and we know how you'd end up spending it, don't we?"

"Hehe . . . yeah, well, that's my business now, isn't it?"

Gil just shook his head at Billy. "I suppose it is, William. I've certainly seen worse happen in here over the years, much worse than a little paid companionship."

Billy gave a deep throaty laugh that turned into a cough. "Truth be told, stranger," he said. "I was ready to leave you out on the Wastes, fingerless at our doors."

Gil tsk-tsked him. "That's not very nice, William."

"Yeah, well, you didn't hire me to be nice now, did ya, boss?"

"You have a point," Gil said.

"So . . . ?" Billy could barely contain his excitement, his heart pounding away in his chest like a tiny motor trying to power an entire city block.

"As you said, I can't rightly throw him back out there," Gil said with a sigh. "What kind of a host would I be then? I'll hook the taps up to my special brew and we'll see what we can do here about firing up a good time."

The stranger looked relieved.

"Thanks, boss," Billy said, turning his girth around and waddling back to his stool. Billy didn't understand what the secret to Gil's special brew was, but it was enough to know that when Gil served it, the bar's crowd was happy.

Only a few things made Billy happy. The company of a good woman and the money to afford her. The second part looked well on its way to happening. Now he only had to work on the first part, which would depend entirely on raising more of the second part. His night was shaping up, after all.

The man Billy had let in stepped up to the bar. "Name's Wade," the stranger said. "You the owner of this place?"

Gil nodded at him. "For now, anyway. Why? You looking to buy a place?"

The stranger shook his head. "Afraid it would interfere with my nomadic nature . . . also, my lack of funds."

Gil actually looked a little disappointed. "Too bad," he said. "So William said you're a musician?"

The stranger reached over his shoulder and patted the covered guitar neck poking out of his pack. "I wouldn't exactly define myself as one thing," he said, "but yeah, since it got me in here out of the Wastes, that's who I am tonight."

"Where you coming from?"

"I was up Cummington way, down from Albany over the Berkshire Mountains."

"How's it going up there?"

"They're surviving," the stranger said. "They run a good kitchen up in the hill towns and they know how to take care of their talent. Left me happy and satiated when I moved on."

"'Tis a noble pursuit, the life of the bard," Gil said.

The stranger looked around at all the long faces. "Looks like you could use a bard for all your bored."

Gil laughed. "You play the classics?"

The stranger nodded. "Sure. Hendrix, Marley, Cobain . . . the crowd pleasers."

Gil looked to Billy, who nodded his approval.

"So that's who passes for classic these days, eh, William?" Gil asked.

"You're not from around here now, are ya?" the stranger asked. "Got a bit of an accent."

"Yes," Gil said. "Yes, I do."

The stranger stared at him expectantly, but Gil didn't offer up anything more.

"Okay," the stranger said. "Now about that meal. . . ."

"First things first, stranger," Gil said. "When you're in my bar, we seal a deal with a drink." Gil picked up a mug from underneath the bar, tipped it to a slant under the spigot and pulled at the tap. A deep dark brew poured out, forming a perfect glass with just the right amount of foam at the top. "You should probably let that sit a second and settle."

"No thanks," the stranger said. "I try not to drink before a show. I know it calms some people's nerves, but not mine."

"We drink," Gil said, pushing the mug over to the stranger, "or Billy here shows you the door. It's our custom and as master of the house, I insist."

The stranger looked over at Billy but the bouncer only stared back at him, dead-eyed and stoic. Maybe Billy had made a mistake letting the guy in. He had no doubt in his mind that Gil would make good on his promise to throw the guy out, but Billy didn't want that . . . not if he was gonna roll the guy for his guitar later, anyway. Still, whatever the boss said goes, and that was as good as law around here, but there was hope yet. If he had to give the guy the bum's rush, he might still be able to get the guitar away from him.

Billy watched the guy with suspicion. He didn't think the guitar player was going to take the drink at first, but after a long moment, he reached for the mug and brought it to his lips.

"Fine," the stranger said. As he drank, his eyes rolled back into his head and after a few long swigs, he put the glass back down, empty. "Is that a house blend?"

Gil nodded. "The one and only."

"Damn, that's good stuff," the stranger said, pounding one of his gloved fists down on the bar. "The way beer was meant to be made, if you ask me."

"Glad you liked it," Gil said. "Now we can get down to business. You play the night, get the crowd going, and you get protection from those monstrosities outside and a free meal. Plus if they all keep drinking, you drink for free."

"Sounds decent enough," the stranger said, "especially if the food is half as good as that beer."

Gil smiled. "Can't promise that. Brewing is my real specialty, but I'll see what I can do. I've picked up a few recipes over the years. Should be suitable enough."

"You have any fruit?"

"Fruit?" Billy said, laughing. "Why, boy? You feeling fruity, are you? You came to the wrong bar for *that*, son."

Gil shot him a look. "William," he said, and it was enough to kill the raspy laugh in Billy's chest.

The stranger ignored Billy, but his eyes were lit up now. "I've been dying for a little fresh fruit, is all. It's hard to harvest anything when you're traveling solo out there in the Wastes, you know? I'd kill for an apple, all nice, juicy and red. I got me an appetite tonight and that would just about be the icing on the cake."

Gil nodded. "I can oblige, mister. William here will see to it all when you're done playing."

Billy swore under his breath and was about to tell his boss he wasn't about to start taking orders and delivering food around like some goddamned waitress, but after that last look the boss had given him, it died on his lips.

"Much obliged," the stranger said. He looked off at the tiny platform at the far end of the barroom. An old worn stool and a rusted mic stand stood on top of it. "You sure that thing can hold me?"

"Don't worry," Gil said. "It'll hold. You're a performer. The stage is what you make of it, right?"

The stranger smiled at that. "I suppose it is," he said,

"but then again, I ain't no miracle worker." He pulled the wrapped guitar off of his back and unwound its covering. He pulled out a gorgeous six-string acoustic with a sunburst finish across the front of it.

Billy whistled. "How the hell do you keep it that nice traveling across the Wastes? I haven't seen one intact since . . . well, hell, I don't know when I've seen one *that* intact."

"The tool of my trade," the stranger said, patting its body. He picked it up and headed for the stage. "Make sure those portions are big, though. Performing works up one hell of an appetite."

Billy watched the stranger as he took the stage, barely able to resist the itch rising at the base of his brain again. Something like that guitar had to be worth a pretty penny these days, right?

The stranger took to the stage in front of the bored crowd and without even introducing himself launched into Hendrix's *Little Wing*. From the first chord, the crowd reacted, their enthusiasm growing through the next several hours with each passing song as the guy worked through a lengthy catalogue of crowd pleasers.

As the night wore on, Billy did more than his fair share of slinging drinks while the boss worked at superhuman speed to keep up with the demands of the thirsty crowd. The dingy joint of sad drunkards transformed as the evening progressed, the crowd becoming friendlier as they joined in on songs from the old days, songs of a simpler time—songs from before the Wastes.

Even the bar itself seemed to change. Every time Billy ran drinks, he seemed to notice something new about the place, something he had never noticed before. The way Billy was running around, he felt the goddamned place might even be larger than usual, but laughed it off as simply being overworked. Still, he had managed to eye several women in the crowd who might be worth a sweaty grunt or two once things died down. The tips flowed in and for a brief period of time they killed the greedy itch he felt at the back of his brain. The crowd was song-drunk when the stranger finally stopped.

Billy watched the stranger work his way through the still clapping crowd, dozens of patrons slapping him on the back or forcing money into his hands as he went. All the love and respect they were giving the guy caused Billy's brain itch to deepen, especially with the stranger getting all the attention from the ladies in the crowd. Billy was pretty sure that if the stranger wanted, he could have his pick of any of the women in the room. He was also pretty sure that none of them would dare charge the guitarist for their services, which only irked Billy further.

As the crowd finally settled down, the stranger made his way to the bar. "Wow," he said. "This place really came alive, didn't it? I mean the crowd, the energy … hell, at one point I thought the entire bar was actually changing! I thought maybe you slipped something into my drink earlier, but I swear this is not the same bar I walked into. . . . I mean, that microphone was rusted when I came in and look at it now. It looks like it just popped off an assembly line." The stranger paused and cocked his head at Gil. "This place really *is* different, isn't it?"

Gil shook his head. "It's amazing how the crowd can change a person's perception of a place." Gil said. "But no. Izdu-Bar is just a bar."

Billy could tell the stranger that he wasn't quite buying Gil's explanation. His boss stared at the guitarist until the stranger looked away.

"Right," the stranger said, then changed the subject. "So about that meal . . . ?"

Gil relaxed. "Ah, yes," he said. "The bargain we struck in exchange for your entertainment this evening. I live to serve. Give me a few minutes to whip something together. The crowd got a little out of control while you were playing, and well . . . the customers always come first."

"You got a place I can sit down for a spell while I eat?" the stranger asked. He held his guitar by its neck, balanced its body on his foot. "I'm worn."

"Sure," said Gil.

The stranger looked around the bar again. "Something off the floor, preferably," he said. "I need a little downtime after a show, you know?"

"Not a problem," he said. "Believe me, I understand the desire for a little privacy, especially in a bar. You can head down the stairs out back here behind the bar. I keep a table and chair down by the brew works for my off hours. I'll send William down with what you desire when it's ready."

"Great," the stranger said. "Thanks. And hey, don't forget that apple, William!"

Him and his apple, Billy thought. Yeah, the guy was definitely fruity. Just one more reason to liberate the guy from his guitar . . . and maybe all those tips as well.

The stranger grabbed up his guitar and reclaimed his pack before heading off towards the stairs. Gil went back to the kitchen area and Billy scoped out the bar. The crowd was still drunk off the power of the evening, which was great. It at least meant Billy was more likely to get a deal on whichever one of the girls was willing to give him a tumble later.

When Gil presented him a tray stacked with a sizable meal—complete with a ruby red apple, of course—Billy headed over to the stairs with it. As he descended the staircase, however, Billy's mind switched back to some of his darker thoughts from earlier in the evening.

A drifter passing through, no matter how talented, was the perfect victim. If the stranger disappeared, others would assume that he had simply moved on as drifters do. The stranger's guitar would no doubt fetch a good price, but a new thought struck him, making him a little bit angrier with every step down the stairs.

A guy like that stranger, a guy who played that good . . . he *had* to be loaded, right? Billy thought so, especially after having seen the tips people had been slipping the guy once he got off the stage. Multiply that money by the number of towns the stranger must have played in his travels . . . the guy had surely been crying poor at the door earlier. Billy's blood began to rise. *The stranger had tricked him*, Billy thought, *no doubt about it. . . .*

The more Billy thought about it, the more convinced he became that he had been made a fool of. Hell, the guy probably wore one of those hidden money carriers on his body, the ones Billy had heard were popular in surviving the lawless plains of the Wastes. Thinking about how the guy had played him, Billy clenched his hands, his nails digging into the side of the steel dinner tray. The itch at the back of his brain was overpowering now, and goddammit if Billy didn't want to hurt the guy for making a fool of him.

The sounds of the brew works became more and more pronounced as Billy got closer to the bottom of the

stairs. The hiss of steam through the twist of copper tubes
leading from the water tanks to the mash tun, hopback,
and copper kettles filled the air, as did the grind of the
old stone wheels that helped to fire the kiln and drive
the heat exchanger. Billy stepped into the brew works,
passed the wall of noise that seemed to die back down
once he was past a large stone tablet the boss kept near
it all, and headed toward the back of the room where the
stranger sat at a long wooden table with his back to him.

"Here you go," Billy said, dropping the tray on the
table next to him, letting it ring out with a sharp clang.
"You even got an apple, as requested."

"Thanks," the stranger said, ignoring the tray as he
fiddled with a small wrapped pack on the table, "but the
apple's not for me."

"Oh no?" Billy asked, checking over his shoulder to
make sure the boss hadn't followed him down. The path
back to the stairway was clear.

"No," the stranger said, shaking his head, "but we'll
come back to that. Let me ask you a question."

"Go ahead," Billy said, welcoming the chance. He had
been so busy planning how he was going to spend the
stranger's money, he hadn't worked out how he should
go about the deed of killing him first. Answering questions would give him a moment to come up with a plan.

"That red stone thing about the size of my chest," the
stranger said. "What the hell is it?"

"Beats me," Billy said. He stifled a laugh as a near
perfect idea struck him. *Beats you too, stranger.* Billy
headed back over to the object and examined all the
tiny marks, squiggles, and symbols on its face. "Looks
Egyptian or something. Boss says it's the family recipe
for his home brew here, but I think he just likes jerking

around the help when they ask about it. I'd tell him to piss off, but the job market ain't what it used to be ever since those brain munchers took over the outside world. Filthy creatures."

Billy put his arms around the hefty piece of stone, lifting it off its display stand. The damned thing weighed a ton. *Oh yeah,* he thought. *This will do the trick. No question.*

The stranger scoffed as he continued fiddling with that package of his, paying no attention to Billy whatsoever.

"What would you know about what's happening in the outside world?" he asked, a hint of anger in his voice. "You're all just a bunch of shut-in's, sitting here, drinking your swill, passing your time, talking crap about a world outside that you don't even *know*. You think the world stopped when the zombies came? No. . . ."

That's it, Billy thought and he lugged the thing across the floor towards the stranger. *Just keep talking.* There was no doubt in the bouncer's mind that the stone tablet would get the job done . . . and quick. Roll the guy, store the guitar away until he could safely get it out of there, and drag the body out back, maybe leave it to the brain munchers. . . .

"What do you expect us to do?" Billy asked, trying to distract the stranger as he moved closer. "Run around the Wastes town to town like you, hoping to avoid them?" Billy raised the stone up, hefting the heavy thing in the air using every ounce of strength he had. The damned thing was likely to crush the dumb bastard's head flat. Billy looked at the back of his target's head and caught sight of the stranger's package, which was now open, its contents spread out on the table in front of him. It was a collection of small tins, tubes, and pads, along with a variety of brushes. "Is that . . . makeup?"

The stranger paused for a second. "Yes. For my performance."

One swift swing, Billy thought, *and it will all be over, save for the cleaning up.* It was a risk rolling the bastard in the basement of the bar, but it wasn't every day an opportunity to profit like this fell in your lap. And even if Gil caught him before he could drag the body up the back stairs and dispose of it in the Wastes, Billy already had a cover story forming in his mind. He'd tell the boss that the stranger really *had* turned out to be fruity and came on to him. When Billy told the bastard where he could go, the stranger had become violent and the situation had escalated. Billy was simply defending himself . . . against a wiry guy who was a full head shorter than himself. *Right.*

Okay, it wasn't the most perfect plan for killing a guy he had ever concocted, but opportunity was not a lengthy visitor these days and just living in a world where the wandering dead filled the Wastes made life a little chancier anyway, didn't it?

Billy readied the stone for its downswing, then paused as some small light bulb in his brain clicked on. "Wait . . . why would you need makeup *now*? That doesn't make sense. You already played."

"The makeup wasn't for my performance onstage," the stranger said, spinning around in his chair. "It's for my performance *now*." His face was normal except for a small gray patch along his left cheek that was the color of those undead bastards out in the Wastes. The stranger dabbed a pad into the tin in his hand and smeared a swatch of flesh-colored makeup over the spot, giving the stranger the appearance of humanity once again.

Panic rose in Billy's heart, the strength leaving his

arms, causing the heavy stone tablet to fall towards the stranger's head. The stranger, however, was quicker, and raised one hand to meet the tablet, stopping it mid-fall. How he was supporting it with just one hand, Billy didn't know . . . then it hit him.

"Stinking zombie," he said with a sneer.

The stranger shook his head, still holding up the stone tablet. "Just another of your stereotypes, I'm afraid." He stood, taking the tablet away from Billy, and flung him back.

Billy crashed against a stack of barrels, his mind fighting to make sense of everything going on. "But . . . but . . . the zombies can't talk, and. . . ."

Billy fought to find words, but nothing more came to him and a second later, it really didn't matter anyway. The stranger adjusted the tablet in both of his hands, flipping it around like it weighed nothing, and then slammed it down on Billy's feet.

Billy heard the sound of his toes crushing before pain shot up his legs. He went to scream, but the stranger grabbed up the apple off the dinner tray and slammed it into Billy's mouth, knocking out two of his teeth in the process. Billy, dazed and in shock, slumped to the ground.

"I'm capable of a lot of things you wouldn't expect my kind to be able to do," the stranger said, crouching down next to Billy and meeting his eyes. "As you've seen. But you're quick to stereotype, aren't you?"

Billy shook his head in uncontrollable panic as the zombie musician stared down at him, examining him. He could taste the sweetness of the apple mixed with the saltiness of his own blood.

"The world keeps on evolving," the stranger contin-ued, picking up the stone once again as if it were made of paper and replacing it on its stand, then walked back over to Billy. "I am a product of that evolution, friend. I don't quite understand why I'm not like the rest of those zombies out in the Wastes, but I have a theory. They say a musician's got music in his soul. They also say that 'music doth have charms to soothe the savage beasts,' so maybe that helps even me out. I'm not sure exactly. Either way, I'm still human enough to walk both worlds, even if it does take a bit of makeup to cover up the gray to accomplish it. I've evolved, but fat, greedy you hasn't, have you? No. You just stay the same." The stranger stood up and kicked Billy's already broken toes.

Pain shot straight to the core of Billy's brain and he screamed again, the sound muffled by the apple.

"Shh," the stranger said. "We can't have any of that now, can we? You know, there's one stereotype that does hold true still about my kind . . . you know, us *brain munchers*." The stranger leaned down over Billy, grinning from ear to ear. "Your boss promised me a meal, but it wasn't that tray of food I had in mind."

The stranger moved out of sight just above Billy's line of vision, a strange and cooling sensation filling his brain as the sounds of slurping and crunching filled his ears. Bouncer Billy would have prayed, if he believed in that sort of thing, but he didn't bother. He doubted that a God who had created these damned monstrosities in the first place was a God he wanted to meet, anyway. The only consolation was that the itch at the back of Billy's brain all night was finally fading, along with everything else. . . .

ABOUT THE AUTHORS

The only dog **Barbara Ashford** ever owned was a dachshund. He didn't say much. After stumbling through several jobs in educational administration, she ran away to the theatre, working as an actress and later as a librettist/lyricist. Her first trilogy was a finalist for the Mythopoeic Society's award for fantasy literature. Her new novel—*Spellcast*—comes out in May 2011 and is set in a summer stock theatre far more magical than any she worked in. She credits her husband for inspiring "The Tale that Wagged the Dog" and for keeping her supplied with single malt whisky. Visit her at www.barbara-ashford.com.

Patricia Bray originally intended to write a completely different story, but when she opened her word processor, she heard the voice of George Harker recounting his adventures and was compelled to record them. Drawing upon her knowledge of Georgian England and love of nineteenth century fiction, she's fairly confident that George and his adventures are entirely the work of her imagination. Well, mostly confident. To find out what she's up to now, visit her website at www.patriciabray.com.

S.C. Butler is the author of the Stoneways Trilogy: *Reiffen's Choice*, *Queen Ferris*, and *The Magicians' Daughter*. A relative once complained to him about all the underage drinking in his books, but who ever drank the water in the Middle Ages? His favorite drink is a glass of Pinot Grigio, and his favorite place to drink it is the bar deck of the Lawrence Beach Club on a summer evening, with two hundred yards of sand and fifty miles of the Atlantic Ocean spread out before him.

Jennifer Dunne is the author of over fourteen fantasy and paranormal romances. While traveling in Italy last year, she fell in love with Venice, and the more she read about the city, the more she wondered. Why would one of the two most powerful men in the world at the time sneak into Venice in disguise, only announcing that he had been there after he was gone? What was he *really* hoping to accomplish? And, because she believes in happy endings, of course in her story, he gets one.

Laura Anne Gilman has a history of writing short stories that aren't quite as-expected. This is nothing new: she wrote her first original novel, *Staying Dead,* when everyone said that urban fantasy was dead, and, in 2008 she wrote *The Vineart War,* an alternate-historical fantasy, when everyone was looking for urban fantasy. She thinks being contrary's a pretty good way to build a career. It should be noted that, despite *The Vineart War* being about wine-magic, and despite the story being set in France, the story for this anthology does not reference wine, but rather a specifically evil sort of cocktail popular at the time . . . the author does not encourage consumption of more than three in an evening!

D.B. Jackson also writes as David B. Coe, the Crawford Fantasy Award-winning author of the popular series The LonTobyn Chronicle, Winds of Forelands, and Blood of Southlands, as well as the novelization of Ridley Scott's *Robin Hood*. The first D.B. Jackson novel, *Thieftaker*, will be released in 2012. It is a historical fantasy and mystery, which, like "The Tavern Fire," is set in pre-Revolutionary Boston. D.B. likes any bar that serves dark ales on tap.

Jackie Kessler writes about demons, angels, the hapless humans caught between them, superheroes, the super-villains who love to pound those heroes into pudding, vampires, ghosts, and the occasional Horseman of the Apocalypse. Her favorite drinks include a semi-dry Riesling and, when at conventions, rum and Diet Coke. When beer is the thing, her favorite bar is the Peculier Pub on Bleeker Street in New York City. For wine, it's got to be The Wine Bar in Saratoga Springs, NY. For more about Jackie, visit her website: www.jackiekessler.com.

Seanan McGuire was born and raised in Northern California, which explains a lot about her approach to venomous reptiles and the concept of "weather." She's been writing since she was nine, driving everyone around her crazy; her first book, *Rosemary and Rue*, came out from DAW in September 2009. More have followed. Seanan lives with two blue cats (Siamese and Maine Coon), too many books, and a great many horror movies. Her favorite drink is the Corpse Reviver #2: gin, Cointreau, Lillet blanc, lemon juice, absinthe, a cherry, and defiance of nature's laws. Delicious, delicious defiance. Seanan doesn't sleep much.

Juliet E. McKenna has always been fascinated by myth and history, other worlds and other peoples. After studying classical history and literature at St Hilda's, Oxford, she worked in personnel management before a career change to combine book-selling and motherhood. Her first novel, *The Thief's Gamble*, was published in 1999. That series, the Tales of Einarinn, was followed by The Aldabreshin Compass sequence and her current trilogy, The Chronicles of the Lescari Revolution. Living in the Cotswolds of England she is lucky enough to have the Wychwood Brewery within easy reach, home of Hobgoblin and Wychcraft beers.

Avery Shade is an author of paranormal and urban fantasy of both the adult and young adult variety. Though grounded in a small upstate NY town, she lives vicariously through her stories. When not busy writing, she is probably off searching for the real meaning of life, the universe, and... well... everything. If you can track her down (try her website: www.averyshade.com) you might offer to go for drinks somewhere. She's all too eager for a bit of escapism. Maybe one of these times she'll find the Ur-Bar and Gil will mix her a drink that can give her some more time.

Maria V. Snyder switched careers from meteorologist to fantasy novelist when she began writing *The New York Times* bestselling Study series (*Poison Study*, *Magic Study*, and *Fire Study*) about a young woman who becomes a poison taster. Born in Philadelphia, Pennsylvania, Maria dreamed of chasing tornados, but lacked the skills to forecast their location. Writing, however, lets Maria control the weather which she does in her new

Glass series (*Storm Glass*, *Sea Glass*, and *Spy Glass*). Readers are invited to kick back with her favorite drink, a Long Island Iced Tea, and read more short stories on her website at www.MariaVSnyder.com.

Kari Sperring grew up dreaming of joining the musketeers and saving France, only to discover that the company had been disbanded in 1776. Disappointed, she became a historian instead and as Kari Maund has written and published five books and co-authored (with Phil Nanson) a book on the history and real people behind her favourite novel, *The Three Musketeers*. Her first novel *Living with Ghosts* was published in 2009 by DAW books and she has recently completed her second. "The Fortune-Teller Makes Her Will" was inspired by the Poisons' Affair that rocked the French Court in the 1670s and by a beautiful named pair of earrings by jeweler Elise Matheson. She's British and lives in Cambridge, England, with her partner Phil and three very determined cats, who guarantee that everything she writes will have been thoroughly sat upon. Her website can be found at www.karisperring.com.

Anton Strout remembers his early days of barhopping in New York City, making The Slaughtered Lamb an old favorite of his thanks to the drinks, dungeon, life-sized werewolves and fake lightning storms. He is best known as the author of the Simon Canderous urban fantasy series including *Dead To Me*, *Deader Still*, *Dead Matter*, and *Dead Waters*. He has also appeared in a variety of anthologies. In his scant spare time, he is an always writer, sometimes actor, sometimes musician, occasional RPGer, and the world's most casual and controller-smashing video gamer. He can be found lurking the darkened hallways of www.antonstrout.com.

Benjamin Tate was born in North-Central Pennsylvania and is currently a professor living near Endicott, NY, teaching at a local college. He began writing seriously in graduate school, using the fantasy world of his novel *Well of Sorrows* as an escape from the stress. His goals in life are to travel Europe, sail the Mediterranean, visit Australia, and preside over a small kingdom from a castle on a hill while occasionally bombarding the villagers below with catapult fire. His favorite drink is a White Russian—preferably with top shelf vodka. www.benjamintate.com.

Ian Tregillis is the son of a bearded mountebank and a discredited tarot card reader. He is the author of *Bitter Seeds*, *The Coldest War*, and *Necessary Evil.* He received a doctorate in physics from the University of Minnesota, but now lives in New Mexico, where he consorts with writers, scientists, and other unsavory types. His favorite holiday drink comes from a one hundred fifty-year old recipe for eggnog. www.iantregillis.com

ABOUT THE EDITORS

Patricia Bray is the author of a dozen novels, including *Devlin's Luck,* which won the 2003 Compton Crook award for the best first novel in the field of science fiction or fantasy. A well-spent youth taught her that the best accompaniment to a fine ale is an equally well-crafted story, a lesson that she drew on for her first foray on the editorial side of the fence. She currently lives in upstate New York, where she combines her writing with a full-time career as Systems Analyst, ensuring that she is never more than a few feet away from a keyboard. To find out more, visit her website at www.patriciabray.com.

Joshua Palmatier is a writer with a PhD in mathematics. He currently resides in New York while teaching mathematics full-time at SUNY College at Oneonta. His novels include *The Skewed Throne*, *The Cracked Throne*, and *The Vacant Throne*, all part of the Throne of Amenkor trilogy. His short story "Mastihooba" appeared in the anthology *Close Encounters of the Urban Kind*. This is his first stab at being an editor and it required the consumption of many, many White Russians. But he'll do it again given the chance. www.joshuapalmatier.com.

Patrick Rothfuss

THE NAME OF THE WIND
The Kingkiller Chronicle: Day One

"It is a rare and great pleasure to come on somebody writing not only with the kind of accuracy of language that seems to me absolutely essential to fantasy-making, but with real music in the words as well.... Oh, joy!"   —Ursula K. Le Guin

"Amazon.com's Best of the Year...So Far Pick for 2007: Full of music, magic, love, and loss, Patrick Rothfuss's vivid and engaging debut fantasy knocked our socks off."   —Amazon.com

"One of the best stories told in any medium in a decade. Shelve it beside *The Lord of the Rings* ...and look forward to the day when it's mentioned in the same breath, perhaps as first among equals."
             —*The Onion*

"[Rothfuss is] the great new fantasy writer we've been waiting for, and this is an astonishing book."
             —Orson Scott Card

ISBN: 978-0-7564-0474-1

To Order Call: 1-800-788-6262
www.dawbooks.com

Sherwood Smith

Inda

"A powerful beginning to a very promising series by a writer who is making her bid to be a major fantasist. By the time I finished, I was so captured by this book that it lingered for days afterward. I had lived inside these characters, inside this world, and I was unwilling to let go of it. That, I think, is the mark of a major work of fiction…you owe it to yourself to read *Inda*." —Orson Scott Card

INDA
978-0-7564-0422-2

THE FOX
978-0-7564-0483-3

KING'S SHIELD
978-0-7564-0500-7

TREASON'S SHORE
978-0-7564-0573-1 (hardcover)
978-0-7564-0634-9
(paperback)

To Order Call: 1-800-788-6262
www.dawbooks.com